THE
BANDIT
MASK

Written by
Justin Biegler

Courtland Printing House
Raleigh, North Carolina

Published in the United States by Courtland Printing House

ISBN: 978-0-9986785-1-1

To Kate, my ever-cheerful companion through all life's adventures.

Proceeds from your purchase of The Bandit Mask support Raleigh-centered groups digging wells and building schools in some of the world's poorest communities.
Thank you!

THE
BANDIT
MASK

CHAPTER ONE

"Get out of the way!"

The chilly September morning made Sam's shouts come out in foggy puffs. He waved his arms and hopped up and down, making a commotion.

The squirrel just blinked at him from where it sat in the street, confusion in its black, bead-like eyes. Oblivious to the several tons of school bus throttling straight toward it.

Sam's shouts and gestures became more frantic as he tried to break the squirrel's concentration. It remained in place, transfixed on Sam, sitting perilously still beside the road's center stripe.

A diesel engine roared as the bus barreled toward Sam's stop.

If only Winnie, Sam's dog, were here. She would have frightened it off with one mighty bark. Squirrels ignored Winnie at their own peril.

That thought gave him an idea. Sam's backpack, filled with way too much homework for just the fourth day of school if you asked him, shifted on his shoulders as he stooped. His cold fingers pawed at the gravel lined roadside while his eyes remained locked on the squirrel's stare.

The bus was now a carnival of yellow lights flashing warnings, and only fifty yards away. Still the squirrel didn't budge.

Sam straightened and gripped a rock like he was going to throw a pitch. Only one chance.

"Sorry little guy," Sam thought aloud.

He wound up and flung the stone.

The rock was smaller than the baseballs he was used to throwing, but

Sam's aim was true. It struck the asphalt three feet wide of the squirrel to skip past harmlessly.

Startled, the squirrel snapped to with a sudden hop. It spun in mid-air and, in a blur of silver and orange fur, dashed back to the long grass lining a ditch on the street's other side. A fat front tire missed the squirrel's tail by inches.

The bus jerked to a stop in a puff of air brakes and exhaust. When the diesel belching engine didn't sting his nostrils, Sam realized he was still holding his breath.

Metal bus doors folded open. Sam gulped and hesitated while the bus driver stared down at him from the top of the stairs impatiently.

Sweat rose on the back of Sam's neck. In the commotion of saving the squirrel's life from certain doom, he'd forgotten about the necessity of preserving his own.

Going unnoticed, Sam had decided, was the best way of surviving at a new school. Certainly someone on the bus must have seen him waving his arms like a madman. They might have even taken pictures.

Sam's heart hammered as he climbed the steep steps.

A laugh like a baying mule met him at the top, and Sam instinctively ducked his head. Its source came from a boy with spiked blond hair and a mouth too big for his face.

Bradley Banks.

Just yesterday, in the cafeteria, Sam had made Bradley's acquaintance - if that's what you called Bradley shoving you as you walked past with a loaded lunch tray. Sam had staggered forward and managed to keep his balance, but gotten ketchup all over a new shirt in the process. Bradley had simply strode away to stalk other prey in the halls, laughing the same laugh that now filled the bus.

Now Sam stood frozen in the aisle way. Bradley's hulking form leaned against a window near the back, an audience of kids in surrounding seats paying him all their attention. Bradley spoke with wild hand gestures and punctuated every few words with his sharp laugh. The din of other voices and a rumbling engine made his words indecipherable, but Sam had no doubts Bradley was bragging about some cruel act of bullying. It could have even been about Sam's ketchup-stained shirt.

But the important thing was that Bradley hadn't witnessed Sam's antics with the squirrel. And he hadn't noticed the new kid climb aboard the bus either.

The bus lurched forward and Sam grabbed the top of a seat back to keep his balance. Keeping his head down and trying to remain inconspicuous, Sam flung himself into the first open aisle seat and listened.

The laughter continued from the back, uninterrupted. He'd done it. Bradley hadn't noticed Sam at all. Then a new voice startled him.

"What are you doing?" A girl in a pale blue jacket said from the window seat. Her dark hair hung in a braid over her shoulder, bound at the end with a ribbon that matched her coat. She stared Sam down with narrowed, fierce eyes.

Sam's tongue went numb as he stammered for words. "Sorry... are you... saving this seat?"

"I saw you. Throwing rocks at that squirrel." Her words came out sharp as the morning's chill. "Make you feel tough? Picking on something smaller than you?"

"No, I-" The words caught in Sam's throat.

"I don't want to sit with someone who throws rocks at animals." She jerked a thumb, pointing back to the aisle.

Sam shot a glance over the top of the seat. Bradley still stood against the window stretched across the seats, in the midst of his tale. If Sam were to stand up now, Bradley and his gang were sure to notice him and focus in on new prey.

Sam took a deep breath, gulped down the lump in his throat, and spoke as fast as he could.

"The squirrel. He was in the road, just sitting. I heard the bus coming, but he wouldn't move."

The dark haired girl's accusing stare didn't waiver, but she also did not interrupt.

Sam felt his face flush as he went on. "I didn't want it to get smashed, so I tossed a rock near him. Not at him. Just to scare him, to get him to move. Honest."

He panted, out of breath from nerves and spitting the story out so quickly.

She studied his face. "You're new in town."

Sam, breathless and trembling from the last few minutes, could only nod.

Finally, after what felt like an eternity of silence, she rendered her verdict. "I don't know if I believe you, but you can stay."

Sam's tense muscles melted into the seat with relief. "Thanks," he offered, unable to think of anything else to say before adding, "I'm Sam."

"Lia," she replied, and spun away from Sam and to stare back out the window at the passing trees and fields.

Lia. He repeated it in his head. Sam felt like a deflated balloon, but he decided he liked that name.

* * *

Dad had said moving to Mapleton would be a 'new beginning' for their family, and so far he'd been spot on. On this, Sam's fourth day of a new school year at a new middle school, in a new town with new teachers, new classmates, and a new locker combination to try and remember, Sam longed for something familiar.

Even the landscape rushing past Lia's window was new. Gone were the storefronts and brick office buildings he was used to seeing on his commute to school. Instead of a city's familiar gray, everywhere Sam looked was green.

Where he expected to see sidewalks and bus stop benches, Sam saw lawns and fields and patches of trees. Ranch houses and open fields zoomed past the window where apartment buildings and stoplights should have been. The distant high rises of downtown skyscrapers were replaced by far away purple shadows of the Appalachian Mountains, as a carpet of deeply colored forest seemed to stretch from the mountain's base all the way to the road their bus bounced along.

Gradually, the forested hills and sloping fields shifted to more houses and side streets branching off the main road.

They crossed a bridge built above a creek with a wide swamp on each side. Dad had called it Willow Creek, which seemed like an odd name considering their new town was named Mapleton.

After a few more blocks, the bus slowed and turned into a parking lot beside a large wooden sign that read 'MAPLETON MIDDLE SCHOOL - A GREAT PLACE TO BE'.

"As long as you don't get mauled while attending," Sam muttered under his breath, with another hesitant glance over his shoulder toward Bradley.

Their bus crept forward and fell in line with several others, all identical and yellow, full of students and belching diesel fumes.

Sam turned to Lia as the bus slowed. "Thanks for letting me sit with you."

She said nothing, and just gave him another hard stare.

When the bus stopped, Sam kept his head down as he shouldered into the crowded aisle and shuffled outside into the chilly morning.

Milling students crowded Mapleton Middle School's front sidewalk. Sam maneuvered around different groups, making his way toward the front doors to be beneath the watchful eyes of teachers. The last thing Sam needed was to get caught out in the open by Bradley Banks.

He wasn't fast enough.

"Well well, if it isn't the newest member of the nerd herd!" A meaty arm wrapped around Sam's shoulders. Bradley fell in step beside him, walking like they were old friends. "I don't think we've officially met. What's your name, wimp?"

"Sam," he muttered through his teeth, continuing as quick as he could toward the front doors.

"We're going to be best pals, you and me." Sam could hear the sarcasm in Bradley's voice and felt his arm constrict like a snake as Sam tried to pull away. Bradley towered over Sam and was as thick as some adults. There would be no escaping his choke hold unless Bradley allowed it.

"No thanks." Sam mumbled.

Bradley's squeeze tightened, and Sam was surprised not to hear any of his bones breaking. "No back talking, wimp. Just for that, you're buying me lunch today."

From a throng of kids, a girl in a powder blue jacket with a matching hair ribbon pushed her way forward. Bradley jerked to a halt but didn't let go of Sam's shoulder.

"Leave him alone, Brad." Lia said, with the same scolding tone she'd used when interrogating Sam about suspected squirrel abuse.

"Aloha cutie. Need a dance partner for tonight?" Bradley danced in place, jostling Sam beside him.

"If you don't back off, I'll make sure you're not allowed in."

"What, is this nerd your date?" Bradley's baying laugh rang out through the frigid morning, and some of the surrounding students turned to watch the exchange. "Which one of you is wearing the grass skirt?" He laughed again and waved her away.

But Lia didn't budge. Instead, she seemed to plant her feet as she put her hands on her hips. "Keep it up, and the only place you'll be dancing tonight is in the parking lot. By yourself."

Bradley's smile sagged as he narrowed his eyes at Lia and stared for a long moment. Sam felt certain Bradley was about to take a swing at her. But Lia didn't flinch, but Sam expected Lia was ready to punch right back.

The silence of their stand-off grew thick.

"Whatever," the bully finally grunted, and pushed Sam aside before stomping off. "Like I'd want to go anyway." Sam staggered a few steps, Bradley's push magnified by Sam's heavy backpack.

Before he could hit the pavement, Lia grabbed one of Sam's shoulder straps and helped him steady his feet.

"Do you always start off on the wrong foot with people?" Lia asked. Her eyes and expression had softened, just a little, and Sam spied a hint of a smile.

Sam shook his head and tugged at the sleeves of his jacket, rumpled from Bradley's embrace. "I don't think he likes new kids. Or maybe he's a big squirrel fan and just needs to hear my side of the story too." The bit of cleverness came out without him even thinking the words

Lia covered her mouth at an unexpected giggle. "Maybe you're onto something." The five minute warning bell sounded with a shrill ring. "Come on, don't want to be late."

Sam walked side by side with Lia, no longer worried about being noticed. She would protect him.

Together they joined the multitude of students migrating up the handful of concrete steps toward Mapleton Middle School's front doors. The Vice Principal, Mrs. Betty, stood facing the flow of foot traffic, greeting students as they made their way inside to start the school day.

Mrs. Betty was easy to spot. No one else at school looked like they could have once been a professional linebacker. She towered over even the tall, lanky kids that seemed destined to play on the high school basketball team, and she had shoulders like an Olympic power lifter.

"So…" Sam took a deep breath, mustering up the courage to ask about something mentioned in the Lia versus Bradley showdown. Now that he was no longer fearing for his life, Sam remembered that talking to girls made him incredibly nervous. "Did you say there's a dance tonight?"

"Sure is. The Harvest Social."

"Good morning Lia." Mrs. Betty called as they passed beneath her broad shadow. The Vice Principal's eyes turned to look down on Sam. "Good morning, young man."

Lia waved to Mrs. Betty while Sam nodded his head and mumbled a greeting. Despite her imposing stature, Mrs. Betty was always as friendly as could be, but Sam imagined she could be pretty intimidating when she wanted. For now, he had more important things on his mind.

He gulped and his legs wobbled, feeling rubbery as they shuffled closer and closer to the front doors. They'd be inside soon, off to different classes. He might not see Lia again all day. Who knows when he'd have a chance to speak with her one-on-one again.

It took all his courage to spit out the words, "Are you going?"

"Of course. I'm on the committee. We've met every few weeks during the summer to plan it all, and the committee members are all staying after school to decorate." She stopped before the front doors and turned toward Sam, her eyes wide with excitement. "You're new in town, you should come and meet everyone!"

Sam had never been to a dance before, but then he'd also never been directly invited to one either. Would Lia expect him to dance with her? The very thought of it made his knees tremble even more. That didn't stop him from blurting out an answer too loudly. "Of course!"

He felt his cheeks burn as he blushed.

"You'll have so much fun," Lia continued, emphasizing, "It's going to be great!"

Sam couldn't think of how to respond, so he just smiled and nodded.

They walked through the front doors to where the hallway split off in both directions. "Where's your locker?" Lia asked.

Sam pointed to the right.

"Ok, well I'm that way." Lia walked backwards in the other direction down the hall. She waved and shouted, "See you tonight!"

Sam watched her as she spun around and disappeared down the crowded hallway before he could think of anything else to say.

He floated toward his locker like he was riding on a cloud. Somehow he'd not only talked to a girl without making a fool of himself, but she'd even invited him to a dance. Things were looking up!

Then he remembered the run-in outside with Bradley Banks. Sam's shoulders slumped as his eyes darted across unfamiliar faces at their lockers. He didn't see any sign of Bradley, but that didn't mean he was safe.

A shrill ring sounded. The warning bell. One minute to get to class. The school day was just beginning, and now that he'd gained the school bully's attention, Sam had to figure out a way to survive the long hours between now and the Harvest Dance.

CHAPTER TWO

The bell rang to conclude fourth period English class. Sam snapped his textbook closed and dashed into the hallway.

He kept his head down as he hustled through the mass of students. Four out of six classes complete and he'd managed to avoid Bradley entirely. Now came the biggest test of the day, surviving lunch period.

When he safely reached his locker, Sam tossed his books inside and slapped a few dollars and loose coins onto the shelf. If Bradley caught him, at least the brute wouldn't get the satisfaction of finding anything to take.

Sam grabbed the lunch he'd packed at home - even before that morning's run-in with Bradley, he'd planned on avoiding the cafeteria - glanced both ways to make sure the coast was clear and, slamming his locker shut, turned to find a safe place to spend his lunch period.

He passed the Computer Lab, full of students playing games on dusty old machines, but it had a big 'NO FOOD OR DRINKS' sign on the door. A few classroom doors were open, but Sam didn't think introducing himself to a strange teacher and asking if he could get crumbs all over their desks was that great of an idea.

He'd nearly resigned to crouch down and just eat in the hallway when he saw the perfect hideout.

For the last three days, the door to the school library had been closed and the windows too dark to see inside. He'd even wondered if maybe the library was shut down for renovations.

But today was different. The door hung wide open. It was still dark inside, empty of either librarians or students, but enough light spilled in from the hallway and windows that Sam saw it was just an ordinary school library.

Bookshelves stuffed to overflowing lined the walls. Reading-themed posters filled any gaps, including one with a cartoon owl in glasses that read "I like books, how about WHOOO?". Several large tables stood like islands over the dark carpet for reading and studying.

Or maybe lunching.

Sam checked over the posters and signs taped to the wall beside the heavy wooden door. His eyes lingered on a flyer promoting that night's Under The Sea-themed Harvest Dance, but otherwise nothing that caught his attention. Nothing about forbidding food inside or declaring the library was off limits for lunch.

Sam quickly made sure he hadn't been followed, and then ducked inside the dark room.

He picked a chair deep in the shadows that faced out at the hallway. Sam didn't want to be noticed, but being caught unaware in a dark room would certainly be even worse than getting hassled in the lunch line.

He'd just taken a big bite from a peanut butter and honey sandwich, his favorite, when a shadow swooped through the doorway.

The shadow slapped a panel of light switches as it passed without slowing down. Fluorescent lights flickered to life. Sam blinked against the sudden brightness as the newcomer stopped abruptly at the sight of him.

Sam squinted as his eyes adjusted to the light. For a moment the figure looked hazy as a ghost, a white oval face in a swirling blur of darker shadows. He blinked again and saw it was just the effect of the woman's grey, curly hair blending in at the shoulders of her similarly-colored overcoat. The coat's hem nearly brushed the floor. She stared at him through white horn-rimmed glasses that made her dark eyes look too big for her face. An arched eyebrow rising above her glasses formed a wordless question.

Sam tried to smile and say hello, but through his mouthful of peanut butter it came out "hnn-uh".

"Who are you?" the woman asked. The words weren't the sharp tone of a teacher scolding a student, but warm like the voice of a grandmother or favorite aunt.

Sam held up a 'just one second' finger, and took a drink of water to wash down the sticky sandwich. "I'm Sam," he said once his mouth was no longer full. "Is it ok if I eat in here?"

"No trouble, none at all," the woman said, stepping into the library and turning to the right toward a still dark doorway. An office, Sam realized, though he'd not noticed it as he'd entered. A pile of books and papers appeared from beneath the crook of her arm where they'd been buried in the folds of her overcoat. She flung these inside the office, swept the coat from her shoulders to toss it inside as well, and then fluttered over to the table.

"I am Ms. Quick." She said with a slight bow of her head. "It is a pleasure to meet you, Sam." Her voice was soft, and the corners of her mouth curled as she spoke, as though she were remembering a fond memory.

Without the coat she looked smaller, no doubt shorter than Sam. Ms. Quick wore a cardigan sweater that also seemed to blend together with her hair, and an ankle length skirt the color of rich soil.

Sam waited for her demeanor to shift, for her mood to take on that of an authority figure giving a child directions, and for her to announce that he had to leave. But those words never came. She simply stood there watching him, as if waiting for him to speak.

"Are you the librarian?" Sam finally asked, more to break the silence than anything.

"The closest thing this school's got to one, I'm afraid." She pulled out a chair and sat down. "I actually own a store in town, selling knick knacks, and trinkets, and other curiosities to tourists. But budget cuts and other concerns that children shouldn't worry over threatened to close this library down!"

She paused, then shrugged. "Couldn't stand to see that happen. Too many of my own fond memories included libraries, I suppose. So I did the only thing I could, and volunteer two days a week."

Sam had taken another bite of his sandwich while Ms. Quick was talking, so he just nodded.

"What about you? What is a young man doing, eating his lunch alone and in the dark?"

"It's complicated." Sam mumbled. Ms. Quick arched her questioning eyebrow again and stared at him with unconvinced eyes.

"Ok," he started. "I'm hiding from someone."

Ms. Quick nodded slowly. "Of course." Then her eyes narrowed as she studied him. "A teacher? Unlikely, you seem too well mannered to be in trouble this early in the school year. A girl? No, I imagine you'd welcome that attention. An adversary? Close, but not quite. Ah ha!" She snapped her fingers. "You're hiding from an oppressor."

Sam shrugged. "Something like that." He muttered, stuffing the last bit of sandwich into his mouth.

Ms. Quick sat back in her chair and folded her arms. "Well, you're welcome to eat lunch here any Thursday or Friday that you like. But, if you want my opinion, the fastest way to deal with one of these," she made a face as she waved her hand with a flourish, trying to think of the right phrase before settling on "juvenile tormentors, is to make friends with other students and stick together."

"I already thought of that," Sam said with his mouth mostly full, but Ms. Quick still understood his words. "I'm not any good at making friends."

"Nonsense, I won't hear that. Mark my words, Sam. A bully will always pick on a loner, especially one who is new in town. But if you have allies at your side, they quickly show their true, cowardly, colors."

"Sure, that's good advice." Sam said, faking agreement. He'd heard all that before, and it was easier said than done.

She chuckled, then said, "Well, if you've got it all figured out then, I'll let you finish eating." Ms. Quick looked up at a clock on the wall. "The lunch hour is nearly gone, and you'll not want to be tardy for fifth period Science class." She stood and scampered to the office without another word, flicking the lights on in the small alcove and disappearing inside.

Ms. Quick was odd, Sam decided, but he was glad she'd let him stay. It felt good to eat his lunch in peace without having to watch his back the entire time.

Sam finished his lunch and stood up to go. He almost walked straight to the hallway without stopping, but at the last second turned and stuck his head into the office.

Ms. Quick sat behind a cluttered desk. She held a newspaper, THE MAPLETON GAZETTE, stretched before her. She took no notice of Sam standing in her doorway.

Her friendly face had changed composure. Now her brow was furrowed and her eyes narrow behind glasses as they scanned the words on the page. She shook her head as she read, as though disagreeing with the article. Her mouth had become a pinched, narrow line on her face, all traces of the warm smile gone.

"Ms. Quick?" Sam asked, against his better judgment.

Her angry eyes flashed up at him and Sam flinched against the stare.

Then she took a deep breath, calmly closed the newspaper and laid it down on the desk. Her face softened back to that of a kindly librarian, but he saw too a sadness in her eyes that hadn't been there before.

Sam's instincts said to run away, to not get involved. Instead, he cleared his throat. "Are you alright?"

Ms. Quick sighed and nodded her head slightly. "Just reading of things that should not come to pass. When you get to be as old as me, it's hard to watch beauty being taken from this world. More troubles that children shouldn't have to fret over, I'm afraid."

"What do you mean?"

"If you must know, some men in town mean to destroy a section of the forest. Apparently Mapleton needs a new shopping mall."

The hair on Sam's arms stood up and he felt goosebumps on his neck.

The night before, at dinner, his parents had discussed that very topic.

"Did you know they're planning on building a new shopping mall just off the highway? Not even five miles from here?" Dad had said, pointing at a map printed on the newspaper.

"Isn't that area mostly woods?" Mom asked as she'd dished up.

"That's right. Smack dab in the middle of old growth forest. Unbelievable." Sam had grabbed a scoop of pasta from the kettle, dropped it on his empty dinner plate, and drowned it in tomato sauce while his father's rant continued.

"This little town already has one mall. I thought we'd put this kind of mindless urban sprawl behind us when we moved to Mapleton?"

"You know, I'd heard that the existing mall was basically abandoned. Shut down, overrun with rats, condemned or something." Mom said, adding, "Sam, make sure to get some green beans too."

"They're supposed to start construction next week." Dad shook his head. "Some citizens are planning a protest, and I have half a mind to go join them."

That was all they'd said. Mom had changed the subject after that to ask how Sam's day at school had been.

When Ms. Quick spoke again, her voice jogged Sam back from the memory of the previous evening.

"There are trees there that have been alive since even before this country was founded."

"Whoa, really?" Sam tried to imagine how big a tree that old might be. Is that what Dad meant when he'd said 'old growth forests'?

She nodded sadly. "A forest teeming with life, and we humans think we can just knock it all down whenever we see fit. There is still magic in this world, and it pains me to think that younger generations will not get to enjoy the bit of it that's still out there. And it's harder still to think that maybe no one even appreciates it at all anymore, that none even care."

For a moment, Sam forgot about Bradley Banks and school dances, and instead felt sad for this nice lady. It was troubling to see her upset, especially after she'd been so kind to him.

"Is there anything I can do to help?" he finally asked.

Her smile broadened a bit even as Ms. Quick shook her head. "Unlikely, Sam, but I do appreciate the sentiment."

"Well, I just wanted to say thanks. For letting me eat in here, I mean."

"Of course." Ms. Quick slowly nodded once, squeezing her eyes closed as she did so. Then she looked up at him. "I commend your courage, Sam. It's never easy being the new kid in school. But you'll be fine, I can tell. You're tough and clever. You're almost like-"

Ms. Quick stopped abruptly and rubbed her chin. She spoke quietly, almost to herself. "Like a raccoon."

"They're often loners, you know," she continued, her voice returning to its regular volume. "But get a few of them together, and you never know what manner of mischief the little rascals might cook up."

She popped up from her desk, quicker then Sam was used to seeing people her age move.

"Anyway," her words came out in a rush as she scooped his arm into the crook of her elbow, "you should be off to Science class. Would hate for you to be late, get in trouble, and miss the dance". Her arm felt bony against his, and though Sam was a half head taller, she pulled him easily toward the library door. Ms. Quick was stronger than she looked.

She ushered him to the doorway, let go of his arm, and Sam's momentum carried him into the hallway.

"Thank you for coming by, Sam. I'm looking forward to speaking with you again."

He turned to wave, but the library door slammed shut. An instant later, the door's glass window went dark.

Sam looked around to see if anyone else had noticed the strange behavior from the part-time librarian. The other students were fumbling in their lockers, too preoccupied with their own conversations and with getting to class to notice Ms. Quick's commotion. He hurried away from the library.

What had suddenly gotten into Ms Quick, and why had she turned out the lights?

He was halfway through spinning in his locker combination when he stopped. Two questions popped into his head.

How had Ms. Quick known he had Science class next? And how had she known about his concerns with getting to the dance?

CHAPTER THREE

The inside of Mapleton Middle School had been transformed. Lia and the dance planning committee must have worked fast.

Sam walked beneath a banner that read 'Under the Sea' and hung across the hallway. Fluorescent lights covered in blue tissue paper cast the school in an ethereal glow while faint Calypso music filled the air. Sam stepped in time to the steel drums as he followed a group of dressed up classmates past clusters of construction paper fish taped to the lockers.

Lia appeared at his side. "What do you think?" She held her hands wide, looked up to the ceiling and gestured around at the hallway decorations. For a moment, looking at Lia, Sam forgot all about the dance.

She wore an emerald green dress with slender sleeves that went down almost to her elbows. Plastic combs in the shape of seashells held her long dark hair at the temples.

Sam almost blurted out that she looked like a mermaid in reply to her question, but caught himself, realizing she was asking about the decorations and not her outfit. "It's... it's like I'm in an aquarium."

Before he could react, Lia grabbed him in a lung-wringing octopus hug.

Sam gasped for breath when she let go. Lia hopped in place with a gleaming smile across her face. She darted away to welcome another group of classmates, but called back at him "Come find me for a dance later!"

Sam pulled at his collar. His tie suddenly felt too tight, like it was trying to choke him, and his legs felt wobbly. Whether it was caused by oxygen deprivation from Lia's suffocating hug or excitement at the prospect of dancing with her, Sam couldn't say.

It took Sam a second to collect himself and his mind drifted back to earlier that night.

"There's a school dance tonight. Could you drive me?"

Sam still could hardly believe he'd said those words. Based on his parents' stunned expressions, neither could they.

The only family member who hadn't been phased was Winnie, their dog. The move to Mapleton had transformed the big boxer-mix from the laziest dog Sam knew to one that always wanted to be outside. Right now she was laying by the front door, no doubt ready to rush out and continue her search for groundhogs in the grass or raccoons in the trash.

They'd been happy to take him, of course, and Dad had cooked dinner while Mom helped him pick out what to wear. And then Dad got out his favorite tie, navy and silver and patterned with paisleys, and showed Sam how to properly knot it.

"For good luck," Dad had said with a wink.

Now Sam floated toward the cafeteria, passing pink and green streamers pinned to the ceiling tiles that swayed like tendrils of seaweed and coral, and got in line with the rest of the students.

When it was his turn, Sam stepped up to the square card table where two women were sitting with an attendance list. The first was a smiling lady in a red sweater that Sam had never seen before. But the second he immediately recognized, surprised to see her here.

"Name?" Ms. Quick said without looking up. The part-time volunteer librarian's grey hair took on the color of the blue filtered light, and her glasses were down her nose as she traced a finger along the list of 7th and 8th graders.

"Hi, Ms. Quick."

"Oh! Sam!" she straightened in her chair and adjusted her glasses. "I'm so glad you were able to make it. Great place to make new friends." She winked at him.

"Sure, I guess." Sam said, clicking the plastic student ID card onto the table.

She nodded, found his name on the list, and put a check beside it. Sam scooped up his ID card, but Ms. Quick put a hand on his wrist. Again, her grip felt surprisingly strong.

"Just a moment, Sam." She turned to the woman in the red sweater. "Would you cover for me for a minute, dear? Thank you." Ms. Quick stood, scooped a weather beaten leather purse from the floor beside her seat, and pulled Sam after her.

She led him away from the cafeteria line, far enough that their voices were drown out by the hum of student conversations and tropical music. Sam glanced back at the line to make sure Lia or Bradley weren't watching, but he didn't recognize any of the faces in line and none of the unfamiliar students paid him any notice.

"I had a thought after our conversation today. It seems we've both been troubled," Ms. Quick said, opening her purse. "A young man, even one so clever as you, might need a hand discovering the confidence you already possess inside. At the same time, a silly old thing like me may want to share a bit of what I appreciate so much. We may be able to help each other."

Sam hadn't ever been the most popular kid. Not at his old elementary school in the city, not on his baseball teams, and things were off to a rocky start at Mapleton Middle School. He'd never been able to unlock the formula for popularity, but even he knew that an elderly librarian's help probably didn't factor into the equation.

But Ms. Quick had agreed to let him hide out in the library whenever she was around, and he remembered feeling bad when he'd stuck his head in her office and seen something so deeply troubling her, so he just smiled and listened.

"This is for you." She pulled an item from her purse and handed it to Sam.

It was soft in his hands, and it took Sam a moment to recognize it as a knitted winter stocking hat; charcoal colored, tipped with hints of silver, and constructed of yarn and felt.

Sam turned it over in his hands as Ms. Quick continued. "It's a rare thing, this hat." She mused, "Not the most fashionable, perhaps. But I think, Sam, that you are the one to whom it may bring a certain amount of luck."

He found himself staring into black button eyes that gleamed with the blue glow of the filtered fluorescent lights. Black felt patches were stitched to the front of the hat beneath the buttons, and a pair of triangular points stuck up from either side of the hat's rounded top.

Sam recognized the face. "A raccoon?"

"I can think of no better totem for you, young man." Ms. Quick said with a smile.

The hat was built for warmth, that was for sure. If he were to pull it on, which Sam was not about to do in sight of other students, a pair of side flaps would cover his ears and the sides of his face. At the end of each of the side flaps a two-foot strand of braided yarn draped down and ended in a ball. Three triangular pieces of black felt were stitched to each ball, giving them a faint resemblance to clawed front paws.

"What's a totem?" Sam wondered aloud.

"Some cultures believe that everyone has a spirit animal. A creature of the wild that mirrors or compliments one's own traits. A totem." Ms. Quick said, sounding like she were reciting from a library book.

"You, Sam, are clever, independent and, I'm guessing, possibly a bit too smart for your own good at times, yes?" She chuckled. "That would describe the roguish raccoon to a fault. They're the bandits of the forest, resourceful and bright, with just a little too much confidence. It's that confidence I think you lack. Maybe some of this raccoon's will rub off on you?"

Sam shot another wary glance back at the line of students checking in for the dance. It didn't seem anyone had noticed him speaking with the librarian, or the odd gift she'd given him. "Well, thanks. I guess." Sam quickly muttered as he stuffed the hat into his back pocket.

"Don't mention it." Ms. Quick replied. "And a bit of advice. If you decide to wear the hat, others may look at you a bit… differently. In event of that, act with kindness and be yourself. You may be surprised by what happens."

Ms. Quick hadn't exaggerated when she'd remarked the hat wasn't fashionable. In fact, it was downright childish. Sam knew he couldn't wear it, not unless he wanted to damage his reputation at Mapleton Middle School beyond repair. He'd never hear the end of it.

Later he'd stuff it in his locker or stash it back safely at home. For now, it could stay in his pocket. The line of students had thinned, and the dance would be starting soon.

"Oh, and Sam," Ms. Quick said as he pulled open the doorway to the cafeteria. "Nice tie!"

The cafeteria had undergone a similar sea-themed makeover. There were more streamers and blue light filters, but also clumps of balloons in shades of teal and green tied to chair backs like underwater bubbles. The aroma of baked goods wafting from a dessert table overpowered the smell of fried food that usually lingered in the cafeteria even when lunch wasn't being served.

Seventh and eighth graders milled together in clumps and cliques, girls in dresses of every color and boys fidgeting with their ties. Most kids stood approximately where they'd normally sit, if their tables hadn't been pushed to the edges of the room to clear space for the dance floor.

Without a familiar group of friends to latch onto, Sam went to stand by the dessert table with a few circling scavengers waiting for permission to fill their plates. A teacher stood guard to make sure no one touched the food prior to the official start.

Sam scanned the room, recognizing a few faces from his classes or the bus, but no one he'd spoken to or gotten to know. Lia was nowhere to be seen, probably still in the halls playing greeter. There also was no sign of Bradly Banks. Had Lia made good on her threat and gotten him banned from the event?

Sam's thoughts were interrupted by a soft whimper behind him.

"Not until after announcements," sighed a boy with red hair, half to Sam and half to the dessert table.

Sam turned around. "What's that?" he asked.

The boy stepped closer to Sam. "They said no desserts until after Mrs. Betty makes the opening announcements," and then, holding up a hand to his mouth to shield his words, "I snitched one of the double-chocolate chip cookies when no one was looking." His dress shirt was too big, and a baggy sleeve half enveloped his hand as he gave a covert thumbs-up. Sam saw incriminating brown crumbs on the boy's collar. The shirt's pale yellow color seemed to clash with his neatly parted red hair.

"I'll make sure to try one." Sam said.

"I'm Charlie," the boy volunteered. "Are you new here?"

Sam nodded and introduced himself.

"In that case, you'll need the full tour." Charlie waved Sam over to the table and proceeded to point out baked goods of interest, rattling off names Sam didn't recognize.

"The brownies are Jamie's mom's special recipe and are always wonderful. I think my friend Stevie brought the coconut cake. His dad's a great baker. Avoid the rice krispy treats though. Mrs. Stewart's hair is thinning, and I found a hair in one at last year's Halloween party."

The teacher on dessert table patrol finally shushed Charlie, and pointed toward the center of the room.

Mrs. Betty strode through the crowd around the dance floor. The Vice Principal was easy to spot towering over everyone. She carried a clipboard in one hand and picked up a microphone as she reached the DJ booth in the other.

"Welcome Mapleton Middle School to your Under the Sea fall dance." She said in a no nonsense voice. Then Sam and everyone else in the room winced as feedback from the microphone screeched over the speakers.

Mrs. Betty turned and made a 'turn it down signal' at a teenage DJ behind the booth. The boy rolled his eyes before adjusting a few dials. Mrs. Betty patted the microphone with an open palm and said, "Testing. Testing. Alright, that's better."

She gestured to a group of nine students lined up along the edge of the dance floor. Lia stood at the far left of the line, sequins in her green dress catching some of the light and all of Sam's attention.

"Thank you to our dance planning committee for making this such a magical evening. These student volunteers have done a wonderful job. Remember, if you'd like to help plan our next event, there will be a sign-up sheet in the office."

Sam had a sudden thought. Maybe Lia would be planning the next event, too? Would it be weird for a new kid to sign up to help?

As Sam considered what joining the committee might do for his popularity, a scolding voice interrupted his wandering thoughts.

"Charles! Wait until Mrs. Betty is finished," hissed the teacher on dessert table patrol. Charlie spun away from the table, still chewing.

"And finally, a few safety announcements." Mrs. Betty continued. "There is to be no wandering or loitering away from the cafeteria. Students are to stay out of the hallways unless going to or coming from the restroom. And please check out with me before departing for the evening so that all students are accounted for." She waved the clipboard over her head for emphasis. "Now," her businesslike tone shifted as she raised her voice, "let's get this party started!"

A screech of feedback filled the room again before the frowning teenage DJ hit a button. From the speakers thumped a Top 40 song that Sam guessed he'd heard a hundred times over the summer. The bass was so heavy Sam felt it in his stomach.

He watched Lia and the planning committee rush onto the dance floor while the majority of the crowd hung back on the fringes. Lia hopped around in circles, smiling and waving her hands overhead.

Now was his chance. Sam clenched his fists and tried to tell himself to get out there and not be timid.

He took one big step toward the dance floor, then someone tapped him on the shoulder.

"Here!" Charlie shouted over the music, presenting Sam with the recommended double-chocolate chip cookie pinched in a napkin.

Sam mouthed 'thanks', and took it. He'd eat one cookie, he decided, and then go dance.

One cookie became two. And then he needed a drink.

By the time Sam finished his punch, Lia had disappeared from the dance floor. Sam circled the room, weaving between tables and clumps of kids, avoiding the dance floor as though it were made of lava. He tried to look cool, indiscreet and casual while he searched for Lia and their promised dance.

In truth he felt very self conscious, circling the underwater dance like a timid shark, feeling certain that other kids were noticing his aimless drifting. He thought about waiting at one of the empty tables. Then the fear of other kids thinking he was a weirdo for sitting by himself made him reconsider. He still didn't see where Lia had wandered off to.

He needed to stall, to kill some time, so he slipped out the back door of the cafeteria next to the dessert table and into the hallway, heading toward the bathroom.

Only the faint red glow from overhead EXIT signs lit the way through the halls. There were no streamers, balloons, or construction paper fish taped anywhere, there'd been no reason for the planning committee to decorate this side of the school. Any traces of the island music that had greeted him when arriving for the dance was lost beneath the heavy thump of bass coming from the cafeteria behind him.

No matter how lightly he tried to step, Sam's shoes echoed down the long empty hallways. Windows into empty classrooms stared at him like black eyes as he passed. His skin tingled and the hair on the back of his neck stood on end. At that moment, he felt alone, like he were the last person on earth.

He decided to turn back, even taking a backwards step toward the cafeteria and away from the silent emptiness of the dark hallway, when he heard a faint commotion ahead; words he couldn't make out and then a locker door slamming.

Sam shook his head at his own foolishness. The sound of another student in the hallway brought reassurance, and chased away the creeping fear that had almost overtaken him. It was just Mapleton Middle School. He continued forward.

He reached the bathroom, a water fountain separating two doors labeled Boy's and Girl's. Sam was in the midst of a long drink from the fountain, cool water washing the taste of cookies and punch from his mouth, when he heard muted voices from ahead and around the corner. Faint laughter, too, and then another locker closing.

Was it burglars? Party-crashing high schoolers?

Whatever the case, Sam knew he should turn around. No one was supposed to be in the hallway. Mrs. Betty had made that clear in her opening speech. He needed to retreat back to the cafeteria.

Instead, Sam swallowed his fear with a last gulp of water, and his curiosity drew him toward the sound.

The voices grew louder with each step. Sam peeked around the corner.

The sound earlier hadn't been someone closing a locker. It had been someone shoved into one.

Charlie's face was pressed against the wall of lockers lining the hallway, like a suspect on a police show. Two looming shadows held him there by the scruff of his too-large yellow dress shirt. Sam recognized one by both his hulking size and spiky hair. Bradley Banks.

"There's always a bathroom toll, piggy." Bradley's tone was taunting.

"Sorry guys," Charlie said through his pinched face. "I didn't know the rules applied outside of official school hours. I don't have any change, honest."

"What do you think, Mitch? Is he holding out on us?"

The other kid, Mitch, said something but it sounded indecipherable through dumb laughter.

"I agree," Bradley said. "Check his pockets."

Mitch started patting Charlie down. Sam's breath stuck in his chest, fearing the two bullies would hear him. His fists clenched and his jaw tightened. He knew he should step in. Maybe they'd back off if the numbers were even, or if there were a witness? Or maybe they'd abandon harassing Charlie and choose to chase Sam? He might be able to outrun the pair. Maybe.

But instead of acting, instead of moving forward to help, Sam took a careful step back, retreating from the confrontation.

He spun around, and started hustling back toward the cafeteria. Then his stomach tensed with guilt, tying in a tighter knot than the tie around his neck, and his legs wobbled like they were made of pudding. He scolded himself.

Coward.

Wimp.

Sam felt like he might throw up.

Friends were supposed to stick together, to help each other through tough times. They'd only just met, but Charlie had been nice, friendly, welcoming and eager to talk to Sam.

And now Sam was abandoning him. He staggered sideways, bumped against a classroom door, and slumped to the ground, feeling like a slimy puddle.

"Gross!" a voice echoed from around the corner. "He's got cake in his pocket!"

The familiar sound of Bradley's baying laugh filled the darkness. "Piggy, you're always good for a laugh. Beat it, but don't let me catch you out here again."

Rapid, clapping steps grew louder, and Charlie came into sight. Charlie's arms pumped and his cheeks puffed as he scampered down the hallway, his baggy shirt billowing behind him. If he even saw Sam, slumped there on the floor against the door in the darkness, Charlie made no indication.

"Sorry," Sam whispered as he watched Charlie disappear into the darkness.

Sam knew he needed to get up, follow Charlie and escape. But the guilt weighed him down. He'd had a chance to stand up for Charlie, to be a friend. Instead he'd balked.

"I guess it's my lucky day," Bradley said. Sam turned to see Bradley and Mitch standing over him. They glowed red in the auxiliary lighting from the EXIT signs. Lost in his own thoughts, he'd not heard them approach.

"Go away," was all Sam could manage.

Bradley's face bent into a wicked sneer. "Grab him."

Mitch lunged forward like a trained dog. Sam tried to duck away, but Mitch gripped his arms with frosting smeared fingers.

Why had he left the safety of the dance floor, the dessert table, and Vice Principal Mrs. Betty?

Mitch hauled Sam to his feet and slammed his back against the locker. His big hands were like clamps on Sam's arms. Mitch wasn't much taller than Sam, but was twice as wide.

Bradley stood back with his arms folded across his chest watching Mitch work, like a mentor critiquing an apprentice. "I think it's time for an initiation." In the dim red light, Bradley's eyes and mouth made deep shadows, like a reverse jack-o-lantern.

Bradley kicked open the bathroom door. Fluorescent light spilled into the dark hallway. Mitch spun Sam around and marched him toward the light. Sam tried to resist, but Mitch dragged him along easily and the door banged closed behind them.

Sam thrashed against Mitch's iron grip. "Help!" his voice echoed off the tiled walls and metal bathroom stalls.

"Nobody's gonna hear you over the music, Wimp." Bradley balled up a wad of paper towels from the dispenser. "You just need to *chill* out." Bradley stuffed the wad of paper towels into the sink's drain and turned on the water.

With a precision that must have come with lots of practice, Bradley and Mitchell scooped Sam into the air and flipped him upside down.

Their shouts and laughter mixed with Sam's cries for help, echoing to a wordless din in the bathroom.

The first jolt of cold water on Sam's head felt like an electric shock.

CHAPTER FOUR

Though he'd crouched beneath the hand driers until his legs burned with the effort, Sam's shoes still felt squishy as he stomped across the cafeteria.

Eight couples swayed to a slow ballad out on the dance floor, their stiff arms and tense shoulders betraying nervousness. The rest of the students sat with their elbows on the lunch tables ringing the dance floor, leaning with chins on their hands and watching the dancing couples with a mix of boredom and jealousy. No one noticed the disheveled Sam marching toward Mrs. Betty.

She raised an eyebrow as Sam approached. "What in the world happened to you?"

"I'd like to report a crime," Sam said, grabbing his ruined tie and holding it in a right angle out from his neck. It was fat and water-logged, looking more like a stubby earthworm than his father's favorite. "Destruction of property." He didn't care what being a tattle-tale would do to his reputation at Mapleton Middle School. Enough was enough.

She clicked her pen and readied her clipboard. "Tell me what happened."

Sam spared no detail, telling her about heading into the hallway to use the restroom, and seeing another student pressed against the locker. He omitted Charlie's name. No sense in him suffering any further harassment that might come from Sam being a snitch.

"It was Bradley and Mitch. Then they grabbed me and…"

At the mention of the names, Mrs. Betty stopped writing. She'd looked up from the clipboard to stare at him, and Sam's story lost its momentum.

"I think I see what happened here." Mrs. Betty clicked her pen closed and holstered it beneath the clipboard's clamp, "You boys were goofing off in the hallways when I explicitly instructed you not to."

"No, I was-"

"When your games resulted in this," Mrs. Betty gestured at his still damp clothes, "you felt foolish, and thought to make yourself feel better by getting others in trouble. Yes?"

"That's not-"

"Young man. I'm not sure how things were done at your old school, but here in Mapleton we understand boys-will-be-boys. And I'm not about to punish one party just because the other participant decided they didn't want to live with the consequences of their rough-housing."

Sam grit his teeth. If Mrs. Betty would let him get a word in edgewise, he could explain that's not what happened at all.

Bradley and Mitch had held him upside down, dunking his head over and over into the sink, yowling like baboons the entire time. Only when Sam went stopped shouting or fighting back and went limp had they grown bored with their game and dropped him to the floor.

Sam tried to start over. "You don't understand. That's not what happened."

"I've heard just about enough. I'll not have you come into this school and immediately start throwing around accusations and causing trouble over some misunderstanding with another student."

Misunderstanding? Sam's mouth hung open, slack in disbelief.

The beats of a faster song replaced the ballad, and the dance floor flooded with students hopping up and down in unison.

Mrs. Betty waved a dismissive hand as she went on. "I'm sure you're as much to blame as poor Bradley and Mitch. It seems just because they're bigger than most kids they get accused of almost anything."

Sam said nothing. He hung his head, defeated and stunned.

"Now if you'll excuse me." Ms Betty hurried away to go scold a boy sitting with his feet up on a table.

"I can't believe it," Sam thought aloud.

Lia appeared from the dance floor. "There you are, Sam! Come join us!" As Lia approached, she got a closer look. "Wait, what happened? Are you alright?"

Sam felt numb, far from alright. "She didn't believe me."

Lia followed Sam's eyes to where they stared at Mrs. Betty's back in stunned disbelief.

"Oh." Her mouth curled to a forced, sad smile. "I think I understand."

Sam shook his head trying to get the jumble of thoughts to straighten out. Anger. Disappointment. Fear. Betrayal. Embarrassment. They all bounced around in his brain, screaming for attention.

"I've got to go," he finally said.

She squeezed his arm, in the same place Mitchell had grabbed. Sam could tell he'd have a bruise. "Did you want to dance?"

Sam absolutely did, more than anything. But he felt pressure in his eyes, tears that he fought to keep back. All he needed was to start crying on the dance floor with Lia to complete his night and become the laughing stock of the entire school.

"Next time," he managed to say, barely keeping his composure as he slipped out the cafeteria's front door and into the hall.

Lia was not so easily evaded. "Sam, wait." Her shoes clicked after him. Sam stopped, sniffled, and wiped his eyes with his sleeve before turning around.

The card table where Ms. Quick and the red sweatered woman had sat checking attendance was empty, and someone had shut off the Calypso music. Sam and Lia were alone.

"It's going to be alright," she said.

"No it isn't." Sam shook his head. "You don't understand."

Lia shook her head. "Actually, I think I do. Let me show you something."

She led him down the decorated hallway. They passed more empty classrooms, cork bulletin boards, and trophy cases. The music from the dance faded with each step.

"Bradley always picks on the new kids," Lia said unprompted.

"Then why doesn't Mrs. Betty do something about it? Why didn't she believe me?"

They approached the front office. A wall of glass windows separated it from the hallway. During the day it would be bustling with activity, the long desk staffed with several attendants assisting students, giving information to parents, and accepting deliveries. Now the windows were as dark and empty as the classrooms.

"Over here," Lia said, pointing to a wall full of faculty portraits. Sam looked at frame after frame of smiling faces, only a few of which he recognized. But when he got to Mrs. Betty's portrait, his hands clenched to fists.

It was unmistakably her, with the short blond hair and wide smile. Beneath the portrait was a brass plaque label.

Betty Banks, Vice Principal.

Sam couldn't believe it, though he could suddenly see the resemblance. From hair color, to smile, to gargantuan size.

"She's Bradley's mom." He muttered, wanting to punch the picture.

Lia put her hand on Sam's shoulder. "I was new to town two years ago. My family moved from…"

"Hawaii?" Sam guessed. Bradley's taunting 'aloha' from that morning when Lia had stuck up for him by the bus suddenly made sense.

Lia surprised him with a laugh. "No, actually. Florida. Bradley's pretty ignorant, and doesn't seem to know the difference. But no matter how many times I tried to correct him, all I heard was 'where's your grass skirt? Hula for me island girl. Why don't you bring me a pineapple' the whole year. Relentless."

"What a jerk."

"Yeah, but I could just ignore him. Other kids had it worse. At least he didn't try to steal my lunch money or, you know, dunk me in a sink. You're not the first new kid I've seen soaked, if that makes you feel any better."

"So what about Mitch?" Sam asked, and then putting emphasis on her actual name, "*Mrs. Banks* let's him run wild too?"

"As long as he's partnered with Bradley when breaking the rules, he seems to fall under the same umbrella of protection."

Sam's shoulders slumped. "What should I do?"

Lia shrugged. "Ride it out. Avoid them until they decide to pick on someone else. That's what I did. I stopped being scared of him and just ignored his name calling."

Sam made a face. A year was an awful long time to keep his guard up. And then it would just be some other poor kid, like Charlie, that had to take the abuse from Bradley, Mitch, and whatever other goons might run with them. "That sounds like a crummy way to handle it."

"Not much else we can do." Lia said, and then added while motioning down the hallway. "We should go back."

Sam eyed the doors leading outside. "No, I think I'm done for the night."

Lia reached out and squeezed his hands. "It'll get better. I swear. Sit by me tomorrow on the bus?"

"Sure," Sam managed a smile. "Thanks for showing me the picture, and telling me about your own experience."

The sad smile danced across her face. Lia nodded once, and then turned back toward the cafeteria as Sam slipped out the school's main door.

Crisp autumn air jabbed at him. A line of SUVs sat idling along the side of the school. He didn't see his parents' hatchback, and the hallway clock had said it would be almost 20 minutes until they arrived.

The steady September breeze quickly reminded Sam of his still damp clothes and hair. Sam crossed his arms, wished he'd brought a jacket, and shivered. For only a moment he thought about going back inside. But he'd had his fill of bullies, dances, and corrupt administrators. He'd rather shiver.

A short brick wall separated the sidewalk from landscaping that lined the school. It was mostly decorative, only three feet high, but kept students from trudging across the flowers and lawn along the school's front. Sam found a spot to sit down and wait for his parents.

It felt like he was sitting on something. An uneven section of the wall, a lump in the bricks. Then Sam realized it wasn't the wall, but rather something in his pocket.

He tilted sideways, realization and remembrance dawning on him as he pulled the forgotten hat from his back pocket. He'd been so preoccupied with dances, snack tables, and Bradley that Ms. Quick's gift had slipped his mind entirely.

Sam turned the hat in his hands until he stared down into the black button eyes of the raccoon face. There was something unsettling about how the hat felt to his fingertips.

The hat wasn't wet, not even damp. It should have been soaked like the rest of him after his run-in with Bradley and Mitch.

As clouds passed rapidly overhead, the moon's glare made the button eyes glimmer as though they were alive.

"Too weird," he said aloud.

It really was a dorky hat. Childish, too. For someone ten years younger than a seventh grader.

The breeze stiffened. Its ever-changing direction poked at Sam's damp clothing from every angle. Far away night birds sang mournful songs at the chill of a fast approaching autumn. An owl, stealthy and invisible somewhere overhead, called out "who who, who-who-who?"

Sam looked up and down the sidewalk but didn't see any other kids outside. None of the parents in the SUV line were paying attention either, their silhouettes had a pale glow as they stared endlessly at their phones.

It would be easy to just toss the silly hat into the shrubs.

But it had been a gift. He remembered Ms. Quick's sad and angered eyes in her office as she read the newsaper and decided he couldn't just throw it away.

"I cannot think of a better totem for a young man." Ms. Quick had said. Sam shook his head remembering the words as his fingers fiddled with the braided strands that were meant to represent paws. He could use a little cunning, a little cleverness, and a little confidence after this night.

The wind gusted harder, sending clumps of dried lawn clippings and discarded candy wrappers tumbling down the sidewalk. His teeth started chattering. Sam turned away from the cold, and looked down again at the hat, into the eyes. Still just buttons catching moonlight.

He looked both ways. No one was watching.

Against his better judgment, Sam pulled the hat over his damp hair.

Immediately warmth enveloped him. The hat fit like a hug. His teeth stopped chattering, and his shivering limbs steadied. Even the breeze seemed diminished, though the flurry of debris still drifting down the sidewalk suggested otherwise.

He reached up and touched the hat. The delicate material seemed even softer than when he'd held it in his hands. It didn't pinch or itch. The perfect size.

He forgot about the cold as Sam's mind raced. He wished he could fix it all. His own troubles, for starters, but other things as well. Stop Bradley from picking on everybody. Fix whatever had made Ms. Quick so sad. But how?

Sam hopped to his feet atop the wall, and started pacing along the narrow bricks. No longer distracted with freezing, he perceived the night with clearer eyes. His ears picked up the crisp sound of dried grass blowing along pavement and how that sound differed from the artificial rustling the plastic candy wrappers made. If he concentrated, he swore he could hone in on the scent of each idling SUV's distinct exhaust fumes.

And from the corner of the brick school, Sam saw a pale, ghostly face staring down at him.

Sam's pacing stopped and crouched down on all fours to meet the gaze of the moonlit face.

The face slowly rotated until its eyes, black and deep as pits, lined up vertically, as if they were stacked one on top of the other instead of side-by-side.

The mournful hooting hadn't been from a passing owl, Sam realized then, but from an owl perched atop the school. A barn owl.

It watched him for a moment more. Then, with a flourish, the owl spread its wings and leapt from the school. Its feathers caught the breeze as it wheeled skyward. Sam's eyes tried to follow, but the owl disappeared into the night's twirling clouds.

"Hey wild man," a familiar voice called.

His mother was smiling, leaning out the rolled down car window.

Sam hopped down from the wall. "I didn't see you pull up."

He fell into the back seat and buckled up. His father adjusted the rear view mirror. "Sam, what the heck happened to your tie?"

★ ★ ★

He could almost taste their disappointment in the air. Their sadness, too. That was almost worse than them being angry at him.

"Who did this, Sam?" Mom asked as they drove toward home.

"I don't know, I'd never seen them before," he lied. The last thing Sam needed was his parents raising a stink at school. Right now Mrs. Betty, no, *Mrs. Banks*, was only ignoring what her son was doing to Sam. What would happen if Sam got on her bad side? He'd end up in detention, or worse, for no reason.

That was it, they'd said. The three of them would go to Mapleton Middle School together in the morning and get to the bottom of this with the principal. Mom worked at her phone to rearrange her next morning's schedule, and Dad said he'd need to send some emails when they got home to do the same.

Gravel crunched beneath their tires as the car pulled down their driveway. Dad sighed as they stopped, looked back at Sam in the mirror and said, "Sorry buddy. I thought you'd have an easier time here."

Sam didn't respond, and just hung his head away from his father's reflected stare. Why couldn't he just fit in? Dragging his parents into it would only make things worse, he was convinced.

He hurried upstairs without any more discussion to get ready for bed.

Winnie pushed her way through the cracked bathroom door as Sam brushed his teeth. She sat down, leaned against Sam's leg, and whimpered as she looked up at him with long, sorrowful eyes.

"It's ok," he said, scratching Winnie's chin. "Tomorrow will be better. Maybe."

Sam went to his room, changed out of his dance clothes, and put on his pajamas. He draped his father's ruined tie over the desk chair before hitting the lights and crawling under the covers.

A whispering rustle made him roll over to stare out the window.

The forest bordering their backyard had become a swirling mass in the wind. Their leaves rippled like a river's rapids, and the gusting wind sent waves through the wood. Sam put his head to his pillow and the window to his back.

A tassel tickled at his neck and he realized the raccoon hat still covered his head.

Mom and Dad hadn't said a word about it. Too focused on his ruined tie and formulating a plan, he guessed. That should have been Sam's first clue that something strange was happening, but he was too exhausted from his day to think on it.

Exhaustion made his eyes heavy as bricks as memories of the day tumbled through his mind, and he fell asleep without pulling off the strange raccoon hat.

CHAPTER FIVE

Bizarre dreams troubled him.

First there was one where Sam found himself suspended upside down in an aquarium. Talking fish kept floating by, all speaking at once. An angelfish with Lia's voice sang him songs from the radio before a pair of walruses chased her away. The smaller walrus had Bradley's smile and the larger one carried a clipboard beneath a shiny brown flipper.

Sam's next dream took him to a narrow cave passageway. He followed it deeper and deeper into the earth, phosphorescent mushrooms glowing red providing the only light. Fat earthworms the size of his arm crawled along the walls. In the crimson light he saw they were patterned with paisleys, plaids, and stripes, like water logged neck ties. Hundreds of them. They squished and squirmed through the tunnels leaving gooey, dye stained trails behind.

Sam shot up in his bed. Cool moonlight shone across his blankets, strong enough to cast shadows in the room. The wind had ceased its roaring and all was quiet. His throat felt dry as sand, and he climbed out of bed to get a drink.

The room felt wrong. Everything was too big.

Another dream, he guessed. His bed loomed overhead like a house and cardboard boxes on the floor, still waiting to be unpacked from their move, were the size of cars.

When he went to the door, he had to stand on his tiptoes to reach the doorknob. He tried turning it, but the door was stuck in the frame and did not swing open.

The floorboards creaked in the hallway outside. Slow footsteps approaching. Something large. Sam let go of the door.

The creaking stopped just outside Sam's bedroom.

THUMP. It sounded like a battering ram against the door. The door shook in the frame but remained stuck. Sam backed away. Dream or not, he didn't want to face what was on the other side.

THUMP. Coins, pencils, and knick knacks littering Sam's desk rattled at the impact. The door stayed closed.

THUMP.

POP.

The door flew open and banged against the wall. A hulking, four-legged creature filled the doorway. Teeth and claws and bristly hair, all crouched in shadows. A deep growl, like the engine of an accelerating school bus, rumbled from the beast.

Sam bumped against the wall, not realizing he'd still been backing away from the door.

The creature tensed, ready to pounce. It growled again, and then-

Wiggled its butt?

An instant too late, Sam recognized the monster. It lunged forward and Sam leapt straight in the air, only to land on the beast's back.

Winnie's back. He scrambled across the dog and ran to the door.

Sam couldn't believe it. What kind of an idiot dreams of their own dog trying to kill them?

The dream made his legs feel odd, wobbly and off balance. His bare feet didn't seem to have the right traction, either. It was like the floor had iced over.

Sam banged against the wall's wooden molding as he slipped rounding the corner into the hallway. Then he found his footing and sprinted down the hall. Moments later he heard another thump that could only be Winnie hitting the wall, too. He didn't look back and he just ran harder for the stairs.

He jumped onto the wooden banister and rode it like a sled toward the living room. At the bottom the railing turned up like a ramp, and launched Sam into the air. The couch broke his fall as he tumbled across cushions and pillows.

Winnie reached the bottom of the stairs as Sam struggled to reorient himself. The big dog was having a hard time getting traction, too. Her feet slipped and slid on the polished hardwood floor like a baby deer on ice. Menacing white teeth glowed in the moonlight as she finally rounded the front of the couch.

Sam grabbed hold of the towering couch back, like his room it was three-times its usual size, and pulled himself up to the top. Winnie jumped up, landing where he'd crashed just moments before.

Outside of dreamworld, Sam would have shouted at Winnie for being on the furniture, and she would have sheepishly gotten down. This dream version of Winnie had monstrous teeth, so Sam didn't take any chances stopping to scold her.

Sam scurried on all fours along the couch back. Winnie lunged for him, paws first, so hard it started tipping. Pushing with all his might, Sam launched himself at the kitchen table.

He fell short, tumbling underneath the table and banging his head against a stout wooden leg. The couch tumbled like a felled tree onto its back. It pitched Winnie forward and she rolled off.

"Winnie!" a shout came from upstairs.

That distracted her long enough for Sam to find his feet and scurry out from under the table. He ran on all fours through the kitchen. Cabinets, the stove and refrigerator rose around him like houses. Sam sprinted toward the back door. He knew he couldn't reach the handle, but he had a better idea.

Sam hit the rubber-flapped doggy-door with his shoulder and burst outside. He rolled down the three wooden steps leading to the back yard, somersaulted once, and then scrambled away from the house without slowing to look back. In the waking world they hadn't been able to coax Winnie through the doggy door, but Sam wasn't taking any chances.

He was halfway across the moon drenched grass and picking up speed before Sam realized he was still running on all fours.

The woods swayed as if waving hello as he ran down the hill toward them. Sam shuddered as he slipped beneath their long moon-shadow and then into the darkness beneath their boughs.

Sam jumped a rotten old log and landed in a puddle of mucky, stagnant water. He spat out the retched taste from his mouth as he continued, deeper into the woods.

The trees became a blur as he ran further and deeper into the dream. Sam didn't dare look back for fear that the Winnie-shaped monster would catch him.

Long fingered branches with leaves at their ends slapped for his face while roots and rocks tried to trip up his toes. But Sam was too quick on four feet, his balance too steady. He ducked the branches and skipped over stones. He tasted the wind and could hear it urging the branches to move faster. They whipped and swiped but came up empty.

Sam did not slow even when his legs and lungs began to burn, though he couldn't remember ever being tired in a dream before.

He came to a stream, just a small creek a few inches deep and not much wider, trickling between smooth stones and exposed roots. Sam ran through it, his fingers and toes tasting the water's chill.

He raced through woods and dreams beneath a bright autumn moon. Great trees towered over head, reaching for the heavens with uncountable fingertips, but even they could not fully hide the moon's glare. Sam weaved between the trees, running from one patch of moonlight to the next, using them like a path.

Miles and hours passed in an instant, the time and distance distorted by his mind in ways that only dreams can conjure.

At once the forest parted and made way, as if keeping a respected distance from some royal figure. Sam found himself in a clearing, and his feet finally stopped fleeing from the ferocious dream-Winnie-monster. He walked, still on four feet, through a great circular clearing, illuminated almost bright as day beneath the moon's unobstructed gaze.

He pushed through grasses as tall as his chin that ended in tiny flecks of seed husks. Vibrant bushes grew in clumps, their deep green leaves and red fruit glowing beneath the moon's light. He didn't stop for a snack or to rest,

Sam pressed on toward the clearing's center as if he were pulled by a magnet.

A dozen playful squirrel faces looked at him in delight as they wove in and out of the foliage. Their heads tilted with curiosity at this newcomer to their glade. They didn't run from Sam, in fact they seemed to be flocking towards him. The dozen became fifty, then the fifty became a hundred and more. They chittered with laughter as they followed him forward.

At the clearing's center a great oak rose from the ground. The moon touched each of the oak leaves and gave it a shimmer. Sam stopped, his mouth falling open. It could have been due to the oak's isolated stance with no other trees to compare it against, but it seemed to stretch higher into the sky, twice the reach of the woods he'd passed through.

Round, symmetrical, perfect. The oak stood unchallenged by pine or maple, and untouched by lightning, disease, or man.

Sam had only a moment to gape before something grabbed him by the hands, pulled him to his feet, and spun him around.

A squirrel, almost tall enough to look Sam in the eye, held him by the hands. The squirrel bobbed its head back and forth as if to some song Sam couldn't hear, and together they spun around and round.

The fact that there was a squirrel large enough to hold Sam by the hand should have sent him screaming in a panic, fleeing from the clearing, away from the kingly oak tree, and its over-sized squirrel subjects. But instead Sam could only laugh.

The sound startled his squirrel dance partner, and it darted away. Sam was only abandoned for a moment before another enormous squirrel took the first one's place. Its nose twitched as it caught Sam's hands, and the spinning continued.

When the second squirrel let go, a third quickly replaced it. Then a fourth, and many more. The squirrels cut in more quickly now, sometimes after just one spin.

If only the Mapleton Middle School dance had been this much fun! Sam thought about Lia, and hoped she might appear in this wild, dancing dream. But trying to make something happen in a dream never worked, so he just let go and enjoyed where his sleeping imagination would lead.

Another squirrel jumped in, bobbing its head back and forth and smiling with a wide-toothed face.

And then over the rustle of his own feet on the ground, Sam heard the forest's song.

The cicadas rattled the night like living maracas. Crickets provided an accompaniment of fiddle playing. And tree frogs lent a throaty vocal section, singing in wordless harmonies. The normal chaos of night sounds combined like an orchestra. Sam found the rhythm, and swayed his head back and forth in time with his latest squirrel dance partner.

The squirrel winked at him, as their heads bobbed side to side. Then the squirrel let go, making way for the next dance partner to step in.

But this time no squirrel came forward. Sam's momentum carried him another half-turn before dizziness caught up with him. With no partner to hang on to, Sam stumbled before toppling to the soft ground. The clear sound of laughter from a thousand voices filled the night. Usually, being laughed at would have made him panic. But there was not a hint of cruelty or mockery in the squirrels' tone, just joy. Sharing delight and mirth and celebration together.

Sam tottered onto his back to look up at the night sky. Stars in unimaginable numbers twinkled down at him. A smile widened on Sam's face until he thought his cheeks might split, and then he too laughed at the craziness of his dream. There'd been a lot jumbling around in his head these last few days, after all.

He wondered how often his dreams were this intense. Maybe they always were, but they just disappeared from memory the moment his eyes opened? Sam hoped he'd remember this one. His parents would probably love to hear about his new-found interest in squirrels and forests and outside stuff.

Sam rolled over on the soft ground, and wondered if he was tossing and turning back in his bed. One more dance, he decided.

Sam went to push himself back to his feet, but the startling sight of his own hands made him slip and topple back to the ground. Sam rolled to his back to better examine himself by moonlight.

His human hands were gone. In their place were a knobby mess of monstrous-looking fur and flesh. He turned them over, back and forth.

The backs of his hands were covered in a fur as bristly as an old hairbrush, and his palms were black as charcoal. At the end of each finger was a dirty, rectangular claw, longer than any woman's nails he'd ever seen.

He saw then that the coarse fur ran up his arms, too. What kind of monster had he become?

Dozens of the giant squirrels crowded around where he lay, still grinning and chittering in high-pitched voices but now looking less like docile dance partners and more like wild animals.

The dream was quickly turning, become a nightmare. He leapt to his feet and covered his ears to keep out the suddenly frightening multitude of squirrel voices, feeling thick fur beneath his monstrous hands.

"Wake up!" Sam cried aloud, trying to will himself from the dream.

When that didn't work, he ran once more. Back into the forest, deeper into the dream. He didn't slow down until the woods and all their sounds faded away into a darkness that swallowed him.

CHAPTER SIX

"Hello? Wake up!"

Sam groaned and turned away from the voice. "Leave me alone," he said and pinched his eyes tighter against the intruding daylight.

A finger jabbed Sam in the ribs. "Good morning! Time to rise and shine!"

It didn't sound like Mom or Dad. The voice was squeaky and high pitched, like a cartoon character on Saturday morning. Not real. Still dreaming.

"Go away" Sam grumbled, swiping over his shoulder toward the voice.

"Are you alright? Did you fall out of a tree?"

What on odd thing to say. Sam's eyes lazily drifted open. He didn't see pillows, a cluttered desk or even walls. He didn't see Mom or Dad or Winnie, or a backpack overstuffed with books on the floor. There was no light in the hallway shining in his eyes, and there was no telltale scent of coffee brewing to hint that his parents were awake.

In fact, there was no sign of a house at all. Most of what he saw was green.

Sam bolted upright and looked around. He stood on a patch of soft moss, apparently where he'd slept. In every direction great trees stretched to the sky, like they'd erupted from the very earth, narrow wooden volcanoes spewing eruptions of leaves. Morning sunshine filtered through the leafy canopy as songbirds whistled and fluttered through the branches, their song giving melody to the trickling gurgle of a nearby stream.

A stream. Hadn't he crossed one of those in his dream?

And at Sam's side, sitting on hind legs atop the green moss, was a squirrel. Amber fur tipped here and there with silver covered its body, except for a bib of white running down its chest and stomach like a baker's apron. The squirrel's tail curled like a question mark and, strangely enough, it had a piece of yellow paper rolled up like a scroll and slung across it's back.

The squirrel didn't dart away. In fact it seemed to be waiting, its front paws folded together and nose twitching.

"Hi!" the squirrel said, a bucktoothed smile coming to its face.

"You can talk?" Sam asked the obvious.

"Of course I can talk! Mother always said the only thing faster than a Ric's feet was its mouth."

"And you can understand me?"

"What a silly thing to ask." The squirrel pointed at the trees overhead. "You fell out of a tree, didn't you?"

"I don't think so…"

"Never seen a raccoon sleeping on the ground before, out in the open. It's unnatural." Its paws drifted to clutch at an over-the-shoulder band of interlaced grass, like a backpack strap. It must have been what kept the rolled yellow paper strapped to its back.

Wait. What had the squirrel just said?

Sam looked down at his hands. He must still be dreaming.

In the daylight, the paws looked less grotesque than they had beneath the moon, and the fur on his arms had a sheen to it. As he flexed the fingers and rotated his wrists, Sam thought they didn't feel any different than his human hands.

The same bristly charcoal-colored fur covered his chest and stomach. He touched his face, feeling a pointed nose and ears. Over his shoulder he saw the incriminating sight of a fat, black-ringed tail.

"It's impossible…"

"Said the same thing myself," the squirrel put its hands on its hips, "coming across you here sleeping on the ground. Thought you must be sick or injured." The squirrel talked in an excited blur, not stopping for a breath between sentences, his back paws fidgeting like he couldn't sit still.

Sam pinched his furry arm, hard. He didn't wake up.

Then he had an idea. The hat. Was this some trick of Ms. Quick's?

He grabbed a pointed ear in each paw and pulled, grunting and tugging until pained tears welled in his eyes.

"Are you feeling alright?" The squirrel's smile swayed, and his eyes shifted back and forth nervously. "You're sure you didn't hit your head?"

How was this possible? He was a raccoon!

Sam spun around in place. In every direction the forest was dense and full. He felt like he might faint. Questions filled his head all at once.

If last night hadn't been some crazy dream, how far had he ran? Which way was home?

How safe were these woods? Could he have been eaten by a bear last night?

What would Mom and Dad do when they came to wake him and found an empty bed? The sun was already up, they'd already know he was gone. Were they freaking out?

How could he understand the squirrel's words and speak the same language back? Why was the squirrel carrying a piece of paper on its back?

And just how had he become a raccoon?

He sat down and took several deep breaths until a calm replaced the questions. Sam looked up and squinted against ray of sunlight shining in his eyes. The sound of songbirds filled his ears. Soft moss felt like a pillowey mattress beneath him.

"Guess I'm not going to school today." Sam said quietly.

The squirrel's head tilted to the side, in puzzlement. "School?"

"Never mind."

The squirrel cleared his throat into his tiny balled up fist. "It's a lucky thing I ran into you. If you don't mind me saying."

"Yeah, thanks for waking me up," Sam said patting at the cushy moss that had been his bed. "Not sure what I was doing sleeping out in the open."

"Not lucky for you, lucky for me. You see, I'm on a mission of extreme importance. Life and death! But I'm nervous. So nervous. Could really use your help!"

Sam looked all around at the trees and the broken patches of clear blue sky just visible through the canopy. Transforming from boy to raccoon, and a talking squirrel on an important mission - how was this not a dream again?

"Not sure how I could help," Sam shrugged, "but I don't have any other plans out here."

"Oh thank the Fleet Feeted Four!" The squirrel jumped in the air with a pumped fist, then quickly gathered himself and stuck a tiny paw out to Sam. "I'm Zip Ric, a pleasure to meet you."

Sam shook the paw, his own was roughly four times bigger than Zip's, and introduced himself.

"Sam? That's a strange name for a raccoon." Zip Ric tilted his head, and then reached over his shoulder to pat the piece of rolled, yellow paper. "No matter. Need to get going, we're on a tight deadline!"

A nagging thought in Sam's head said he should be more concerned with figuring out how to get home, how to turn back into a boy, and how to keep his parents from grounding him for the next year. What important business could Zip Ric be handling? Acorn shortage? Chipmunk invaders?

Sam looked back down the hill, and thought about trying to retrace his steps back home.

Less than a week at Mapleton Middle School had almost gotten him killed. He'd made no friends and his parents were embarrassed with him. He'd chickened out on dancing with Lia, Bradley was going to torture him all year, and his stomach still twisted in a knot when remembering how he'd abandoned Charlie with the two goons. And now Mrs. Betty Banks, the vice principal, would probably have it in for him too since he'd tried to rat out her son.

Sam turned to Zip Ric. "Alright, I guess. Lead the way."

Zip Ric needed no more encouragement. He pumped his fist once in the air and then shot into the underbrush like he'd been fired from a gun.

Sam scrambled to follow, his first steps clumsy on four feet. It took a moment to find the easy running rhythm that had come naturally last night when he'd fled for his life from Winnie.

He followed Zip Ric's trail, a furrow of disturbed leaves. Sam slalomed between thick tree trunks and clumps of underbrush.

The wind whistled through Sam's ears, flat against his head, as he picked up speed. His paws bit into dirt and dried leaves. He was far from home and running further, deep into the very woods he'd hesitated to step more than a few feet as a boy. Still, a smile came to his face.

The forest air tasted like freedom, the leafy branches above hid him from worries, and the thrill of adventure took the burn from his legs. It felt good to be following danger this time instead of fleeing from it like usual.

Sam caught glimpses of Zip's bushy tail, like a submarine periscope rising from a sea of dried leaves.

"Where are we going?" Sam shouted, loud enough for Zip to hear over the ruckus they made stampeding across the forest floor.

"Important mission. Matter of life and death." The squirrel squeaked without looking back or slowing.

"You already said that. What's our objective?"

"Delivering a message. To the Wood Seer."

"Wood Seer?"

"Wisest creature in the whole forest. It's said he knows every corner of these woods, and watches over every creature in them. I'm to give him a message and get his advice."

Without slowing, Zip Ric leapt over the rotting trunk of a fallen tree. Sam fell a few steps behind as he struggled to climb over. "What kind of advice?" Sam shouted when he caught back up.

"Not sure, depends on the answer to the question."

"Ok, so what's the question then?"

"That's easy. I'm supposed to ask 'how do we get rid of a dragon?'."

Dragon? It was one thing to accept a boy-to-raccoon transformation and talking squirrels on important quests. But dragons? In the foothills of North Carolina? No way. Sam laughed. "You're joking."

Zip Ric stopped. "No really. I've seen it. Big and ugly and sleeping." He patted the rolled up sheet of yellow paper.

"It left a message, stuck to a tree, before it went to sleep. It had already destroyed a score of trees or more, not far from my home. I've got to see if the Wood Seer can read dragon script, figure out what the dragon wants, and then ask the Seer to use his magic to make the dragon go away before it wakes up again."

It was all incredibly silly. There were no such thing as dragons or wizards or magic. But then Sam scratched his head, right where a knitted raccoon cap should have been if he were still a boy, and had second thoughts about his conclusion on magic.

"Well lead the way then, before the dragon wakes up."

Zip Ric clapped his paws together, pointed with both his index fingers to the right, and took off through the dried carpet of leaves. Sam was right on the squirrel's heels as the ground slope shifted, and they now ran downhill.

"So how far away does this Wood Seer live?"

"I don't think much further. Just need to keep going this direction, and look for the Wood Seer on the opposite side of a creek in a Tearful Tree."

"Tearful Tree?" Sam asked. "What's that?"

"Beats me, some kind of riddle. That's one of the reasons I needed your help. Raccoons are way more clever than us squirrels."

The Tearful Tree? Sam doubted he could be much help with that. He wasn't very good at riddles, and he wasn't feeling all that clever. The forest felt foreign, full of new smells and sights, and if a squirrel didn't understand what kind of tree would be sad or weeping or whatever, how was Sam supposed to puzzle that out?

They ran on through the woods. After several more minutes of trying to keep up with Zip, Sam thought of another question.

"You said the riddle is one of the reasons you need my help. What's the other?"

Zip Ric stopped, and turned to look back at Sam. He answered without a hint of fear in his voice. "For protection. To keep me from getting eaten."

The squirrel spoke the words as nonchalantly as Sam's mother might say "Don't forget to grab your lunch", or "Could you let Winnie outside?"

Even in bright sunlight with the merry song of birds filling the air, the woods suddenly felt dangerous again.

"Eaten? By who?" Sam couldn't take care of himself when facing bullies at school, and bullies didn't have claws or fangs, like most things in the forest.

"By the Wood Seer, of course. Squirrels are one of an owl's favorite foods." Then Zip waved an arm in a wide windmill gesture. "This way, let's go!"

Zip burst forward again, scattering a wake of weeds and fallen acorns.

Talking squirrels that'd seen a dragon, tree riddles, and now an owl wizard. Sam didn't try to guess what might be next as he hurried to keep up with Zip Ric.

CHAPTER SEVEN

To Sam's eyes, the creek looked more like a river, and his quivering legs weren't cooperating.

"One foot in front of the other!" Zip Ric shouted from the opposite bank. "You can do it!"

Easy for him to say. The squirrel had bounced across the fallen tree that bridged the creek without giving the rushing current and scattered rocks below a second thought.

Sam had taken a different approach, stepping carefully to the edge of the embankment and peering over the side. It was a ten foot drop to the racing water. The creek wasn't too deep - a few large rocks, slimy with algae, broke through the water's surface - But it was at least fifteen feet wide and flowing quickly. Too dangerous to try and wade through.

That left the toppled tree trunk forming the makeshift bridge as the only way across.

"You're sure this Tearful Tree thing is on that side?" Sam called over to Zip Ric. His claws left gouges in the soft wood as he held on tight to keep from slipping.

"Absolutely! Great Grandpa Ric said so, and he's the smartest one in the whole family!" Then Zip rubbed his chin. "Or maybe he's just the oldest. I forget."

Sam inched forward, shuffling more than stepping. It was hard to take the 'don't look down' advice so often referenced in movies and books when, on all fours, he essentially was facing downward.

Sam's nose twitched. A vaguely spicy scent, almost like root beer or tea filled his nostrils. His stomach growled at the thought of food. He tried to focus on the smell and his hunger, if only to keep his mind off the churning waters below. The aroma seemed to be coming from the tree trunk.

"What kind of tree is this?" Sam shouted over the water's roar.

"It used to be a sassafras. Smells delicious, right?"

Sam tried to think about root beer floats as he continued forward. Then, trembling from his feet to his tail, Sam finally stepped off the tree trunk and back onto dry land. Zip Ric patted him on the back.

"Always thought raccoons were good climbers. Guess you can't believe everything you hear." Zip Ric adjusted the band of braided grass across his chest, the rolled up yellow paper making a scraping sound against his fur as it shifted.

Sam looked back at the long log laying across the creek. From this side, it looked even narrower. Sam felt something in his chest. His heart still pounded from the danger, but it wasn't that.

The log crossing had been dangerous. He could have fallen and sprained an ankle, or even broken something. But he'd done it. He'd stepped out onto the tree and made it across.

It was pride that he felt. A surge of confidence.

They turned right to follow the creek's flow and to search for the Tearful Tree.

Sam's stomach rumbled again, so loud he heard it over the gurgling creek.

"Zip, are you getting hungry?" With all the escaping from Winnie, moonlit dances, and keeping up with Zip, Sam had really worked up an appetite. The sweet smelling sassafras had only woken it up.

Zip Ric sat up on his hind legs and craned his neck to study their surroundings. His nose twitched this way and that.

"It's your lucky day, Sam. I think I smell some mulberry trees just over there. Follow me!"

They scurried along the creek bank, following the water's flow, and came to a clump of trees with spreading branches low to the ground. Among the green, egg shaped leaves Sam saw dozens of plump berries. In a few short hops, Zip Ric was at the base of the tree. He shrugged off the woven grass harness holding the rolled up note and disappeared up the trunk.

Sam had never seen a mulberry before, and thought they looked similar to blackberries or raspberries from the grocery store. Most were red, but higher up the tree he saw some that were deep purple, almost black. Sam's mouth salivated with anticipation.

The closest branch nearly touched the ground. Sam stretched as tall as he could and grabbed a pair of red berries with each paw and stuffed them greedily into his mouth. The sudden tartness made his cheeks pucker up and his eyes water.

The branch where Sam had harvested the berries shook, and Zip Ric's head popped out from between the leaves. "You ate a red one, didn't you?" He clutched a mulberry in his paw so purple, ripe and plump it was on the verge of bursting. "These are better." He dropped it to Sam's awaiting paws.

Zip Ric wasn't kidding. Sam smacked his lips at the sweet taste. Delicious.

He realized the last thing he'd eaten were snacks from the school dance cookie table. After following Zip over rough terrain for the last few hours, it was no wonder he was hungry.

Today was Friday, Sam reminded himself. He wondered what Lia had thought when he hadn't shown up for the school. Did she decide he was a coward, that he was hiding from Bradley Banks and his vice principal mom?

It all made him so mad. Bradley, and Mitch too. They'd wrecked his father's tie and they'd made him so scared he couldn't even run when cornered by the lockers. That their reign of terror extended to others, like that nice Charlie kid who'd been so friendly, was even more maddening. Why didn't someone do something about them?

Sam's stomach knotted, and not due to hunger. He should have stepped in and said something, at least tried to stick up for Charlie when Brad and Mitch had him pinned against the locker. It might have still earned Sam a dunk in the bathroom sink, but at least he wouldn't be carrying regrets about how it all went down.

Maybe that was the underlying reason he'd not accepted Lia's invitation to dance? Because he knew he didn't deserve it? He'd acted like a coward, trying to save his own skin, and abandoned someone in danger when he could have stepped in.

While Sam was lost in thought, Zip Ric returned to the ground and sat on a rock nearby. His cheeks were full as he chewed with his mouth open. "You should eat more." Mulberry juice ran down Zip's chin and stained the white fur bib on his chest.

Sam went to the next low to the ground branch. He had to stand on his hind legs and hop in order to grab a purple-black mulberry. Most of the fruit that low to the ground were the sour ones.

"You'll never get full like that. The best berries are higher."

Glancing back in the direction of their bridge over the creek, Sam said, "I think I'd prefer to keep my feet on the ground right now, thanks."

"Leave it to me," the squirrel said. Zip wiped his front paws in the grass, stretched his neck one way and then the other, and rotated his front arms one at a time in a circle. He reminded Sam of an Olympic swimmer getting ready to dive in for a race.

"It's ok, I'm not even that hungry," Sam lied. "I'll be fine with the red ones."

Zip Ric chittered with laughter. "No sense meeting an owl on an empty stomach. Besides, we Rics are the best gatherers in all existence. Watch this!"

Without another word, Zip Ric leapt lighting fast into the depths of the mulberry tree. He flew through the web of branches, grabbing ripe mulberries by the armful. Every few seconds Zip would drop to the ground and deposit berries in a pile where Sam sat.

Sam idly bit into a mulberry as his eyes tried to follow the streak of gray, red-brown, and white. It was easier to tell where Zip was harvesting by the shake of branches.

After ten trips, and a pile of mulberries as tall as Zip Ric, the squirrel stopped his harvest. "Think that's enough?" Zip wasn't even breathing hard.

"That was incredible!" Sam looked at the pile, eyes wide within his black fur mask. "How did you do that?"

With a wave of a paw Zip Ric tried to deflect the compliment. "It was nothing. Like I said, when it comes to harvesting, we Rics are unmatched!"

They ate a while longer before continuing downstream. Sam felt like he could burst and was glad they were no longer running through the woods. They both kept their eyes peeled for a Tearful Tree, whatever that might be.

Sam pondered the question. Maybe it was a pine tree, leaking a large amount of sap as if it were crying? Or a big sugar maple, drilled to make maple syrup, drops like tears falling into a bucket?

The woods thinned as they walked beside the creek, changing from leafy hardwoods to long needled pines.

Gradually the creek's sharp embankment flattened from the cliff-like ledge where they'd crossed to a shallow slope up from the water. Dense patches of prickly briars grew along the hill before the towering pines edged them out. They walked on a soft bed of fallen brown pine needles.

Sam had a thought. "Does this creek have a name?"

"Dunno. I've never been this far from home before."

Sam looked up through the pine boughs at the patches of blue sky and tried to get his bearings. Since meeting Zip, they'd ran with the rising sun on their right shoulders. That gave their initial sprint through the woods a north-easterly direction. When they crossed the creek, they had made a hard right to follow the flow of water, so that meant they now were heading southeast.

"Of course..." Sam nodded to himself, more sure of his idea. "I think this creek flows into Mapleton, and I think I know what we're looking for."

"What's a Mapleton?"

They continued along the creek for another twenty minutes. It widened in its bank until the ground turned muddy. Sam left mushy footprints as he walked. Zip Ric moved in graceful arcing hops, three at a time before stopping and landing with a soft plop.

For only a moment Sam thought about how they should have waited to cross the creek. Here it was wide enough to have waded through and not chanced the log crossing. But he'd survived the risk, felt a surge of confidence, and been rewarded with a belly full of mulberries on the other side. Plus, he wasn't soaked to his shoulders. Given the choice, Sam would have done it all again.

The pines didn't grow in the muddy marsh the creek had created. Knobby trees and cattails dominated the soft soil, but grew low to the ground. Which made it easier to spot the Tearful Tree.

Rising like a lonely mountain from the marsh, a green-gray mound of leaves towered above the small plants and grasses. It looked less like a typical tree than it did an enormous round shrub or miniature fertile hillside.

"I think that's it!" Sam said. "That's where we'll find the Wood Seer."

"It's incredible." Zip Ric said in an awed tone. "I've never seen such a tree, and I'm a bit of an enthusiast. But why do you think it's the Tearful Tree?"

"This creek. My dad called it Willow Creek when we drove…" Sam paused. It wasn't the right time to bring up the fact that he wasn't really a raccoon. Zip Ric wouldn't be able to understand. "Uh, that's all. He called it Willow Creek."

"I still don't get it." Zip Ric stopped to look at the Tearful Tree and rub his face.

"Haven't you heard of a weeping willow tree before?"

"Why would it weep? Poor tree. Does it not like living in a swamp?"

"Look at its branches. The way the leaves droop down, kind of like tears? Tearful Tree?"

Zip Ric's eyes widened and he jumped in the air. "Oh, wow! You're right!"

Together they hurried toward the willow. Low, drooping branches that grazed the ground formed a leafy perimeter wall. Up close, Sam thought the willow looked more like a head of long hair, with bangs hanging over the face, than anything else.

Then a familiar feeling found him. Sam recognized it by the knotting in his throat and stomach.

"Hold on." Sam stopped and put his paw on Zip's shoulder. "Are you sure this is a good idea?" Apprehension tinged with fear filled Sam as he looked up at the tree rising before them.

"Great Grandpa Ric said I needed to bring this message to the Wood Seer. We've got to find out what that dragon wants. This is the only option."

"I mean, is this wise? To disturb an owl at home? What if he tries to eat you?"

"He won't be allowed to eat me, of course. He's a predator. If he wanted to eat me, he'd have to hunt me down. No eating guests, that's the first rule of the forest. Imagine what his friends would say if they found out."

"I'm thinking he'd eliminate the witnesses by, I don't know, eating them, and then say whatever he wanted."

"We'll be just fine. Trust me. Come on!" Zip Ric hopped onward.

From this close he could see the willow's leaves were narrow and slender, the opposite of the plump mounded tree as a whole. They were dark green on top, and colored in a lighter, silvery sage green on the underside. A slight breeze caught them and made them flutter. To Sam, the tree almost sounded like it was hissing.

Knobby roots had broken free of the ground. They twisted and coiled above the surface, wound up from years of seeking soil and water, and Sam had to step carefully to avoid tripping.

He reached the base of the tree and looked up at the hundreds of branches that extended from the trunk. Zip Ric bounced past Sam, stuck to the tree like velcro, and disappeared with his note into the branches.

"Wait, Zip Ric." Sam said in a hushed voice, trying to keep his voice down so as not to alert any sleeping owls.

The squirrel reappeared. His claws kept him stuck to the side of the tree, headfirst toward the ground, like Spider-Man.

Sam pointed at the willow tree. "I've never climbed anything this high before. I'm not sure I can."

Zip Ric dropped to the ground beside Sam, and took Sam's front paw in his own. Like a tailor taking measurements for a new suit, Zip Ric tapped at Sam's claws, flexed his raccoon fingers, and ran his hands up Sam's arms.

Zip completed his inspection, and nodded in approval. "These will work just fine." He jumped back against the side of the tree. "Come over here."

Sam obeyed. Zip Ric, who so far had climbed trees in a blur, too fast to see, now moved each paw with deliberate precision. He inched a dozen steps up the tree, as if reminding himself of the basics of climbing.

"Alright. Tree climbing essentials!" Zip Ric dropped back to the ground again, landing inches in front of Sam. "First, use your claws to hang on."

Sam looked at his paws, and nodded his understanding.

"Second," Zip Ric now counted off the points with his fingers "use your back legs to climb. You'll tire yourself out if you pull with your front paws the whole way. Hold on with the front, push up with your back, and then move your front paws to a new grip."

That made sense. Sam's human legs could run around all day, but the monkey bars always made his arms burn after only a few minutes. As a raccoon his arms were no doubt stronger than they'd been as a boy, but his back legs were still stouter.

"Third, watch out for bugs. Ants and bees like to live in tree hollows. You don't want to put your paw into one of their nests."

"Fourth, and most importantly, remember one simple fact," Zip Ric adjusted the roll of yellow paper against his back and leapt onto the side of the tree trunk. "Climbing is the best!"

Sam forced himself to take a deep breath to try and steady his nerves.

"Here goes nothing" he said to himself, dug his claws in, and slowly followed his tiny friend.

CHAPTER EIGHT

Somehow, Sam found climbing the weeping willow tree to be less difficult than crossing the creek on a fallen sassafras.

He moved at a careful but steady pace. Sam concentrated on pushing with his legs instead of pulling with his arms, like Zip had said. Though he didn't dare look down, Sam guessed he had to be thirty feet up.

Maybe it was Zip Ric's pep talk, or maybe he was getting used to his raccoon body, but Sam was actually enjoying the climb.

He looked up at a sudden commotion overhead. Zip Ric charged down the tree, head first, straight toward Sam. For a fleeting moment Sam thought the squirrel had fallen, maybe knocked from the tree by an ornery owl. Then Zip Ric stopped on a dime, ran in a quick circle around Sam, and declared the findings of his search.

"I found him! The Wood Seer is sleeping, tucked in a small hollow." Zip Ric shot up to the next branch almost too fast to see. "I'll lead you there. Follow me!"

Sam wondered again how Zip Ric thought waking up a sleeping owl was a good idea, but he kept the concern to himself. Zip was determined to help his family. Also, hadn't Zip claimed that he'd seen a dragon just a day or two before? Owls were relatively safe by that comparison.

Zip Ric led the way, from one branch to the next through the jumble of willow limbs. They reached a fork where one wide limb angled to the left and then skyward as another shot out to the right and grew at a flat angle to lean out toward the creek.

Only now did Zip Ric keep his voice down. "Here we are." Even through a whisper, Sam could hear the excitement in Zip's voice.

Sam had to climb the last few steps to the fork in the willow's trunk before he could see the shadowy opening right where the limbs split apart.

In the fork was a hollow that looked unnaturally perfect. It sides were too straight, the arch over the hole too symmetrical, almost like it had been carved. Despite its rounded top, the dark doorway reminded Sam of the doggy door he'd narrowly escaped through the previous night.

But that wasn't what Sam found most unsettling.

Something was draped before the opening. Twenty or more individual, lumpy strands hung over the barrier. They swayed in unison against a breeze Sam couldn't feel through his fur, and reminded him of the beaded curtains fortune tellers in movies and cartoons always had at the entrance to their lairs.

As Sam drew closer to the doorway, he saw these strands weren't strung with something as innocent as beads. These were made from the remains of small animals, rodents and lizards. Skulls and bones and teeth, all bleached white by the sun and digestion. The remnants of an owl's hunting, and a warning to trespassers.

The grotesque sight didn't slow Zip Ric. Without hesitation, he hopped to the doorway and tapped lightly on the trunk.

At first nothing happened. Then after a long moment, Sam saw a stirring behind the bone curtain and within the darkness. A noise that could only be a yawn groaned inside the hollow. A great wing stretched out from within, dried bones rattling against each other where they'd been pushed aside.

The wing's intricate pattern was astonishing. Broad, individual feathers were striped in alternating bands of tan and chocolate. The feathers overlapped to form a network of larger, broken stripes that ran from the tip of the owl's wing to its shoulder. As the stripes narrowed and converged, new patterns began. Staring at the wing, Sam felt mesmerized as he tried to trace the colors and patterns with his eyes even as it was pulled suddenly back inside the hole in the tree.

A face peaked out from the darkness, just behind the swaying bone curtain that was already slowing as it settled from the wing's disturbance. Great golden eyes squinted against the daylight, and the owl used its wing as a visor, like a soldier holding a salute. Tufts of feathers resembling pointed cat ears lay back against the owl's head. A sharp black beak opened to say something, but instead it coughed and hacked for a moment.

"Who's there?" the owl finally said in a voice raspy with sleep.

Zip Ric pulled the rolled up note from his back and tucked it beneath his arm. He swept into a bow so deep that his tail came up over his head to touch the tree branch before him. Zip Ric held this position, like a delegate seeking courtly favors from a king, as he spoke.

"Oh wise Wood Seer, I am Zip of the Rics. I come to seek your counsel and your aid."

"Yes, yes. I could tell by the cut of your teeth that you were a Ric." The owl's head bobbed up and down while the rest of his body stayed cloaked in shadow. "There's not been a Ric in this tree for many seasons, and the last one had the sense not to wake me after a night of hunting." The owl's threatening voice had a gruff edge to it, as well as a hint of a British accent. "Tell me why I shouldn't eat you where you stand?"

Sam's grip tightened on the tree branch. He knew this had been a terrible idea. How could he protect Zip Ric when they were up in a tree? Sam was just a novice at climbing and the owl could fly.

Zip Ric was either extremely brave or an excellent actor, because he showed no hint of fear as he straightened to meet the owl's eyes.

"Your wisdom is often spoken of among the Rics, great Wood Seer. But so is your mercy. I come seeking advice, and want no trouble."

The owl made a sound similar to a cough, but it could have also been a laugh. "Well what of him then?" The tip of the striped and speckled wing straightened and pointed through the bone curtain at Sam. "Why have you brought a trickster to my home? All creatures must keep their wits about them when dealing with conniving raccoons. You say you don't want trouble, and here you've brought trouble to my very door."

Zip Ric looked back with wide eyes at Sam. The question seemed to have startled the little squirrel, and he looked at a loss for how to respond.

"I am no raccoon-" Sam started to say.

The owl burst from his doorway. Its great wings spread like a parachute, and its vicious beak parted. Zip Ric almost dropped the yellow paper from beneath his arm as he dashed behind Sam.

The owl stopped only inches from Sam's face, looming over him like a scolding parent. Dried bones still rattled like dice in the doorway. The great bird's golden eyes were wide, gleaming, as it glared down at Sam's face.

Sam had been too stunned to move an inch. The owl's sudden lunge had startled him, but he wasn't sure what was worse - the owl's razer sharp beak and talons, or losing his balance and falling forty feet to the ground. His paws gripped the branch so tight he thought his fingers might dislocate, but Sam stayed rooted to the tree and met the owl's gaze.

Finally, the owl sagged from his attack stance. "Contrary to my initial fears, raccoon, I discern no trouble in you. Liars and cowards are one in the same, and both would wilt before the wrath of Humphrey the Great Horned Owl." The owl paused. "But you... You kept your feet and your wits when accused."

It seemed, for once, Sam's petrifying fear had been just the action required. He felt like he needed to lay down for a minute and collect himself, but instead kept a tight hold to keep the wind and any great horned owls from knocking him to the ground.

The owl, Humphrey, backed away without turning, his talons finding places on the branch to grip without having to look. Humphrey perched against the willow's trunk and folded his wings calmly at his sides. He looked too large to fit in the dark hollow behind him, it only came up to his shoulder. If Sam hadn't already seen Humphrey within the dark doorway he never would have guessed the owl could wedge inside.

"Alright, now that we've exchanged pleasantries, Master Ric, you may proceed." The edge had left Humphrey's voice, and he spoke now the way Sam imagined kindly shopkeepers in London did. "Tell me the aid you seek, and I'll decide what help I may be."

Zip Ric patted Sam on the shoulder as he scurried forward to again stand before the owl.

"My family, the Rics, have lived in the same oak tree for two hundred and eighty-seven years, more than five hundred generations. It stands where two hillsides meet, its top rising above the heights of any tree in view. A wide meadow of berry bushes and tall grasses spread beneath its boughs and wherever its shadow touches."

As Zip gave the details of his home, Sam realized the squirrel was describing the kingly oak tree from his dream. Despite his accepting the reality of his transformation into a raccoon and then being chased into the woods by Winnie, somehow his brain had still filed the dance with the squirrels beneath the great oak as merely a lump of dream, and he'd not given it a second thought.

Humphrey nodded. "I know your tree well. It lies at the very edge of my stead."

Zip continued. "There is a danger coming. For weeks humans have been prowling in our fields during the day, marking trees with X's, even placing one upon the base of my family's home."

"Most troubling," the owl agreed.

"And then, just two mornings ago, we heard a great roar and smelled smoke. The sound and stink continued for hours. At dusk the noise finally stopped. My brothers and I went toward the source of the sound to investigate. A chunk of forest, less than a five minute hop from our family oak, was gone."

"Good heavens!" Humphrey held a wing before his mouth.

Zip Ric went on. "The ground was chewed to pieces. In the middle of what had been forest, a huge yellow dragon slept. And it left these," Zip held up the rolled piece of paper now, "pinned against several of the remaining trees. Quiet as we could, we stole one of the notes and took it home. But none of us Ric's could read it, not even Great Grandpa. We think it's in dragon script."

"Dragons… dear me," muttered Humphrey as he rubbed the place beneath his beak where a chin would be. Then, with a flip of his wing, Humphrey gestured for the note.

Zip Ric took the roll of yellow paper, its edges smeared with dirt and mulberry juice from their travels, and unrolled it. Sam pressed the top of the paper to the tree limb to keep it from curling back on itself.

The message was short, spelled in block letters that weren't written in dragon at all, but in words Sam could read, even when holding the note upside down. His heart sank as he read through the message.

Humphrey stroked the side of his beak with a feathered wing as he studied the note. "As you may have guessed, I have traveled far, seen many things, and unlocked many mysteries in my life. This paper, this note, even this particular shade of yellow, they are all familiar to me."

Zip Ric's head nodded with excitement. "Yes, great wise owl. That is why I was sent. We knew you would know its meaning and what to do!"

"It says 'Warning'." Humphrey traced the top word with his wing for effect. Zip Ric followed Humphrey's gestures and waited for more.

"These next words here are unknown to me, but this one says 'trees'."

"Warning, trees? Who needs warnings about trees?" Zip Ric scratched his head but let the owl continue.

"Finally, this last word here is 'Monday'." Humphrey pointed again to each word he could read. "Warning. Trees. Monday. That is the end of the message." Humphrey folded his wings across his speckled chest and looked rather proud of himself.

Sam didn't say anything as he re-read the message to himself. It wasn't a long note, more of a posting against trespassers than anything. But Humphrey had missed the meaning entirely.

"Amazing!" Zip Ric said, his head tilted sideways looking down at the note. "What does it mean?"

"Even one as wise as I cannot begin to understand the madness found in the words of dragon's and men. Probably just inane babbling. As mother always said, the only thing more loony than a human is a chipmunk."

Zip Ric sighed in relief. "Well I feel better."

"Wait." Sam couldn't keep it to himself any longer. His stomach knotted. He didn't want to read the note aloud, he didn't want the message to be true, but he couldn't let Zip Ric go home unwarned. "That's not all it says."

Humphrey snorted. "Ah yes, here we go. Now the raccoon trickery begins, some scheme for his own gain? Perhaps I misjudged your benevolence after all." Humphrey waved a dismissive wing. "Go on then. Tell us what it really says."

Sam coughed into his paw to clear his voice, and read the black block letters printed on the yellow paper.

WARNING

THIS AREA SCHEDULED FOR TREE CLEARING TO FACILITATE CONSTRUCTION OF THE ARBOR HILLS MALL. NO TRESPASSING. WORK TO COMMENCE MONDAY, SEPTEMBER 16th.

The bottom of the note wasn't signed, but stamped with a logo. Sam pointed at it. "And this says 'Banks Development Company - Serving Mapleton for 30 Years." The name couldn't be a coincidence. It seemed that no matter what he did, even turning turning into a raccoon, Sam could not escape Bradley Banks or his family.

The silence hung heavy in the air. Even the song birds seemed to take notice and quieted their tune.

"What's a mall?" Zip Ric said after a long pause.

"I believe it's a state of mind, an idea of-" Humphrey started, but Sam cut him off.

"Buildings. They're going to clear the trees to build stores and parking lots."

Zip Ric's mouth dropped open as he stared at the note in disbelief. Sam patted the squirrel's shoulders.

Humphrey shook his head. "This sounds like raccoon mischief to me. He means to trick you, Master Ric, but to what end I've not yet deciphered. Tell me, raccoon, how is it that you can read these words?"

"My name is Sam," he said.

Then Sam tried to shout that he wasn't a raccoon at all, even as he backed away down the branch away from the angry owl that was shouting over him.

"More lies! What is your game?" Humphrey's voice boomed through the tree and overpowered Sam's voice as his flashing beak lunged toward him. "I'll have no more of this foolishness! You've upset us all, and it's time you left this tree!"

Sam's back foot reached into empty air. The branch beneath him swayed as he tottered and tried to right himself. A momentary feeling of weightlessness that comes when balance hangs at the precipice, usually when you've already fallen, filled him. Without thinking, Sam squeezed his eyes shut.

"Enough." A woman's voice said. The word wasn't shouted, but commanded sternly, like a school teacher.

Sam felt something unfamiliar. A peaceful calm filled the air. It was like all his fears had evaporated instantaneously with the word.

When he opened his eyes, Sam found he wasn't falling. The branch beneath his feet was stout and sturdy. Only his own legs quivered.

He looked up to see who had spoken with such authority as to quiet Sam's fears and Humphrey's accusations.

The face staring down from a higher branch sent his limbs into a frantic tremble once again.

CHAPTER NINE

The face of a ghost, pale as the moon, with black pits for eyes stared down at Sam. It perched on a narrow branch, just above Humphrey's hollow nook.

A barn owl.

Where Humphrey was large and intimidating, the barn owl was svelte and graceful. She swayed with the moving branch beneath her claws. The feathers of her wings were mottled with swirls of deep brown and auburn. Her body was cream colored, a dingier white than her moon-shaded face. Darker speckles covered her chest like chocolate chips in ice cream.

Her black eyes followed Sam as he carefully repositioned his paws and took a few timid steps back toward Zip Ric and Humphrey. Hadn't he seen those same eyes, not even 24 hours ago, perched on the Mapleton Middle School? It couldn't possibly be the same owl that'd watched him from the roof as he'd prowled around wearing the raccoon cap, right? This barn owl did not look quite as creepy in the daylight, but her presence was none the less unnerving.

Her gaze left Sam as she turned to the others. "Humphrey. Are you over stretching yourself again?" Her beak appeared from the camouflage of her feathers as she spoke, and her face returned to a blank white slate when she became silent.

Humphrey stammered to answer her. "Not at all. This seemed of a trifling concern. I didn't want to disturb you."

Zip Ric's mouth hung open. "You're the Wood Seer," he said, looking up at the barn owl. "The real one."

The barn owl's eyes closed, and Sam thought he could almost perceive a smile among the white feathers of her face.

"I have many names and titles, young Zip Ric. But you should just call me Vera."

Sam retook his place beside Zip Ric as the squirrel performed another one of his expert bows, swooping low until his tail touched the branch past his head.

"They brought a note, mistress. From near the great Ric oak, at the forest's edge. I could make out only a few of the words. The raccoon-" Humphrey stopped, then corrected himself. "-Sam claims to be able to read its words."

Vera's eyes squinted as she looked down at the unfurled yellow sheet. "Sam, if you will, please read to me these words of warning."

Sam repeated the note as commanded.

"Lies," Humphrey blurted when Sam had finished. "I don't understand his scheme, but this trickster is up to something." Vera raised a wing to silence the larger Humphrey. He quieted down, but crossed his wings with a huff.

The barn owl's head swiveled back to Sam. Vera's gaze seemed to look through his skin and to his insides. She studied him in silence for several long seconds before she again spoke.

"What Sam the raccoon has said is true. The humans intend to destroy the Ric's ancestral home."

To Sam's surprise, the great horned owl did not protest. In fact, Humphrey's attitude made a sudden and complete about-face.

"That is terrible!" he wailed. Humphrey waddled out and wrapped a consoling wing around a confused Zip Ric. Zip winced to have the owl feathers touching him. "We must help this poor creature. Tell us, oh wise Vera, what must we do?"

Sam found Humphrey's sudden turn of character suspicious. "You must forgive Humphrey," Vera said, as if she could read his doubts. "He has a flair for the dramatic, with a tendency to fall deep into his convictions, with no shame in immediately changing his position if proved wrong. We probably all could learn from his example of not being too sensitive about our pride."

Humphrey could only shrug his mighty, striped wings. "It is the curse of one who possesses a soul that burns with a fiery passion, but is willing to listen to the reasonings of those he trusts and respects."

Owls, it seemed, could be as varied as people.

"We must save our home." Zip Ric said, getting the conversation back on track. "What must I do, wise Wood Seer?"

Vera's words were measured as she spoke. "First, we must think. Why do the humans wish to build this mall?"

"They need a place to store supplies for winter?" Zip Ric guessed.

"They have a personal vendetta against the Ric family!" Humphrey proclaimed, quite wrongly, with offended shock.

Vera closed her eyes, making her face as blank as a dinner plate. Sam was reminded of scooping spaghetti, two nights past, onto a similarly blank plate. And something Mom had said while Dad was ranting about the new mall.

"The Mapleton shopping mall is shut down. There's no place in town to buy coats or shoes or video games."

"What are 'shoes'?" Humphrey whispered to Zip Ric.

"That is correct, Sam." Vera said. "The humans seek to build a new location to purchase goods, because their current mall is abandoned."

"Well why don't they just un-abandon it rather than using their dragon to destroy our tree?" Zip Ric asked.

"That is an excellent question," Vera said. "Once, that old shopping mall thrived. However, over time as mankind lost interest in the building, decay and other creatures crept in to take their place."

Sam remembered another piece of what Mom had said. "The current mall is overrun with rats, isn't it?"

Humphrey made a face like he'd just bit into something foul. "And vicious ones to boot. Scarcely safe for one to even fly past anymore."

"As the humans and their shops withdrew, a mighty army of rats was all too happy to fill the void." Vera continued. "Now it is known in the woods by its new name. Rodenthold."

"Bloodthirsty creatures." Humphrey said. "Rats are vile, dangerous, and always looking for a fight. Or a new conquest."

Vera raised a calming wing toward Humphrey. "Be careful generalizing, Humphrey. There are always exceptions." Again Sam thought he saw a smile form in the otherwise still feathers that masked Vera's face.

They were all quiet for a moment. "With all that said, to repeat the squirrel's question," Vera said. "How can we convince the humans to preserve the great Ric oak?"

"Brute force!" Humphrey punched a balled up wing-fist into his other wing. "We strike the humans when they least expect it, and drive them from the field."

"Would the rats leave the mall, Rodenthold, if we asked nicely?" Zip Ric wondered. "And give it back to the humans I mean?"

Humphrey stood up straighter on the willow bough. "That settles it. I shall volunteer as diplomat! To broker a peace, negotiate a treaty. Bring all parties to the table. Human and rat, squirrel and owl, and discuss a compromise."

"For starters, dear Humphrey," Vera said gently, "How do you intend to negotiate with humans? They can no longer communicate in the language of All like we here."

"Also, the rats would never discuss such matters with an owl. They view us as even more dangerous than mankind. Night predators are one of the main factors for them seeking shelter beneath a roof."

Humphrey grumbled.

"What if-" The idea had popped so suddenly into Sam's head that he had to pause a moment to gather it. "What if we could do both?"

Humphrey stammered and started to protest, but Vera again quieted him with a wave of her wing. "Go on, Sam. What do you intend?"

"Well," Sam was careful not to say 'we', "if *the humans* intend to destroy Zip's tree in just a couple of days, the squirrels will probably have to fight to scare them off. At least at first. But an army of squirrels can't hope to stand up to the humans for long. No offense, Zip."

"None taken," Zip Ric said. "We Rics are gatherers, climbers, and escape artists. Not so much warriors."

"So what if we convince the rats of Rodenthold to march to war on behalf of the Rics? You said most rats are arrogant and warlike? Maybe we could convince them that their army is mighty enough to face the humans on another front? March out from Rodenthold and fight for the Ric's tree?"

One of Humphrey's eyes narrowed as realization crossed his face. "For the dual purpose of both defending the Ric Tree, and emptying Rodenthold of rats!" Humphrey lunged forward and now wrapped his wing around Sam's shoulders. "Vera, this raccoon is a clever one. I'm glad he's on our side!"

Vera rephrased and repeated Sam's solutions. "Could we somehow convince the rats to leave Rodenthold to join our cause? Would they fight alongside the Rics? Rise against the humans, and prevent them from building their new mall?"

She thought aloud about both sides of the questions. "Taking on the humans by force is risky. And even if we could win the day, would it be enough to change their minds? Humans," Sam swore he saw Vera's eyes flick to him as she said it, "are a strange species that can't be easily understood. One moment they act in balance with the world around them, and the next greed motivates them to do whatever they please."

She continued. "The rats, they are another story. Most rats are prideful and haughty, easily influenced. How else could humans persuade them to run through mazes, the rat always trying to get the prize faster? For years, humans have sought Rodenthold's destruction. This has only strengthened the rats' resolve, and led to their total takeover of the mall. Rats are natural followers, only dangerous when a rare, ambitious rat comes along."

"The ruler of Rodenthold, Emperor Nezearius, is one such rat. Nezearius commands his realm with an iron fist. He's held the teeming mass of Rodenthold together these long years by keeping a careful eye on his rivals, and disposing of them quickly when they begin questioning his rule or otherwise become a threat. It is Nezearius that must be convinced to join the fight."

"But wise Vera," Humphrey asked, "if you and I are unsuitable to treat with this Emperor Nezearius, who is to go?"

Zip Ric sat up. "If a Ric is good at anything, it's talking. We must try. Of course I'll go!"

Vera bowed her head at Zip. "Brave Zip Ric. And what of you, Sam? Will you see your own plan through? Raccoons are as renowned for their clever minds as they are their nimble hands. And this is your plan after all. Do you dare to face the darkness of Rodenthold? To speak with their leader, and convince Emperor Nezearius to leave the safety of his conquered kingdom to face a dragon and the humans?"

Sam gulped as all eyes turned his way.

His thoughts drifted suddenly to his parents. Certainly they were back home and worried sick. They'd be speaking with police and sending out search parties.

In the back of his mind, Sam knew he had to get home and let them know he was alright. It was already past noon, he guessed, and if he turned for home right now it would be almost dark by the time he made it back.

But Zip's entire family was in danger. His home, too. Time was short. Sam couldn't abandon them in their hour of need.

And wouldn't they be proud of him if he could save acres of forest from being destroyed? The fact that he'd be thwarting Bradley Banks' family business also gave Sam an extra bit of incentive.

"Zip and his family need all the help they can get." Sam said. "I will do whatever I can to lend a hand. How do we get to Rodenthold?"

Humphrey clapped his wings together. "Marvelous! Wonderous! Such courage!"

For a moment Zip Ric pumped a triumphant fist, then he slumped. Vera turned to him. "What is the problem, young one?"

"Well, Ms. Wood Seer, it's just that the others. They're going to be disappointed they couldn't help."

"The others?"

"My brothers, sisters, cousins and elders. All the other Rics. They want to save our home just as badly as me. In our legends, the Fleet Feeted Four were always able to swoop in and save the day. I hope my family isn't too disappointed we can't do the same."

"Squirrels, swoop in to save the day..." Vera repeated, trailing off in thought and closing her eyes. "Yes. Those are all excellent ideas."

"What's that, Vera? More plans?" Humphrey asked, his own face looking confused.

Vera dismissed his question with one last wave of a wing. "None that I'm ready to share. More of an idea. But that will be for you and I, Humphrey, to handle. You've given me a grand idea, Zip Ric. One that may be our greatest hope of saving your home yet."

Sam and Zip Ric glanced at each other. The squirrel shrugged his shoulders.

"For now," she said, "only concern yourselves with your part of the plan. Raise an army of rats, and return to the Ric tree with all haste. Humphrey, give them directions on how to find the rat fortress of Rodenthold."

CHAPTER TEN

Zip Ric moved in fits and starts. He'd take a few steps beside Sam, then shoot six feet up a tree before stopping and smelling the air. Then he'd leap to another tree, bounce through a bush, and land back on the ground.

Sam stayed to the ground and followed Zip Ric's erratic movements through the woods. Dappled afternoon sunlight filtered through the trees and seemed to haphazardly highlight points of interest on the forest floor; A rock here, a colorful insect there, or a clump of wild flowers.

They'd set out from the owl's home two hours before, climbing steadily uphill, away from the willow tree and swamp.

Vera had given no clues about her sudden idea involving squirrels saving themselves, or what errand she and Humphrey would be on. She had perched in silence as Humphrey gave Zip Ric directions to the old mall-turned-rat-fortress.

"The trees will begin to peel like paper, and then you'll cross a rocky, old river bed. Should be dry this time of year. You'll notice that the tree tops suddenly…" Humphrey had stopped himself, rubbing the side of his face with a feathered wing. "Oh dear me, no. That won't do. You'll be on the ground after all. Let's see, after crossing a river of stones, look for trees that don't have forgetful squirrels to thank for their placement. Keep going, follow the obvious paths, and you'll know you're close."

"Is that a riddle?" Zip Ric had asked. "What does that mean?"

Humphrey winked. "Sometimes saying things in riddles helps one pay better attention. You're both clever, you'll understand when you get there."

Riddles or not, based on Humphrey's guidance it seemed Rodenthold was in the exact opposite direction of Sam's house. That meant with every step, Sam grew a little further from home.

His parents would be worried sick. Sam was a little surprised not to see police helicopters overhead or to hear sirens and bloodhounds baying in the distance. He'd seen enough television to know that when someone went missing the authorities sent out search parties.

They'd understand, Sam tried to tell himself. Wasn't he supposed to make friends? Even though he was a squirrel, Zip Ric certainly counted as a one. And weren't friends supposed to stick together? Sam figured he was in no more danger out in the woods than he would have been roaming Mapleton Middle School. Short of meeting a black bear, raccoons must be pretty high on the food chain, after all.

Besides, Mom and Dad had been bugging him to go play outside since they'd arrived in Mapleton two weeks ago. Hiking halfway across the county must count for something.

He was still a raccoon anyway, and just turning up at home unannounced and without a plan was probably not the best idea. The circumstances on how the transformation had happened were still a mystery. It had something to do with the raccoon stocking cap, that much was certain. Its eyes had been so startling, almost like they were looking back at him.

Sam pinched himself again on his furry arm and pulled at his ears. Still not a dream, and the ears stayed attached. He wondered once more where a part-time librarian like Ms. Quick had come across such a hat.

Even if he went straight home, it wasn't like his parents could just magically change him back. He also doubted that Mapleton had a local wizard specializing in removing hexes. He'd need a plan, not just to get by Winnie, but to let his parents know the creature that had sneaked through the dog door wasn't an opportunistic pest but in fact their transformed son.

Then Sam stopped and smacked himself in the forehead.

Zip Ric dropped to the ground. "What's the matter? Mosquito?"

Sam shook his head. "The Wood Seer. Vera. Do you think she knows actual magic?"

"Oh, most definitely. I bet she's got some spell up her wing to stop the dragon, protect the Ric tree, and keep us safe for another five hundred-plus generations. Why?"

"No reason."

Maybe Vera could change him back? She probably knew a potion recipe, or a witch with a smoking cauldron living up in the mountains. There was an unspoken wisdom behind Vera's black eyes.

Sam first looked backward at the ground they'd just passed, and then up at patches of cloudless blue sky through the tree limbs. The weeping willow tree was far out of sight, and even if he ran back now, Vera and Humphrey would likely already be gone. Vera had indicated there would be much for the two owls to do on their own, including flying back to the Ric Oak to inform Zip's family of what the note said, but that Sam should watch the skies for their return on Sunday, the day before the dragon was scheduled to rise and burn Zip's home. Hopefully Sam and Zip would have an army of rats at their side to welcome the owls and whatever mysterious help Vera had thought of so suddenly.

He resolved to tell Vera about his predicament at the Ric tree when they met again. By then they would have either saved Zip's home, or it would already be too late for the squirrels. He tried to push the second thought from his head.

They continued on through the forest. Humphrey had indicated that they'd reach Rodenthold before dusk without having to hurry, and that they should wait until cover of darkness to approach the walls anyway.

"Vera and I will refrain from hunting," Humphrey had said, "which shall make traveling by night through our territory a bit safer. However, we're not the only predators in these woods, so you must still keep up your guard."

For now, Sam and Zip didn't run, as they had for most of the morning before crossing the creek and looking for the owl's Tearful Tree, and instead moved across the forest floor at a brisk walk.

"Squirrels usually prefer to stay in the trees, right?" Sam asked, the thought suddenly occurring to him. "Are you walking down here just for me?"

"Traveling by tree is safer," Zip Ric agreed, "much much safer. No foxes, hard for hawks to maneuver through the branches, and fewer cats. Faster too."

"So why have you been running along the ground all this time?"

Zip Ric pointed up at the boughs overhead. "Travel by tree is always better, except if you don't know the way. I've never been to this part of the forest, never ran through these branches. It's easy to get turned around in an unfamiliar tree and, before you know it, you're running with your back to the sun when it should be in your eyes. Or you twist and turn so much that the extra speed didn't matter because you scampered a much further distance."

The tree branches above intertwined like the most complex highway system on earth. They wound and wove together to make a tapestry in green needles and leaves.

"Yep, whenever you want to get anywhere new, you have to travel on the ground. Even the Fleet Feeted Four left the trees when they had a quest or mission to a new land they'd never visited."

"Who are they, the Fleet Feeted Four?" Zip had mentioned them a few times, and the Wood Seer had perked up when Zip spoke of them.

"Wait." Zip Ric stopped. "You've never heard of The Four?"

"It's never come up in school," Sam shrugged. "Who are they?"

"Why they're only the quickest, fastest, and chattiest squirrels ever to walk the woods! It's thanks to The Four that rabbits have long ears, that owls sleep the day away, and even why you have rings on your tail."

Sam laughed. So even squirrels had their own fables and tall tales.

"They were four siblings," Zip Ric went on as they walked, "two brothers and two sisters. There was of course Chikirith, a gray squirrel like me. Shadowed Tilee, her fur as black as your mask. Tiny Stratford, mad as a chipmunk with a temper as red and fiery as his coat. And last was the fair Izel."

Zip Ric went on, his excitement making his words even quicker than usual. "They all had their part to play. Chikirith was the eldest, their leader, and could climb and carry the best of all. Tilee was softer spoken but with a mind for puzzles. Izel's powers bordered on magical, and she could harness the wind with a flick of her tail. Stratford often got The Four into trouble, but just as often saved the day."

"So Vera thought they could help? Are The Four still out there somewhere?"

Zip Ric chuckled and shook his head. "No silly. The Fleet Feeted Four lived at the dawn of the world, when all was new and summer never ceased. Berries and acorns grew from every tree, and their was no need to harvest because winter hadn't yet been born."

"In their day, The Four saw every inch of woods and came to know every tree. Eventually they settled down, retired from their adventures, and each founded their own clan of squirrels."

"Were Rics the family Chikirith started?"

"You raccoons are clever! That's right!"

Zip Ric promised to regale Sam with every Fleet Feeted Four story he knew once they'd saved his tree from smoke-breathing dragons and humans with saws. For now, there was still the business of finding Rodenthold.

They followed the land north and east, through the forest of maples and oaks, pines and elms swaying in the light breeze. The sun had passed its apex and began dipping toward the other horizon. Sam guessed by the light that school would have let out hours ago, the students of Mapleton Middle School adjourning for the first weekend of the school year.

With every step, Sam grew more accustomed to having four feet instead of two. He didn't have to watch his step on slippery wet leaves. Even if one foot slipped, he still had three beneath him. And the benefits didn't just end with balance. He and Zip had walked, ran, and climbed for nearly the whole day, with only the briefest of breaks to chat with owls and eat mulberries.

Despite all that action, Sam's stout furry legs were only just beginning to feel the miles. His raccoon body was covered in muscles that worked just right to keep him moving forward. Sam thought he could travel for another several hours if need be. He couldn't remember ever feeling stronger.

If Sam was a fountain of energy, than Zip Ric was a power plant. The squirrel never stopped moving. He weaved through tree trunks, scurried beneath piles of rotting leaves, and hopped between rocks and logs. Once he'd even bounced across Sam's back as if he were a raccoon-shaped stepping stone.

Gradually the slope shifted and they were again walking downhill. To Sam it was somehow more difficult to go downhill than up. Gravity didn't work that way, and strolling down a hill should have been far easier than climbing up the other side. But in his raccoon form, Sam found he had to consciously slow himself down or he'd soon be out of control and at risk of toppling head over heels.

Stones stuck out from between the fallen leaves more and more the further they descended down the hill. The number of trees thinned, too. Most had a strange, pale bark peeling from the trunk, curling like rolled paper. It was brittle to the touch and broke away when Sam reached up to feel it. He recognized them as birch trees.

As they continued, even the birches thinned. Large rocks broke through the forest floor, like tombstones where trees had once stood. Zip Ric's erratic movement slowed until he was walking carefully, as if on tip toes, at Sam's side.

"This must be the stony old river bed Humphrey described." Sam said in a whisper. He wasn't sure why he'd kept his voice down. Maybe it was instinct.

"I'm not sure I like it here. No, don't like it at all." Zip Ric's teeth chattered as he spoke, his typical exuberance muted.

Sam said nothing else, but kept his eyes sharp for danger. His little friend was right, the forest held an eerie aura that Sam couldn't put his paw on. Even the birch trees swayed differently. They seemed to creak and moan in the breeze. Sam could almost hear them whispering warnings.

Chunks of pale boulders stuck up from the ground ahead like the bleached bones of the earth. Smaller stones were stacked into miniature pyramids by eons of twisting creaks and shifting ground. In the golden, diminishing daylight the rocks cast twisted shadows like monsters from a ghost story.

The smell of the woods changed, too. Like the musky scent of decay from sticking your face in a bag of rotting mulch, but stronger and concentrated and filling the air.

The canopy of trees broke open and an evening sky formed an orange ceiling above the world. Before them was a field of stones in tan and cream and white, as wide as a highway and stretching off as far as Sam could see to the right and left. Large boulders three feet and taller dotted the river bed. A great river had once wound through these stones but now it was little more than a rain-fed brook.

It was empty of trees, any living ones at least. The bare skeletons of long dead trunks and saplings that hadn't survived reached up like twisted fingers from the stones. Here, no birds sang, and the din of the forest was so diminished Sam could hear the faint trickle of water flowing somewhere between the rocks.

"Let's hurry," Sam said, still in a whisper.

They weaved between the taller boulders. In his raccoon body, Sam couldn't see over the tops, and he felt like he was in a great stone labyrinth.

Sam was careful to watch his footing between the rocks and to keep as quiet as he could. He wasn't sure why he was so unnerved. It was just an old river bed. It wasn't like a mythical troll was going to burst from the ground and grab him.

Zip moved quicker as he hopped from stone to stone. He'd gotten a fair distance ahead of Sam, and was nearly halfway across the rock bed, when he jumped to the top of a tall rock pile. But Zip misjudged the footing or his grip, and went sliding right over the top, off the back side and out of sight.

"Zip! Are you alright?" Sam's voice echoed along the old river bed.

There was no answer.

Sam clambered through the field of stones. It wasn't easy. The stones had been rounded by water and time, and they shifted beneath his a weight, threatening to smash his paws and toes, as he hurried.

There was still no sign of Zip Ric. Had he fallen and hurt himself? Hit his head and knocked himself out? Broken a leg, or something worse?

Sam reached the rock pile that Zip had disappeared over and hurried around its base toward the other side. "Zip, where are you? Please be ok." As he reached the other side of the boulder, Sam's voice failed him.

There was his friend, pressed with his back against a stone four times the squirrel's height. Zip Ric's eyes were wide and his mouth hung open.

Just a few feet from Zip, the rocks themselves seemed to move. Pale stones striped with dark black bands rolled as though an ocean wave stirred beneath them.

An almost inaudible voice filled Sam's head. "Relaxss. Sstay sstill. Yess, it ssoon will passs."

The voice was so subtle it could have been Sam's ears playing tricks on him. The breeze perhaps, giving words to his own underlying fears. Then Sam saw the flat, spade-shaped head rise from what looked like a moving sea of stones and knew better.

A rattlesnake, specifically a timber rattlesnake. Sam recognized it from pictures he'd seen when researching how dangerous the woods in his new backyard might be. Mom had teased him, said he was being silly, overly cautious. He'd snapped back that they shouldn't have moved somewhere with venomous snakes.

"Luck and patiensse." Hissed the snake. "Luck and patiensse. Yess. They've alwayss sserved uss well."

Zip Ric didn't move. His body a statue, like he was frozen in place. Only his tail trembled.

"Sstay sstill. Yess. Relaxss. Trembling musscless make for tough meat and poor digesstion."

The snake's words were soothing. Not just soothing, but hypnotic. It's head swayed back and forth like a pendulum, or a watch on a chain.

They held Zip Ric in a trance like state, but the snake's whispered words had not stricken Sam. Yet.

The snake hadn't seen him. Sam's mind raced as he tried to think of how to save his friend while not getting himself killed in the process.

For a flashing instant, Sam had deja vu, a sense that he'd been in this very situation before.

That was of course nonsense. He'd never seen a snake outside of a zoo. Until that morning he'd never met a talking squirrel. And he had certainly never been a raccoon before.

But then it dawned on him. Though it had been less than 24 hours before, it felt like a lifetime away. Crouching in a dark hallway beside endless rows of lockers, watching as Bradley and Mitch shook down Charlie for their own twisted enjoyment. The stakes here were higher, and Sam would admit a poisonous snake was far more dangerous than some over-privileged bully, but the situation was the same. Once again, Sam was presented with a choice.

Would he save his own skin and slink away? Or, in spite of the danger, would he stand up for his friend?

Luckily for Zip Ric, those thoughts passed through Sam's head quicker than an eye blink. Jaw clenched and muscles tensing for a fight, Sam made his decision.

CHAPTER ELEVEN

The rattlesnake swayed back and forth with a calm and soothing effect. Its tongue tasted the air, seeming to savor the scent of squirrel and Zip's palatable fear.

"Eassy." it said, in a slow and soothing voice. "The pain passsess quickly. Yess."

The tremble in Zip Ric's tail slowed. He seemed to sag against the stone at his back, like the squirrel's bones had turned to jelly. The snake's words were working.

The snake drew its head back and stilled its swaying, even as its muscles tensed, readying to strike. The snake's mouth parted a hair's width, its own version of a smile, as its eyes narrowed. Dinner time.

That would have been the end of Zip Ric, entirely entranced by the viper's subtle words and hypnotic movements, when something the snake hadn't expected happened.

The stone flew from Sam's paw. Though it missed striking his target by inches as it whizzed harmlessly past to clatter among the other stones, the pitch was enough to save his friend.

The noise of rocks clapping together snapped Zip Ric out of the snake's hypnosis. Zip leapt straight upwards just as the snake struck, too fast for Sam's eyes to follow. The snake missed and bit only empty air.

Zip Ric spun in mid-hop. His claws found the side of the boulder he'd been backed against. Zip's arms and legs wheeled like windmills as he scrambled to hang on.

The snake worked itself back into a tense coil. It ignored wherever the thrown rock had come from and focused only on the slipping squirrel. Sam knew that once the snake rewound it would strike again.

Sam grabbed another stone from the ground and gripped it carefully in his paw. He eyed the snake and tried to imagine its spade shaped head was a catcher's mitt.

See the target. Rotate shoulders in windup. Plant one foot and lunge forward. Follow through with his other leg and shoulders, and flick your wrist.

The stone whistled as it flew. It smacked like a drum against the back of the snake's head.

The snake's face slapped to the ground. It made a coughing sound as it gasped for breath and tried to right itself.

"Zip Ric! The snake's down! Hurry!"

Zip needed no more encouragement. He gave up trying to keep hold of the boulder and dropped to the ground, only inches from where the snake thrashed. Zip thumped the top of the snake's head with his tail as he passed and in one leap landed at Sam's side.

"Thanks! Let's get out of-"

A chilling noise filled the air. Though nearly unconscious, the snake had enough sense to shake the rattle at the end of its tail, making a sound like bones shaking inside a shoebox. The noise bounced among the boulders and stones, and somehow grew louder as it echoed.

Not an echo, Sam realized, but a response.

The whole riverbed came alive with rattling. It seemed to come from the very earth, no doubt from hidden dens filled with the poisonous timber rattlesnakes. They had to get off the ground.

Zip had come to the same conclusion. "This way," Zip called as he scurried on top of a rock and leapt up onto the the tall boulder he'd moments ago struggled to get a grip on.

Sam followed after him, but his chest hit the boulder with the first jump and knocked the wind out of him. He started slipping back toward the deadly ground. Zip Ric grabbed Sam's paw as Sam looked down to try and find somewhere to push with his feet.

The stony riverbed below was moving. Rattlesnakes poured from the earth to pursue the warm blooded creatures that had ventured into their domain.

With a grunt, Zip Ric managed to pull Sam onto the boulder before one of the snakes could bite him on the backside. Zip Ric then jumped over to the top of the next tall stone. Sam took a couple of breaths before following, this time making the leap without slipping over the side. They didn't need to say it aloud, but together they understood a simple fact; to touch the ground would be certain death. In the shadow of any stone could be three feet worth of rattling, coiled muscle and venomous teeth ready to strike.

They continued hopping from boulder to boulder with as much speed as they could manage when they realized their islands of safety were getting further apart.

"There!" Sam said pointing, but Zip Ric was already ahead of him. The squirrel bounced across two more boulders before sticking like glue to the side of a dead tree. It was bleached white by the sun and only had a single knobby limb sticking out from the trunk ten feet or so off the ground.

Sam followed across the last stones with considerably more effort. When his claws bit with satisfaction into the side of the trunk, he never thought he'd be that relieved to be tree climbing.

He shimmied up the smooth trunk, its bark having long ago rotted away, to where Zip Ric had stopped in the nook of the dead tree's lonely limb.

Sam looked over the side. The ground below looked alive as rattlesnakes milled among the rocks looking for their prey. Zip Ric sat up on his haunches and chittered down at them.

"Have you ever seen a snake that close before?" Sam asked.

Zip Ric didn't take his eyes off the clamoring snakes below. "Never." Zip was breathing hard for the first time Sam could remember. "Well, not never. Knew a garden snake once, but he only ate bugs. No hypnosis, smaller fangs. Couldn't talk. We called him Steve. Nice guy, that Steve."

The urgency of the rattling below lessened and after a few minutes stopped entirely. The snakes were still down there, but they'd quieted their alarm.

Sam slumped against the tree. "So now what?" Time was ticking, the sun was moving quickly through the sky and toward the horizon. They had too much to do, meeting rats and saving Zip's home, to be stranded up a dead tree.

"We have to wait. Until nightfall."

"You want to go down there in the dark? Are you crazy?"

Zip Ric shook his head. "Mother always said snakes are the one thing that are less dangerous in the dark. They move slower. Must not be able to see so well. Its our best chance."

Sam leaned out over the branch again, craning his neck and trying to count the snakes. Their scales camouflaged so well with the broken rocks of the dry river bed that they kept disappearing before his eyes. Counting them was impossible. Zip was right. There would be no way past right now.

Green trees towered over the river bed from their destination on the opposite side, with Rodenthold somewhere beyond. Sam surprised himself, thinking about how much he couldn't wait to be back in the woods. Less than a day ago he was too anxious to step foot beneath the trees. Now they looked as welcoming as home after a long journey.

The sun slipped toward the tops of the birch trees they'd passed beneath to reach the river bed. They waited in silence as the sky turned from orange to red. Speaking would keep the snakes alert, and they needed the reptiles' attention to fade with the falling temperatures and dimming light.

Before the sun could slide from view beneath the fading green leaves of the forest, a blanket of wispy clouds swept in from the west and cloaked the purpling sky in gray. Through the veil of clouds, the sun lost all intensity and color as it dropped out of sight beyond the trees.

"Won't be many stars that can cut through that." Zip Ric whispered quietly. "A shame. Starry skies are good luck."

They waited until night had fully overtaken the forest, and then another hour past that. The creaks and croaks of nocturnal creatures provided an eerie soundtrack to Zip and Sam's next, stealthy moves. The moon appeared, shining like a street light in fog through the haze of clouds.

Wordlessly they crept down the side of the old tree like a pair of ninjas.

All was still on the ground. Nothing moved, nothing shifted.

Sam led the way, stepping without a sound onto a boulder beside the dead tree. He turned and hopped to another rock sticking up from the old river bed, the last elevated spot between the river bed and the safety of the trees. Zip Ric landed beside him. Twenty feet of stony ground lay between them and the edge of the dark forest.

Sam didn't see any sign of snakes below. They had to make a run for it.

He put his mouth against Zip Ric's ear. "Ready?" he whispered as quietly as a leaf falling from a tree.

Zip nodded. Sam counted down on his paw. Three. Two. One.

They leapt from their safe vantage point. Sam had almost expected to feel scaly flesh beneath his feet as he landed, but exhaled in relief when he felt cold stones instead.

Rocks shifted beneath his feet and Sam felt the air rush through his ears as he picked up speed, scrambling as fast as he could after Zip Ric and toward the trees. . Any moment he expected to hear rattles and see an ambush of triangular heads rise up from the stones around him.

The attack never came.

Zip Ric reached the woods first and immediately ran up the base of a twin-trunked maple tree. Sam ran past, deeper into the forest and away from the snake den. He'd never been so happy to feel dirt beneath his feet or to hear dried leaves crunching. Any sound that wasn't a rattle was a welcome noise.

Zip Ric dropped to the ground and fell in step beside him. "Wow! That was close!"

Behind them and far back, Sam could suddenly hear the echo of rattles. Sam tried to run even faster as Zip Ric started howling with laughter.

"They're just realizing we slipped away while they slept!" Zip Ric exclaimed, leaping up as he ran to pump one tiny fist in the air. "You bashed a snake with a rock and saved my life! What a story! Think I'll call it Sam The Snake Slayer. Been working it over in my head the whole time we were in that tree. Hard to keep quiet that long without putting your mind on something else. Did you have a hard time staying quiet with all the excitement?"

"Excitement? Zip, you were almost eaten." The sound of rattles had faded into the distance, stout trunks of trees muffling their rhythm.

"Almost eaten is the same as almost slipped, almost caught, or almost remembering where you put that acorn you socked away yesterday. Every squirrel day is filled with a series of almosts, and we always come out ahead." He winked. "Almost always."

Sam let his feet slow down. "Well I'm glad you're alright with it. Those wicked snakes nearly killed you."

"Not wicked, Sam. They're just snakes."

"Putting you into a trance and trying to kill you sounds pretty evil to me."

Zip Ric shrugged. "It's just what they do. They have to eat. If eating things makes you evil, mulberries probably think we're pretty cruel after how many we devoured today!"

Sam didn't say anything.

"Besides," the squirrel continued, "it was my own fault. I was careless to just go bounding through their home without thinking. Like Mother always said,

'Whether 'neath shade trees or open sky,

always keep a careful eye.

It's always where you fail to look

that the greatest dangers lie.'

Sam muttered, "If you say so." Thinking of the snakes made his skin crawl.

They continued on through the darkness. Every noise to the side or overhead reignited his fear. Something to the left rustled through the underbrush.

"Not to worry," Zip Ric said, "just a field mouse. Right now, the place we need to keep watch on is the sky. Not all owls are as friendly as Vera and Humphrey."

Slowly the forest changed again. It wasn't as obvious as the shift from hardwoods and pine to the marsh where they'd found the Tearful Willow Tree, and it wasn't announced by great rocks sticking up from the ground like at the snake's den. Sam couldn't put his paw on it.

"There's something peculiar about the trees here." He finally said.

Zip looked up. "Really?"

Sam eyed them as they slipped through the darkness between rows of trees. Maples, all of them. Even in the dark he could tell by their leaves, shaped like pointy green crowns, and their odd seed pods.

The maple seeds were pebble sized, each with a blade-like fibrous extension. It looked almost like an insect's wing. When seeds fell from a maple, they wouldn't plummet to the ground like an acorn. Instead the blade caught air and twirled like a helicopter to carry it away from the parent tree and deliver the seed softly to the ground.

Seeds and empty husks from feasting birds littered the ground between the rows of maples. Then Sam realized what was off about the forest.

"These trees line up too neatly. They're in rows." He thought a moment. "People must have planted them."

Zip Ric took an excited breath. "That's what Humphrey meant! Remember his riddle? He said 'look for trees that don't have forgetful squirrels to thank for their placement'. Do you know what that means?"

They spied the end of the trees ahead. Through the darkness, even with the cloudy sky hiding the moon, Sam saw where the rows of maples ended. The forest's edge.

The trees thinned and finally gave way to grass. At least it had once been grass. Now weeds and nettles stuck out several feet tall from the unkempt lawn. Sumacs and other volunteer trees stood proud among the weeds.

Sam's heart beat in excitement as they pushed through the dense brush. At last they came to the end of the overgrown grass.

A dark sea of asphalt stretched out before them, flat and featureless and empty of cars.

Beyond the parking lot, the old mall was square and squat. From this distance its architecture, full of uninspired right angles and uniform heights, looked almost like a scattering of over-sized children's blocks. A dark stain filling the horizon.

Rodenthold.

CHAPTER TWELVE

To Sam, it was Rodenthold's stillness that he found most unnerving.

Forests were meant to be quiet and peaceful, but not shopping malls. They were meant to bustle with shopping carts and traffic, people on cell phones and carrying bags, lights and noise and activity. But the abandoned mall was still and silent.

"It doesn't look all that welcoming, does it?" Zip said, his words whispered as though they might awaken the night.

At each end of the building, the mall's squareness grew to twice the height. Those must have been the department stores, Sam guessed, now empty and unlit. They looked like looming black towers to either side of the main mall building, making the place look every bit the fortress it had become.

The only light came from the clouded moon above, and none from inside the old mall. Silence filled the parking lot like a looming shadow.

Sam's heart hammered in his chest. There was no sense waiting, no matter how much he longed to just stay hidden. "Let's go," Sam whispered. They'd come this far, it was time to get on with it.

He pointed a clawed finger at the closest section of the mall, the side wall of one of the hulking department stores, and Zip Ric nodded a silent affirmative.

Together they stepped out into the open and onto the parking lot, still warm underfoot from soaking up sunshine all day. It reeked of old oil and gasoline. Instinct flared, encouraging Sam to flee back into the tall grass and the cool dirt of the forest. But he dug his claws in and continued forward.

Zip Ric slunk low to the ground moving his feet with deliberate care, like a rock climber scaling a sheer cliff face.

Weeds grew up through cracks in the asphalt to break up the monotony. Towering light poles, their lights extinguished and dead, reached toward the sky like long skeletal arms.

In the distance, Sam heard car engines groaning and tires pushing on asphalt. Traffic on nearby roads. But Rodenthold and the surrounding trees obscured headlights, and the evening commuters passed by without stopping, leaving the old mall lonesome and cloaked only in shadow.

They passed an overturned, rusting shopping cart. The thought that it was likely the only thing with wheels in this old parking lot had just crossed Sam's mind when a new sound filled his ears.

It started as a light and distant scraping against the asphalt, but quickly rose in volume. A harsh grating sound, like his parents' coffee grinder in the morning, scoured at the night's silence.

Sam glanced back in the direction of the noise.

A pair of tall, dark shadows were moving quickly towards them, growing in size even as the volume increased. It took Sam a moment to finally identify the source of the noise, and another moment for him to recognize the shadows. In another instant, he heard a sound that chilled Sam to his bones.

Over the grinding din of skateboard wheels on old asphalt, a familiar laugh echoed across the parking lot as the moon cast its muted glare on a head of spiked hair above an over-sized body. Bradley Banks had found him.

They were sitting ducks out in the open.

"Come on!" Sam waved Zip forward. The squirrel had stopped, looking back mesmerized by the boys on skateboards, but Sam's words woke up Zip's flight response.

They dashed across the asphalt toward the unwelcoming shadow of Rodenthold, all thoughts of stealth and hesitation abandoned. Getting into the safety of the overgrown landscaping that sprouted up along the walls was their only chance.

The noise of the skateboards grew louder, but Sam didn't dare to look back. He tried not to worry about how painful a heavy plastic skateboard wheel rolling over his tail would feel, and kept running, focusing only on reaching the towering walls and finding safety in their shadows.

Sam couldn't believe his bad luck. Miles from home, wearing completely different skin, and he still couldn't put the troubles of Mapleton Middle School behind him.

How had Bradley found him? There was no way the bully would recognize Sam as a raccoon, right? Still Sam felt certain that, if he caught them, Bradley would be as merciless to an innocent raccoon and squirrel as he was towards new classmates.

Side by side, Zip Ric and Sam leapt over a chipped concrete curb, onto the sidewalk and then beneath an overgrown cedar shrub.

Sam spun around and readied himself to dash in one way or another away from pursuit. At least in the foliage his smaller size would be an advantage against the goonish Bradley.

It was only then he realized they hadn't been chased at all. Bradley and the second shadow were meandering around on the parking lot on top of their skateboards and apparently hadn't even noticed Sam and Zip Ric's escape. That was good, because Sam was panting to catch his breath after the sprint.

Bradley was attempting to hop his skateboard over a crack in the parking lot, while the other shadow watched with his own board popped up against his leg. Sam recognized the other boy as Mitch, of course, who fumbled for something in his pocket.

Bradley cursed loudly as he mistimed the jump, sending him staggering to catch his balance in one direction while his board rolled off noisily in the other.

"Want a cigarette?" Mitch asked as he pulled a pack from his pocket. "Stole a few from my dad."

Bradley waved him off as he trotted to retrieve his board. "No way man, those are gross." It surprised Sam to hear there was anything he and

Bradley agreed on.

Zip Ric tucked himself to Sam's side. "What are those?" he whispered through chattering teeth.

"Bullies. Or buffoons. Depends on who you ask."

Mitch lit his own cigarette with clumsy fingers. "Suit yourself." He sucked in a mouthful of pungent smoke before breaking into a coughing fit.

"Yeah, real cool, Mitch." Bradley popped the skateboard into his hand by stomping on its back. "You look like my grandma puffing on that thing."

They exchanged a few taunts and insults back and forth. Mitch kept sucking on the end of the cigarette and coughing immediately afterward. Watching him do it made Sam's stomach queasy. The faint stink of smoke found its way through the night air to make Sam's nose wrinkle.

Mitch point toward the mall. "Think it's really haunted?" he said, changing the subject between wheezes.

Bradley snorted. "No way."

"But I heard-"

"Whatever you heard was wrong. It's just rats. They've wrecked the place though, my dad said."

"I'm not sure. Some tenth graders said they tried to go in and-"

"Dude, its just rats." Bradley cut him off again.

"Alright," Mitch laughed, and then coughed again on the smoke. "I dare you to go and pull on the door."

"What? Don't be stupid. I'm not going in there."

Mitch dropped the cigarette, crushing it beneath his shoe. "You chicken? I didn't say go inside, just go open the door. If it's just rats, what are you scared of? It's probably locked anyway and won't budge."

"Fine," Bradley sneered. "But if I get rat poop on my hand, I'm wiping it on you." They hopped on their skateboards and rolled slowly toward Rodenthold.

Sam carefully maneuvered beneath the cedar bushes until he could see both the bullies and the glass doors with their looming blackness within.

Zip Ric tapped excitedly at Sam's shoulder and pointed upwards. Sam followed his gesture to the old mall's roof.

Above the doors, a shadow moved across the top of the wall. Something not quite as black as the old brick walls, dusk among the dark. Something with fur that caught the filtered moonlight. Sam realized then that it was not just a something, but several somethings.

The rat army, it had to be. The whole section of wall above the door filled with their silhouettes. Shadowy lumps lined up in a row on the wall like a row of teeth. There must have been hundreds of them up there. They made no sound, at least not one that could be heard over grinding skateboard wheels, as they waited there at the edge of the roof line above the doorway.

An ambush. The rats had taken positions and were awaiting Bradley and Mitch's arrival. Sam's eyes swiveled back and forth between his unsuspecting classmates and the rats above them.

Bradley and Mitch made no indication they'd spotted the rats, but they still seemed apprehensive as they rolled up a ramp onto the sidewalk in silence. They popped their boards into their hands and paused before the line of dark glass doors.

The sneer had disappeared from Bradley's face. To Sam he looked visibly nervous, in no hurry to go and test the door handle. So much for all his tough talk.

The rats above didn't budge, staying still as statues.

"Go on then," Mitch said. He took a half step backward as he spoke. "See if it'll open."

Bradley drew in a deep breath and forced a laugh, as if he could fool himself to bravery. He took two long strides to the door and grabbed the metal handle in his meaty hand.

The door swung easily on its hinges and Bradley's mouth fell open in dumbfounded surprise.

A piercing war cry filled the night from the horde of rats massed above the doors. The call came so suddenly and with such a shrill volume that Sam had to cover his ears.

Bradley froze in place, the door pulled half open in his hand as his eyes slowly made their way up the wall to the source of the blood curdling sound. Mitch's mouth was agape as he pointed up at the line of howling rats over the door.

Then as suddenly as it began, the war cry ceased. Bradley, door still pulled partway open in his hand, turned back at Mitch and shrugged. Then a lone voice pierced the night.

"NOW!"

There were no additional shouts from the rats, just the clatter of a sudden rainstorm. Bradley ducked his head and Mitch spun away from the rain.

No, not rain, Sam saw. Raindrops didn't bounce off the sidewalk.

Thousands of tiny pebbles ricocheted off the ground. The rats were hurling them from the roof above.

Mitch turned and sprinted away from the attack with his skateboard under his arm. He never looked back.

Bradley flinched and winced, and then pulled the door all the way open to duck inside for shelter from the shower of stones.

He vanished inside for only a moment, and the rain of stones ceased as suddenly as it had begun.

Seconds later, a different door further down the line burst open. Bradley fell outside, backwards, to the sidewalk. His eyes bulged as he turned over and tried to scramble away on hands and knees from whatever he'd seen inside.

Just then a wave of fur, tails, and teeth splashed out from the wall of glass doors. The rats howled as they charged, leaping onto Bradley's back and scurrying up his legs. Bradley shrieked as ten rats latched onto the back of his jeans and t-shirt.

Somehow Bradley got his feet underneath him and broke into a run.

The rats who'd charged from the doorway, their enemy in flight, then began filing orderly off Bradley's back. With their blitz attack successful, they dropped one by to the pavement as casually as if descending a staircase.

Bradley disappeared into the night along with the fading sound of his terrified shrieks, and only then did Sam feel the wide smile on his face.

A victory cheer erupted from the walls as the rats on the ground high-fived and marched on two legs back toward the glass doors.

As the rats on the ground drew near, Sam could see they were strangely equipped. Each had a band of what looked like a piece of gnawed, black shoelace draped from a shoulder and across their chests like a sash. The sashes connected to a belt of the same material around their waist. Stranger still, each rat bore a piece of twig or unbent wire clothes hanger as tall as their upright height and sharpened at the end. Rat sized spears? It was hard to tell in the darkness. To complete the oddity, each of the rat soldiers wore a rounded helmet formed from bottle caps or ping pong ball halves.

"Reload!" bellowed the mighty squeak from above. The cheering ceased, and the rat shadows along the wall disappeared from the edge. With no skateboard wheels to drown out the sounds, Sam could hear thousands of scurrying claws moving overhead in the night.

The mob of rats reappeared from a service door on the opposite side of the glass entryway from where Sam and Zip were huddled. The service door was painted the same color as the mall bricks and invisible if you weren't looking for it. The multitude of rats swept outside like a tide, chanting as each took a position in one of a dozen long lines that stretched from the service door out into the parking lot. They were similarly equipped as the soldiers that had burst forth from the doorway, though their spears were strapped across their backs by their shoelace sashes. Sam couldn't imagine the rats' helmets would do much to protect them against an exterminator's boot or a cat or whatever else might try to attack the rats, but they looked imposing none the less.

With another barked command, the rats began scooping up stones and passing them shoulder to shoulder down the line and back inside. The lines of rats swayed like tentacles as they bent and swooped to collect every last stone.

In just minutes they'd nearly swept the area clean, harvesting their spent ammo for reuse, more efficient than any broom or vacuum cleaner.

"If I could get my family to work like that," Zip Ric remarked, "we'd finish the fall harvest in an afternoon."

As the rest worked, a smaller rat broke away from the stone collection assembly lines and marched toward Bradley's skateboard, abandoned in his haste to flee.

This rat wore a sash and belt slightly different than the rest, made of a dingy white shoelace instead of black or brown. A sewing needle hung from its hip like a sheathed sword.

Three burly rats with an assortment of scars and notches in their ears followed the smaller rat, each clutching their spears at the ready as they approached the skateboard.

Bradley's abandoned skateboard lay overturned, its wheels sticking up in the air like an opossum playing dead. A flicker of moonlight caught on a blaze of white fur on the small rat's forehead.

The small rat placed a paw on one of the solid plastic wheels and spun it on the axle. The trio of thicker rats stood a step back and looked on as the small rat with the needle sword studied the wheel's movement, watching it wobble.

Behind them, the lines of rats collecting stones finished their work. With ordered precision, they broke from their assembly lines and formed up into two square blocks of rodents standing on two legs at attention.

"Should we stand up and introduce ourselves?" Zip Ric nudged Sam. "I think that rat might be in charge. See how the others all watch what she's doing?"

"She? How can you tell?" Sam whispered back, just as a another big rat ran over to the skateboard and confirmed Zip Ric's inclinations.

"We've completed cleanup operations, Lady Olenthia. What would you have-"

The small rat's tail snapped as she spun around. "You shall address me as General. General Olenthia. I'll not remind you a third time this night, Clive."

"Right. Apologies ma'am." The big rat, Clive, said before hanging his head.

"I've never seen a device such as this," General Olenthia gestured at the skateboard. "We shall bring it before the Emperor. He will know its name, and how to put it to use."

Sam gulped down his fear and whispered to Zip Ric. "Now or never. Here goes nothing," then he stood up from his hiding place in the cedar bush. "It's called a-"

Clive and the other three big rats leapt between Sam and General Olenthia, leveling their spears. The two blocks of rats broke rank and reformed into an arc to surround the shrub Sam and Zip had taken refuge beneath.

Zip Ric slowly rose to his feet in the vegetation. A wide grin spread across his face as he waved at the rats.

"Identify yourselves!" shouted another of the big rats, waving a spear for emphasis.

Sam and Zip both talked at once and over each other so it came out in an unintelligable jumble.

With a horizontal slicing motion with her paw, General Olenthia silenced them both.

She turned to her three bodyguards. "Seize them. They too shall be brought before Emperor Nezearius. He has ways of dealing with spies."

The one called Clive pushed Sam on the shoulder, and pointed to the service door from which the army of rats had emerged. The blocks of rats, every one of them now holding a spear in hand, closed in around what had been his hiding place.

"But we're not spies," Sam said as he was marched toward the service door. "We've come to ask for your help."

"Silence." The small rat said. The rats had flipped the skateboard back onto its wheels, and General Olenthia stood on its sandpaper-like surface. "I, General Olenthia Von Brightwhisker of the Fourth Legion, hereby charge you with seeking to infiltrate the kingdom of Rodenthold. For your crimes you will stand before the Emperor. You may plead for pity before his throne."

"Hmph," Sam heard the rat called Clive say to one of his fellows. "Never seen that work, how about you?"

CHAPTER THIRTEEN

The darkness overwhelmed Sam. He could feel it around his body, tangible, like it was pressing in on his shoulders and chest.

No, it wasn't the darkness he felt. It was the rats.

They pawed and pushed from every side, moving in a wave through the formless nothing the dark created, finding their way through Rodenthold's pitch black entryway not by sight but by instinct and repetition. And touch.

The noise was as thick as the darkness. Gruff rat voices shouted curses as the Fourth Legion bounced against each other on its way through the dark. The shouts mixed with the grinding roll of skateboard wheels on the tile floor ahead. Somewhere behind, Sam heard a voice he was certain belonged to Zip making indecipherable yelps in the boiling mass of rats. The squirrel's shouts sounded pained and only added to the chaotic noise all around.

"Zip!" Sam shouted. This made laughter bloom around him. The rats mocked Sam's distress by sarcastically mimicking his call. Zip Ric either didn't respond or it was drowned out by rat voices. Sam wished he could somehow help, but for now they were both on their own.

Sam's paws treaded over unseen, discarded objects in the dark. There were bits of rubbish that could have been shredded cardboard or plastic packaging, and slimy spots that he told himself were probably just a bit of old food to keep his stomach from retching.

Once he stepped down on what felt like an abandoned electrical cord, and only realized it was someone's tail when he heard a pained grunt just ahead and had an unseen paw smack him across the nose in retaliation.

The sounds from the Fourth Legion grew as the throng pushed through the darkness, frustration at being blind and constantly bumping into each other making the air thick with tension. It seemed like a riot could erupt at any moment.

"Mind yourselves!" the stern command of General Olenthia's distinctive voice rose over the din from somewhere not far ahead of Sam.

The rat army's boiling unruliness was reduced to a simmer at her command. Still, Sam heard a few muffled snickers in the ranks, the way misbehaved children who've just been scolded can't help but giggle when the teacher turns away.

"I wager whatever you jokers think is so bleedin' funny," growled a threatening voice that had to be Clive or one of General Olenthia's other scarred captains, "wouldn't be nearly so if I bit off half your ear."

The threat silenced the laughter and, though he was reasonably certain the threatening voice had come from somewhere to the left, Sam sure hoped he didn't accidentally step on that particular rat's tail.

The choking darkness continued for several more grueling, crowded minutes, before Sam's eyes finally got to see something other than overwhelming black.

Ahead, he perceived a faint, horizontal sliver of pale blue light. It started only an inch or so wide, but grew with each step. The bottom of a door, he guessed, letting in light from the opposite side. They seemed to be marching straight toward it. At once Sam was relieved that he'd soon be able to see again but also terrified of what his eyes might find once they were no longer protected by the darkness.

"Company, halt!" came the General's command before the doorway.

The marching stopped, and for a moment Sam enjoyed a break from the constant bumping and jostling around him. Then came another shout, "Door Team. Forward!"

A rush of rats from around and behind pushed and shoved to get into position. Sam winced when a running rat struck him straight in the back. He reached behind, his paws finding the stunned rat's shoulders in the darkness. "Watch it," Sam grunted as he half guided, half shoved the rat around him.

There was a pause, and for once the company of rats were silent as they waited for the next order.

"Listen up," General Olenthia barked. Her voice came from not more than a few feet ahead. "You are the Fourth Legion of Rodenthold, the most disciplined regiment in this Empire. You are no common rabble, no common rats. Remember this as you march among the citizenry."

The rats remained quiet as General Olenthia continued. "You have the duty and privilege of escorting foreigners to the Emperor's throne. His esteemed judgment will determine if they are delegates or spies, but until then they shall be afforded your best behavior." She paused a moment, and Sam gulped at the thought of being labeled a spy.

"Do I make myself clear?!"

"Yes Ma'am!" the Fourth Legion responded in regimented unison, without a hint of the animosity that had overtaken their attitudes in the dark.

Another command sounded and the pair of doors began groaning on their hinges. A wide open space yawned into view beyond the door. Overhead, skylights lining the ceiling let in the moon's pale glow to light the way.

The sudden burst of moonlight would have been startling if the stink pouring through the doorway hadn't overwhelmed his senses. Sam had never smelled such a stench. Like an overflowing trash can left out in the sun, a dumpster full of used diapers, and a refrigerator stuffed with rotting broccoli all mixed together.

The rabble around him, that had been so formless and disorderly in the dark, fell into a precise rank and file as they began to march forward from the department store and into the main sections of the mall. That was the difference between moving unseen by your commanders versus being under their watchful eyes, apparently.

General Olenthia traveled at the head of the column, still standing atop Bradley's abandoned skateboard.

Though smaller than the rat soldiers to either side of Sam, the General had an imposing presence as she stood arrow straight with narrowed eyes, one paw resting on the eye of her needle sword as she looked side to side at the kingdom around them. The white fur on her brow, he saw now as it caught the moonlight, was diamond shaped and almost seemed to glow with an icy fire.

Sam stumbled forward with the marching rats, through the doorway and into the abandoned mall's main causeway even as he gagged on the odor. He coughed, feeling like he might throw up the mulberries he'd eaten so many hours ago.

A sturdy paw patted his shoulders. "Welcome to Rodenthold," laughed the rat at his side. "Where if her citizens don't kill you, the stench just might!"

Sam suddenly remembered his friend, and spun his head around, looking for Zip Ric.

It took him only a moment to find Zip in the next row back. To Sam's surprise, the squirrel had an ear to ear smile across his face as he marched on two legs in step with the rats. Zip Ric waved excitedly when his eyes met Sam's.

"Watch it!" grumbled rats around him as Sam maneuvered over to his friend's side. Displaced rats quickly filed forward to fill the space Sam had abandoned.

"Are you alright?" Sam asked, looking over Zip Ric with concern. Zip seemed uninjured, but Sam questioned him about the pained cries in the dark.

"Oh I'm fine," Zip said, "just very ticklish. I was getting bumped into from all sides and couldn't contain myself."

They walked together with the tide of General Olenthia's Fourth Legion down the center aisle of the building. Once the aisle would have accommodated mall-walking grandmothers and loitering teens, now it allowed clear passage for the rodent military.

Rodenthold blossomed around them like a rotting flower. Trash, refuse, and scraps lay in heaps and mounds to either side of where they marched. Sam saw tattered furniture, gnawed plastic toys, and the remains of shoes among the piles. Some of the trash piles spilled out from abandoned storefronts to form individual pointed peaks, like a range of miniature, filthy mountains. Other areas seemed deliberately heaped, like clothes racks stacked on top of each other to form rat sized skyscrapers and ramshackle apartment buildings. A tangled web of junk. There seemed to be no rhyme or reason to the chaos, and there, too, seemed no end to the number of rats.

Rats crawled over every surface on both sides. Other things did, too. Roaches, centipedes, and other long-antennaed insects scurried along the floor and walls, careful to stay out of reach of any rat lest they become a meal.

The din of rat industry rose above the noise of Olenthia's grinding skateboard wheels as rats milled among the piles to either side and darted about on endless errands, gathering garbage and chewing at everything, even the walls. Other sounds, unidentifiable cries and screams from further back in the dark made Sam shiver. This was the noise of progress, apparently, as the rats continued to transform the mall into a rodent's paradise.

But they didn't look happy. Sam watched as rats clawed and squabbled their way past each other. It looked exactly how the trip through the dark with the Fourth Legion had felt. He watched as several shoving matches broke out among the citizen rats. One featured dozens of combatants, a full-on brawl. The block of soldiers kept marching, ignoring the upheaval all around them. When they left one uproar behind, another soon replaced it with even more chaos.

"Is it just me," Zip Ric asked as he looked over to the side, "Or do the citizen rats seem a little grumpy?"

Before Sam could respond, a command from ahead reached his ears.

"Prisoners." Olenthia had turned around on the skateboard to face them as they continued through the mall. She gestured for them to draw closer with a calm but stern expression on her face.

This time the soldier rats didn't complain as Sam and Zip shouldered their way through the ranks.

As they reached the row behind the skateboard, General Olenthia dismissed the pair of panting rats that had been pushing from either side of the skateboard and looked to Sam. "Would you mind making yourself useful as we speak?"

Sam gritted his teeth but didn't protest as he pressed his front paws on the gritty, sandpaper-like surface of Bradley's skateboard and walked on his hind legs behind it. The board moved surprisingly easy, and he found he had to change his hand position to keep it from rolling away out of control. Zip Ric stayed beside him while Sam pushed.

General Olenthia gave a satisfied nod as she looked down on them from her perch. "Tell me, prisoners, what do you think of our fair city?"

"It's about-" Sam started to say.

"No." Olenthia's firm tone cut him off. "Raccoons are known far and wide for their cleverness and trickery. Though I've never met one of your kind, I'd rather not be made a fool. Let us hear the squirrel's opinions."

Sam looked down at Zip Ric for an answer. The squirrel scratched his head before responding. "Well, I'm not sure I'd use the word 'fair' to describe it."

Some of the citizen rats ahead and to the left momentarily caught Sam's attention. The rats had noticed the passing block of troops and stopped what they were doing to hurl insults and curses at the marching soldiers. The Fourth Legion ignored them as they marched on.

"To say such words could be construed as treason," Olenthia said, responding to Zip's assessment of Rodenthold, "to the wrong set of ears at least. Explain."

"I guess what I mean, Ms. General, is that when I think of home, I think of open skies and cool breezes, happy family members all around and sunshine. But that's only my opinion. It's alright that rats think of different stuff to make them happy." He'd responded so quickly that Zip's words rang of truth rather than simple appeasement.

Olenthia didn't say anything as she studied the squirrel's face for a moment, then she looked off thoughtfully to the side. It seemed like a good opening to bring up their mission, to convince the rats to join in the Ric Family's fight.

Sam started to speak. "That's actually why we're-"

"Legion!" Olenthia barked suddenly, cutting Sam's words short again as she pointed in the direction of her gaze. "Prepare to repel dissenters!"

The rat soldiers turned as one to the side and reformed ranks in the same direction as the taunting citizenry that had caught Sam's attention. Sam's eyes bulged as a wave of howling rats poured down the side of a pile of filthy clothing toward the waiting line of soldiers. The Fourth Legion was under attack.

Sam glanced quickly back to Olenthia, and was surprised to see her eyes weren't full of fury or fear. Her face held none of the anticipation he felt. In fact, she almost looked sad. The clash of battle drew Sam's attention back to the front.

The soldier rats had taken an interesting formation. The front row held their spears in two hands across their bodies, shoulder to shoulder, to form a horizontal row of spears, almost like a fence. They then dug their feet in and thrust both hands forward to keep the rioting rats at bay, like a fighter holding back a shorter foe. The attackers couldn't get past their upheld wall of spears. Then the second row, holding their own weapons butt-end forward, whacked at the shoulders and noses of the fiercest attackers until the main agitators lost their will to fight.

As the angriest rats retreated back up the side of the laundry pile, the rest of the riot lost steam too. Still spitting and throwing taunts at Olenthia's troops, the attacking rats dropped back, less of a retreat and more like a loss of interest.

The Legion soldiers stayed braced for several more seconds until it became clear the threat had truly dissipated. Then General Olenthia called for them to move out, and the rats fell back in line.

Sam saw the scarred rat named Clive stomp back into place to his left. Clive's eyes were on the hillside of soiled laundry, still swarming with other rats. "Idiots," he muttered.

They resumed their march. The center aisle narrowed the further they went as the trash heaps to either side grew in size. The column snaked through the chunks of debris and fallen ceiling tiles jutting into the walkway. Sam maneuvered the skateboard by carefully shifting his weight enough to turn the noisy vessel but not upend its prestigious passenger.

General Olenthia had turned to face forward again. After a long silence, and without turning back, she said. "Raccoon. You were about to speak, and I believe make some excuse for your presence beneath our walls. Have I guessed correctly?"

Sam just said, "Yes."

"Very good, I'd like to hear this tale recounted before we reach the Emperor. However," She turned to look back over her shoulder, the diamond shaped blaze of fur on her forehead again catching moonlight, "I am not so foolish as to hear a raccoon's carefully delivered version of the tale. Squirrel, you may proceed."

With wide eyes, Zip looked up at Sam. Sam shrugged, as if to say 'why not?'.

Zip Ric cleared his throat into a tiny balled fist. "Well, it all started two-hundred and eighty-seven years ago," began Zip's far too long history of the Ric's Family Oak tree as they continued the long march through Rodenthold.

At least the story might take Sam's mind off the smell.

CHAPTER FOURTEEN

Zip Ric's story wound on even as their path toward the heart of Rodenthold did the same.

Twice more the Fourth Legion had to stop and fight back bands of rioters. One group pitched beads and pebbles at the soldiers, and Sam realized suddenly that the Fourth Legion's helmets were not for protection from humans at all but from their fellow rats.

Zip paused his story telling at each scuffle, and resumed right where he left off when they continued marching.

General Olenthia listened with complete patience, only interrupting when it was necessary to bark an order at her soldiers. Clive shouldered over to Sam's side and muttered, "Doesn't your little pal know what 'skip ahead to the important parts' means?"

Finally Zip Ric reached the point of the story about owls, then snakes, and finally seeking shelter in Rodenthold's shrubbery at the sight of the Bradley Banks.

"Long story short," Zip said at last, "me and Sam are here to get your help to save my family's home."

"Interesting," Olenthia said. "Dizzying at points, but I think I understand the majority of your cause. It seems you were perhaps not in league with the two that tried to infiltrate the walls after all."

"So you'll help us?" Sam blurted. He'd stayed silent, somehow, through Zip's whole long story.

Olenthia shrugged. "Perhaps, Sam," she said, having learned his name from Zip's story, "but that is not my decision to make." Then she spoke no more.

At last the path widened into what had been the mall's food court, and Sam saw a marvel of rat construction.

A great wall rose before them, spanning from a burnt out Hibachi Grill sign on the left side and across to what had been an ice cream parlor on the right. A dozen more skylights high above in the ceiling cast the area in blue shadows.

The wall was built from dozens of flat rectangular panels. Salvaged tables, refrigerator doors, bathroom stall pieces, and other items from inside the mall had been collected and bound together with rat ingenuity and who knew what else. Sam even spied an overturned arcade game laying among the wreckage. The panel faces were stacked, long side down, giving the wall an unkempt, checkerboard pattern that rose over six feet high.

"Welcome, boys," Clive chuckled, "to the Vermin Keep."

A call went up from the wall as the Fourth Legion approached. Shadows scurried along the top, like soldiers behind a rampart.

"Stop here," Olenthia said to Sam. She hopped off the skateboard when it came to a halt. Then Olenthia turned to the wall and swept into a deep bow.

"Who goes there?" came a grizzled voice from the wall above.

"I am General Olenthia, commander of the Fourth Legion." She did not stand as she spoke. "We are escorting a pair of prisoners caught before our walls and seek audience before the Emperor."

A harsh, curt laugh echoed from the top in response. Then muted voices, arguing, drifted down from the wall's rampart.

At last they called down again. "Alright, you may pass. But not everybody! Leave most of that scum outside."

Sam was close enough to Olenthia to hear her issue a frustrated growl before she stood up. When she turned back to her troops, though, she was the picture of composure.

"Vanguard, you'll accompany me and the prisoners inside." Clive and a dozen other large rats stomped to Olenthia's side.

"You remaining captains, stay alert." She continued. "Cycle the watch until we return." Olenthia looked at Sam and pointed at the skateboard. "Bring that inside as well."

A long piece of particle board rose six inches off the ground to expose a shadowed gap for a doorway. Olenthia led the way on foot. Burly rats with crossed arms watched from the walls above as Sam ducked to enter the opening. The tunnel was longer than he guessed, and it was a dozen steps or more before Sam emerged back into the veiled moonlight shining from the skylights overhead.

The food court was as full of trash and refuse as the rest of Rodenthold. Mounds of what looked like mostly food wrappers were stacked haphazardly throughout with clouds of flies buzzing above them.

Thick rats, as big or bigger than Clive and the other members of Olenthia's Vanguard, lounged against the heaps of filth, without any of the hustle and bustle of the rats beyond the Vermin Keeps walls. They eyed Sam and Zip with amusement and joked among themselves.

"Rat nobility?" Sam wondered aloud, making the guess based on the rat's overgrown size and lack of activity.

"Hardly," Clive said, keeping his voice down. "They're the Emperor's Chosen. His personal army. Meanest rats beneath this roof. Even somebody your size would be smart not to cross them."

Olenthia led the way to a bank of restaurants on the far wall. The skateboard's wheels clicked as it rolled over the tile floor. Sam waved flies away from his face as they stopped beneath a tall counter top.

Faded yellow letters above announced this restaurant as PIZZA PETE'S, and featured a cartoon man wearing a chef's hat. The cartoon mascot, obviously 'Pete' Sam guessed, was twirling the side of a thick moustache and wore a smile that made Sam uneasy. In the shadows, even the cartoon face looked sinister.

They waited in silence, staring up at the counter as though a teenage cashier would appear at any moment to take their order. Sam's stomach grumbled. Even with Rodenthold's stench and the Vermin Keep's buzzing flies trying to suppress his appetite, the thought of a stretchy-cheesed pizza made his hunger rally.

"Make way, make way!"

The shout came from within Pizza Pete's, and grew in volume as it continued. "Behold! The savior of the sewers, the titan of the trash pile! Our lord of the laundry heap and magician of muck!"

Zip Ric clapped his front paws together and trembled in anticipation.

"The star of salvage! The chieftain of crumbs!" The voice was getting louder, closer. All eyes looked up at the counter top.

First appeared six giant guard rats. Members of the Emperor's Chosen, no doubt. They peeled off, three to a side, and stood shoulder to shoulder with their spears at attention.

Next came a tiny rat, who scurried to stand in the shadow beside one set of three guards. It wore a purple sash over its shoulder and what looked like a miniature black beret over one ear. Its carefully groomed whiskers stuck out to the side and the rat stood with an air of smug nobility.

The small rat held a paw over his chest. What he lacked in size, he made up for in volume. "All bow," his shouts echoed, "before the ruler of refuse and the vicar of vile. Mightiest rat in the realm!"

"Behold! The great Emperor of Rodenthold, his eminence, his majesty, his highness! Emperor Nezearius!"

Based on that grand introduction, the rat who stepped into view looked nothing like what Sam had imagined.

An ancient, scowling rat hobbled forward. Emperor Nezearius clutched a knobby staff, no more than a twig, using it as a walking stick. In his youth, Nezearius would have likely been as large as his bodyguard retainers, but now his ears, whiskers, and back drooped with age. The paw clutching his staff was missing a finger and the Emperor's fur was streaked in long stripes of paling gray, washed out by time and battle.

Emperor Nezearius shuffled forward to stand beside the now bowing purple-sashed announcer and leaned heavy on his staff. Yellow eyes narrowed as he scanned his line of bodyguards from left to right, and then the formation of soldiers below. Nezearius's eyes hesitated on Sam as they passed, but did not stop for long. There was a tension in the air as this inspection took place, and Sam thought he saw even a few of the bodyguards arrayed along the counter top trembling during the long silence.

Finally Emperor Nezearius snorted, and then reached out to cuff the announcer rat on the side of his head. The little rat staggered, almost losing his balance, but recovered his feet to stay on the counter and resumed his bow. The rat's beret wasn't so lucky. It fell from his head and fluttered to the floor.

"What is the meaning of this?" Nezearius barked to no one in particular. "Stand up, stand up, you fools." The bodyguards, announcer, and members of the Fourth Legion tentatively straightened back to attention. The Emperor's glare swung around among the assembled.

"That one, that one there." A grizzled, crooked finger from the old rat's paw directed his malicious words right at Sam. Sam's heart quickened in his chest. "The raccoon. He did not bow before me!" For emphasis, the old rat struck the counter with the butt of his staff.

Olenthia glanced back to where Sam and Zip stood frozen, before addressing the Emperor in a calm, steady voice. "My lord, I beg forgiveness for the prisoner's insolence. It is my mistake. I failed to brief them on proper procedure when standing before your greatness."

"Do you see? These creatures of the wood, they know nothing of order, of rule, of reason." Nezearius now waved his finger around, gesturing to make his point, his shouts directed at no one in particular. "Too ignorant to even know their betters. Is that what you would return to? Huh?"

Olenthia waited for the Emperor's ranting to cease, and then attempted to change the subject.

"My lord, this night your armies repelled a pair of humans from the walls, and we bring you a gift." She gestured at the skateboard. "A relic of the invaders."

"Yes, yes," the Emperor waved dismissively. "We'll have it delivered to the refinery for hauling mortar and slag. Get to the point, what of these prisoners?"

A trio of scowling rats appeared from the shadows. They looked at Sam with narrowed eyes as they snatched the skateboard from beneath his paws. Even though they were rats, Sam recognized them for what they truly were; he knew a bully when he saw one. That seemed to fit the bill for the

Emperor as well as all his Chosen bodyguards.

As the sound of the skateboard wheels faded into the darkness, Olenthia began. "We then apprehended these two at the foot of our walls following the battle, not more than a half an hour ago. We brought them straight here, to stand before you. We thought they were possibly in league with the human invaders, but-"

"We had nothing to do with them!" Sam blurted before he could bite his tongue. Olenthia spun around, needle sword in hand and a fire in her eyes that she'd not shown before. Sam raised his paws like a captured criminal on a cop show.

When Olenthia spoke to break the tense silence, she kept her gaze on Sam. "Once more, Emperor Nezearius, I must beg forgiveness from your grace. The prisoners' manners are in fact so barbaric," her eyes narrowed as she said through gritted teeth, "that they do not even recognize when someone is about to speak on their behalf."

Sam flinched at the scolding.

"Apologies, my lord." Olenthia turned back to the Emperor, sweeping into a bow and keeping her eyes down as she spoke. "The squirrel here, Zip Ric. He has told me of their errand and I believe they possess no ill will for Rodenthold."

Clive leaned over to Zip and Sam heard him whisper, "A bit long, but great story, mate."

"His home is besieged by humans," Olenthia stood from her bow as she went on. "They seek to destroy his ancestral oak tree."

"The squirrel has come before us to seek our aid, to bring the *might*," Olenthia punched her fist to emphasize the word, "of our illustrious forces against their oppressors. It is my belief, Emperor Nezearius, we should not only set these two free, but also send a pair of legions to aid in their fight."

Zip Ric's eyes widened and his posture went tense with excitement. The thought of bringing two thousand heavily armed rat soldiers back to his oak tree no doubt exceeded his best expectations for the mission.

After a pause, the Emperor cackled a forced laugh. "Should we now? And to what end, oh wise Olenthia who suddenly thinks she can counsel her elders?"

"If I may be frank," Olenthia turned her eyes down for a moment, and Sam saw on her face the deliberate mustering of courage that he so often tried, and failed, to summon. "Master, our home is collapsing in on itself."

Emperor Nezearius cast a cruel smile to the ceiling and raised his arms in false alarm. "Is this true? Is the roof caving in? Has one of the walls toppled?"

"You know what I mean, your majesty," Olenthia's tone stayed even. Sam admired how she kept both frustration and fear from her voice even while being mocked. "The soldiers are losing their edge. Too many rats dwell beneath this roof, with more arriving by birth or by pilgrimage every day. We're barely able to maintain order."

"Nonsense." The Emperor spit at this last comment. "Look around. It is entirely peaceful here."

Sam had spent less than an hour within Rodenthold's walls and knew that to be a falsehood.

Olenthia went on. "With your permission, I can lead the Fourth Legion and another legion of your choosing on an expeditionary mission with three objectives." Now she counted off on her fingers as she spoke each point. "First, it will be a training exercise to work some of the softness from these troops."

There was a murmur of agreement from the members of her Vanguard. Whiskers twitched, paws gripped spears a little tighter, and Clive pinched a spot at his midsection that was a bit too thick and nodded.

"Second, we can forge a diplomatic alliance with the Ric family, additional squirrel clans, and other members of the forest."

The rat Emperor snorted but let her finish.

"And finally, we can conduct scouting operations to determine where to establish an expansion home and secondary city of Rodenthold."

Emperor Nezearius twirled his whiskers with his paw, for a moment bearing a striking resemblance, if a more haggard version, to the yellow Pizza Pete logo. "It is as I thought, Olenthia. Your promotion came too soon, based on your intellect alone, with no consideration for maturity, judgment, or experience. I'm beginning to have my doubts about you, *General* Olenthia." He put a bitter emphasis on her title.

"As if you could lead such a force anyway!" he went on. "Do you think yourself the rival of me, the great and wise Nezearius? It was I who led our people to victory here beneath these walls, who founded our great city before your parents were even born. You think yourself a general, a leader? You're just a sentry,on guard duty along a pitiful stretch of wall on our southern flank. Your words border on treasonous. Overstep yourself again and I'll reassign you to watch over a salvage pile at the back of a grub farm. How does that sound?"

The Emperor's words seemed to sting Olenthia worse than thrown stones. She said nothing in her defense as she slumped, head bowed.

Olenthia, the proud rat general, had earlier that night repelled two potentially dangerous, if completely ignorant, teenagers from Rodenthold's walls. Now she was being berated for voicing that the rats of Rodenthold could both help Zip Ric's family and themselves. She was trying to do the right thing, and she was being ridiculed for it. It wasn't fair, it wasn't right, and it made Sam's jaw tighten.

"And I'm ready to pass judgment on these two prisoners as well. We must make an example of Rodenthold's enemies." The Emperor turned to the small announcer rat. "So that all might hear my decree, you'll repeat the rest of what I say."

"The rest of what I say!"

"Not yet, idiot!"

"Not yet-" Again the small rat was almost knocked from the Pizza Pete's counter top by the Emperor's backhand.

"Wait!" Sam again spoke before thoughts of self-preservation could stop him. He flinched, waiting for Olenthia to again stand him down with drawn sword.

Instead, the brow-beaten general only looked back over her shoulder to watch the next move by the raccoon who'd dared to interrupt the proceedings a second time.

Not a single rat moved. Emperor Nezearius leaned forward heavily on his walking staff, his old eyes narrowing to murderous slits. "We're waiting."

Sam cleared his throat, giving his brain another second to plan. Then he had an idea.

"It's true, we followed the humans straight to your door."

A gasp went up from the assembled rats, as Emperor Nezearius just laughed. "You see? He admits it!" the Emperor said as he nudged the loud, little rat. The announcer rat flinched at the initial contact, but then smirked when he realized he hadn't been smacked.

Sam stood tall on his hind legs and stuck his chest out to try and look confident, trying to think about how medieval knights in the movies always spoke when standing before a king. Flattery.

"The whole of the forest speaks of your legend. The story of Rodenthold and the might of the rats within." Sam's voice rang out through the food court, and with each word he felt his confidence swell. "How a brave band of rats drove out the humans from the great halls, and founded a kingdom all their own."

In truth, Sam didn't know the history of Rodenthold, he was only guessing. But his words made Emperor Nezearius stand up straighter, and seemed to be working.

"My friend and I decided to see it for ourselves, and seek the aid of the noble rats. Together we braved a great journey from the Ric Oak. Over rock and root, through stream and beneath sunlit paths. We faced a den of rattlesnakes and survived. We supped with owls and lived to tell the tale."

"But when we arrived at the edges of your parking lot, we knew not how to present ourselves before your honorable presence, Emperor Nezearius, or how to approach the walls of your kingdom."

That part made Sam feel foolish. Emperors had empires, kingdoms had kings. The rats were all wrong with their labels. But there were more important matters at hand than correcting the rats' choice of words.

"When we saw the two humans approaching on their skateboards-"

Sam overheard heard Clive mumble, "Skateboard... good word for it," as he went on.

"- we saw a chance to behold Rodenthold's fabled fighting force in action. In awe, Zip and I watched them repel the human invaders with stone and spear and claw. The courage of General Olenthia and her soldiers held us in a trance, and it was then that we were found."

"Rest assured, we bring no calamity or chaos with us. We sought only the aid of you noble rats in the defense," Sam put his arm around Zip Ric's shoulders, "of my good friend's home."

It was only when he finished that Sam realized his heart was racing like a freight train and that his legs were trembling with nerves. His jaw soon quivered as well.

General Olenthia, still standing by herself in the space before him, made eye contact and gave Sam a slight bow of her head. Sam nodded back, acknowledging her silent thanks.

"That was awesome!" Zip Ric said in as quiet a whisper as the excited squirrel could manage.

"Yeah!" Clive leaned over to give Sam a thumbs up from the other side of Zip Ric.

All eyes turned to the Pizza Pete's counter top. Emperor Nezearius's staff leaned against his shoulder as he slowly clapped his paws together.

"Well said, young raccoon. Moving words, indeed." The ancient Emperor turned back to the announcer rat. "Echo my verdict so all assembled might hear clearly."

Sam pinched his eyes closed as the little rat's big voice trumpeted throughout the food court.

"The criminals shall be locked in the Rodenthold prison until the wise and just Emperor Nezearius determines their sentence to be complete!"

Olenthia's shoulders sunk, Zip Ric's face was painted in a nervous smile, and Sam stood dumb founded. This couldn't be.

The Emperor stood smug from his perch on the counter above the proceedings, his chest puffed out and his chin stuck high in the air, standing the way European kings and queens always did in old oil paintings. The announcer rat mimicked his ruler's pose just past his shoulder.

A murmur ran through the twenty or so members of the Fourth Legion's Vanguard. For a moment Sam thought they might mutiny, turn against their Emperor's orders, and march Sam and Zip Ric straight to the Ric tree to face the humans. But it was not to be.

"You heard the Emperor's verdict," Olenthia said in a quiet voice as she turned and drew the needle from her belt without any of the speed or flourish of before.

Sam's paws clenched and his first instinct was to fight his way out. For the first time ever, he was bigger and stronger than the bullies trying to persecute him. He probably outweighed each rat four to one.

But as the sad eyes of Olenthia and the assembled members of her Fourth Legion closed around them, Sam felt the fight drain out of him. This wasn't the decree any of them had wanted either.

"Sorry, mate," Clive said as he grasped Zip Ric by the shoulder and turned him around. "Shame. That was a good story, too."

CHAPTER FIFTEEN

Zip Ric got a hopping start, picked up as much speed as he could in the small space, and leapt. His claws scratched and scrambled against the smooth metal walls but could find nowhere to grab hold. He dropped back to the tiled floor for the twentieth or thirtieth time. Sam had lost count.

"Almost had it that time!" Zip Ric's squeaky voice echoed inside the bathroom stall.

"Almost," Sam said without meaning it.

It was hopeless. Soldiers from the Emperor's Chosen regiment had taken over prisoner escort from Olenthia's troops and herded them from the Vermin Keep food court. They'd come to a dark side alcove and Sam found himself shoved past a large wooden door into a Ladies Restroom-turned prison block. The warden, a small rat with shifty eyes, had been stunned to see prisoners ushered into his jurisdiction. Sam got the impression Rodenthold didn't often entertain guests.

A dozen toilet stalls with metal walls painted pea-soup green made the perfect prison cell for a raccoon and squirrel. The rats had built a causeway from repurposed wooden bed frames along the face of the cells, blocking the gap from floor to bottom of stall doors and created an elevated walkway for the warden to patrol. The smooth stall walls stretching to just below the ceiling were high enough to keep even the spring-legged Zip Ric contained.

But that didn't stop him from trying.

Zip jumped again, scratching in vain for a foothold. This time he landed with a splash, inside the toilet bowl. Sam wiped a few droplets from his shoulder as a sopping wet Zip Ric dropped to the floor.

"I think I'm getting closer!" he said, the water doing nothing to drown his spirits. He leapt again, shedding water as he went airborne.

Sam sighed. A frosted glass skylight overhead glowed golden and gave the bathroom its only light. It was Saturday now, the sun was up. This was the second time in three days he'd been captured and stuck in a bathroom. How ironic. At least this time he was right side up and not getting soaked by a couple of eighth grade gorillas.

The warden had pointed the Emperor's Chosen to a cell in the middle of the row. They'd pushed Sam and Zip inside and pulled the door closed. Rat engineers had reinstalled the latches to work from outside, keeping prisoners inside the stall rather than intruders out. A mix of chicken wire, broken chair legs, and metal panels from water fountains blocked the way beneath the stall walls into the adjacent cells. Peering through the small gaps, Sam couldn't see any other prisoners housed to either side.

Sam had listened as the Emperor's Chosen left with a great thump of the heavy wooden door. For a while he'd tried to pry open the rat-constructed barriers between the cells, thinking that maybe the door in the next cell wouldn't be latched if there were no prisoners inside, but the rats had built the fortifications too sturdily.

As the hopelessness of their situation set in, Sam's adrenaline had faded. The weariness of a day spent running through the woods, climbing trees, evading snakes and skateboards, and marching through the kingdom of Rodenthold finally caught up with him. Sam had fallen asleep on the cold tile floor mere minutes after imprisonment.

He'd woken up hours later, with sunshine streaming through the skylight and Zip Ric using him like a big gray pillow.

Now, as he sat slumped against the stall wall, Sam's mind wandered to a surprising place. He didn't fret about being a prisoner, or what tortures the rats might have in store. He didn't worry about his parents or fret over how he was going to change back into a boy and wake up from this dream. He didn't even think about his growling stomach that hadn't eaten anything since being stuffed with mulberries the previous day.

All Sam could think about was that they'd failed.

In two days, Zip's home would be destroyed. The Ric family would be scattered and killed, the supplies they'd spent weeks gathering tilled beneath machinery and boots, or possibly even a dragon if Zip was to be believed, even as chainsaws tore through the limbs of their ancient oak tree like knives through soft butter.

Vera had said Zip and Sam's errand to enlist the armies of Rodenthold was their best chance. The two owls were still out there pursuing Vera's secret idea, but she'd said that was a long shot. A force of rats had been key. And they'd failed.

They'd come so close, too. Whether it was the words of their story or the crumbling state of Rodenthold or a combination of both, it seemed they'd convinced General Olenthia to the merit of their cause. But in the end they'd been no match for the iron fist of Emperor Nezearius and his rule.

Zip Ric's claws fought for a foothold for what seemed like the hundreth time, his spirit undaunted by the failures so far, when Sam heard two sounds. First came the heavy bathroom door banging shut, and then there rose a familiar voice from outside their cell. The words echoed through the bathroom.

"Warden. Report. Have the prisoners been fed?"

"No, General Olenthia. As commanded they've been kept-"

"Your orders have changed. The prisoners are to be provided rations and then I'm to interrogate them further. Do you have supplies here at the prison?"

Sam and Zip Ric, who'd stopped his leaping upon hearing Olenthia's voice, exchanged a glance as they stared at the stall door and listened to the voices beyond.

"We've not had a prisoner here in my lifetime, ma'am, and haven't needed to maintain a food stockpi-"

"Go then. Clive here has the necessary requisition paperwork ready to file. Four day's rations, three to fill the the raccoon and the fourth for the squirrel. Clive will help you carry it back as well."

"But who will watch the-"

"I'm perfectly qualified to keep an eye on a locked door, thank you. Go. Now."

There were no more protests, just the thud of the bathroom door as the warden and Clive were sent on a food gathering errand. Sam and Zip listened as rat footsteps climbed onto the wooden causeway outside, stopping before their door.

Sam shifted his stance and his muscles tensed. Now might be their only chance at escape. Zip Ric seemed to have the same idea. His tail twitched as he braced for action.

They waited several seconds, anticipating the sound of the latch turning, ready to pounce once the door swung inward.

"Gentlemen." General Olenthia's voice was calm through the wall. "Before this cell stand one hundred of my best troops. I am going to open the door and step inside. Do not attempt to escape. Even if my soldiers let you survive the fight, you'll spend the rest of your lives withering away in that cell. Do we understand each other?"

Sam sat back, all thoughts of escape evaporating. "Yes," they said in unison.

"Excellent." The latch clicked and the door swung open only inches, just enough for Olenthia to slip inside before pushing it closed again. She stood on the lip of the wooden barrier above them on her hind legs, her front paws folded across her chest as she leaned back against the door to hold it closed. The thick needle sword hung at her side, and a pair of bandoleers draped from her shoulders to form an X across her torso. Instead of bullets for a machine gun, Olenthia's held pebbles.

"Now that you've had time to sit here and stew, you'll tell me the true purpose of your coming to Rodenthold."

Sam slapped the floor. "We've already told you. I thought you'd been listening? If Rodenthold won't help us, fine, but please let us go so we can try something else before it's too late."

Olenthia studied Sam's face carefully before turning her gaze. "Squirrel, Zip Ric, do you have anything to add?"

Zip Ric sat up and looked at the skylight.

"It's already afternoon out there. That means we're down to a day and a half until my family's oak tree is destroyed."

"It may not be as grand as the Vermin Keep," Zip continued, still looking up at the sky beyond their prison, "and my family isn't nearly as big as the one you've got here. We could relocate, move deeper into the woods, find a new tree. But our oak tree has been home to the Rics for over five hundred generations. If we lose our tree, we'll lose more than just a home. We'll lose a part of ourselves."

The rat general looked down at the floor tiles. Her stern expression did not falter. "It is as I thought." Olenthia stood up straight and grabbed hold of the stall door's edge to pull it open. "Good. Follow me," she said, slipping out of the cell and leaving the door standing open.

Sam and Zip's eyes met again. Was it a trap? Sam shrugged, and they tentatively followed Olenthia out of the cell.

As they emerged, Olenthia pointed at the heavy wooden door that led into the hallway and to the rest of Rodenthold. There was no sign of the hundred other soldiers she'd threatened them with. Just one rat, one squirrel, and one raccoon, alone in the Ladies' Room. "Any moment, the warden and Clive-"

"You were bluffing!" Sam said.

Olenthia gave a quick nod. "I had to be sure of your motivations. And we'll need to use more deception to keep from raising an alarm. When the warden returns with food, play along."

She spoke not a moment too soon. The wooden door opened by a few inches as the warden and Clive appeared, each carrying a large leaf-wrapped bundle in their arms, so big that it obstructed their view.

"Remember," Olenthia looked back at Sam and Zip to whisper, "play along."

Clive and the warden were halfway across the bathroom before the warden saw the prisoners outside of their cell. He dropped his parcel and scrambled back toward the door. "You two hold them off, I'll get reinforcements!"

"Stop him," was all Olenthia said, but Clive was already ahead of her. The big rat grabbed the warden by the tail and tugged him back.

"What is the meaning of this, I should-"

Clive put the warden in a headlock. "You should watch your mouth. That's a general you're shouting at."

Olenthia played it cool. "The Emperor has summoned the prisoners for further questioning. I'm to lead them to the Vermin Keep at once."

The warden wasn't buying it, and he quickly said so, protesting about procedures and orders and protocol as he struggled in Clive's grip.

Olenthia rubbed the diamond shaped spot on her forehead. "That thing I said about playing along?" she said, turning back to Sam and Zip. "Nevermind. Clive, shut him up."

"Sorry mate. Nothing personal. Just, you know, orders." One of Clive's arms windmilled around, his paw forming a fist, and bonked the warden on the top of the head between his ears. The warden crumpled to the floor unconscious.

"Raccoon - I mean - Sam," Olenthia said, "Help Clive with those packages. Zip, follow me." She dashed to the opposite end of the bathroom, away from the exit door.

Sam tucked one of the bundles under his arm while Clive unholstered some netting from his back to wrap around the other package and heft it onto his shoulders like a backpack, and they turned to follow.

Olenthia was already halfway up the wall with Zip Ric right on her tail, scurrying up a plastic conduit that connected an electric wall socket to the mall's overhead wiring. Sam surprised himself when, even with one arm hanging tight to the leaf wrapped bundle, his paws expertly found a good grip on the plastic sleeve. He felt like Spider-Man as he scurried up the wall after them. And to think he'd never even climbed a tree until the day before.

The ceiling tile lifted like a hatch when Sam's head bumped it. Olenthia and Zip each grabbed him by a shoulder and hauled him up above the drop ceiling. Clive followed moments later.

"This is so exciting!" Zip Ric said to no one in particular.

"And dusty." Clive patted at his flanks, making a cloud.

Olenthia shushed them. "There won't be any sentries posted up here, the floor is unsteady and dangerous, but we still need to hurry. When the warden wakes up or if any patrols come to check on you prisoners, they'll quickly figure out how you escaped unseen."

They were standing in a maze of obstacles above Rodenthold. Heating ducts, trays full of electric wires, support beams, metal rafters, and innumerable other features created a tangle that made it impossible to see more than a few feet in any direction. The space was short, too. Sam thought if he stretched to full height he could reach up and touch the roof overhead.

"This way." Olenthia said, "And careful where you tread. Especially you, Sam."

They hurried forward in a line through the dry and dusty space, scampering along the tops of ceiling tiles. Olenthia led the way with Zip Ric at her back. Zip moved as easily through the man-made tangle as he did through thorny underbrush under the open sky. His still damp fur from the failed escape that landed him in the toilet quickly acquired a coat of clinging dust.

Sam came next, and had to squeeze his way through the jungle of obstructions. He was careful to keep hold of the food bundle under his arm while also watching his footing on the ceiling tiles. The tiles shifted slightly wherever he stepped and bowed beneath his weight like an unsteady bridge if he stood too far from the metal tracks providing support at the edges. Black rectangular pits where other tiles had previously broken away reached out from the darkness.

His pulse quickened as Sam imagined a tile crumbling beneath his feet, a new hole opening, and dropping him thirty feet to the mall's floor. If the fall itself didn't kill him, the swarms of barbaric rats below certainly would. He did his best to push these thoughts aside by sticking close to Zip Rip and keeping an eye out for spider webs to avoid.

Last in line was Clive. He kept muttering about dust as he spit it from his mouth. Sam thought that if the rat only kept his mouth closed, Clive probably would keep some of the dust off his tongue.

The only light came from narrow beams of sunshine that found their way through the smallest roof gaps. Though only a hair thick, the stray sun rays illuminated swirling dust like yellow laser beams.

Olenthia gave a wide berth to these columns of sunshine, sometimes climbing over tall sections of duct work to stay clear of them. At first Sam couldn't understand why, until he noticed the ceiling tile under one sun beam. Even in the dim light, Sam could see it was soggy and sagging. Of course. If sunshine could get through a hole in the roof, so could rain water. Dry and solid, the tiles barely supported Sam's weight. A wet tile might break apart beneath even a rat's light form.

Sam bumped into Zip Ric when the squirrel paused before him. Olenthia was on her hind legs, sniffing the air and looking around. "Wait here, I need to get my bearings." She said, her claws scuttling over the false floor in the opposite direction. She stopped over an empty space where a sun beam continued through a pit where there had once been a ceiling tile. Olenthia peered over the side and squinted below at Rodenthold, before dashing back.

She looked to Clive and said, "We're above the western wards, near the Fourth Legion's barracks."

"Cool," was all Clive replied.

"You know the way down from here, yes?"

"Sure," Clive scratched his chin. "But we can't go that way. There's no chance of getting through the barracks with these two in tow. The Fourth might let us pass, but the other legions housed there won't."

"We're not going down to the barracks. Only you." Olenthia pulled two small bits of paper, scarcely bigger than confetti pieces, from her pebble bandoleers. She pressed one into Clive's paws. "This is a full confession, where I take all responsibility for the liberation of these prisoners, explains you were only acting under orders, and should clear you of all wrong doing. If you're caught, present it to-"

"Hold on," Clive said with a laugh. "All due respect, General, but wasn't it me who convinced you that these two hadn't done nothing wrong? That we needed to do something?" Clive crossed his arms. "If anybody ends up punished, ma'am, it should be me. But let's just get out of here and not worry on it."

Olenthia put her paw on Clive's shoulder and looked him in the eye. "You're staying behind, Clive. I have a far more important, and dangerous, mission for you." She held up the other scrap of paper. "Descend back into the barracks, give us an hour's head start, and then assemble the Fourth Legion to read them this decree."

Clive took the papers in his paws, as Olenthia continued. "If they have even a fraction of your courage, they'll do what's right. We will save these squirrels, and in the end, save our own home as well."

The big scarred rat studied the two folded scraps of paper for a long moment before unslinging the food bundle from his back. "You'll be wanting this then."

Zip Ric took it from him and fumbled with the yarn straps until they were over his shoulders.

In unison, the rats stood up arrow straight and saluted each other. Without another word Clive darted away to the left and into the darkness. Olenthia watched him go for a moment before waving Sam and Zip to follow her straight ahead.

As they continued through the tangled web of wires and ducts, Sam thought about the sacrifice Olenthia and Clive were undertaking.

The two rats didn't have to help Zip Ric and Sam escape, they could have left them there in prison to waste away. But instead they were risking their stations, their lives, their families, everything, to rescue a pair of strangers simply because it was the right thing to do. He'd never thought of rats as noble, but Olenthia and Clive's actions were making Sam have second thoughts.

After several more minutes of fumbling through the dark, Olenthia pointed up at the ceiling to a round plastic lid. "Here we are. Sam, can you fit?"

Sam reached up, pushed at the lid, and was almost blinded when it easily shifted against his paws to let in a face full of daylight. With his eyes pinched closed, Sam's paws found the lip above the opening and pulled himself up. His torso lodged in the hole for a moment. Zip and Olenthia pushed against his backside until he popped loose onto the roof of the mall.

He stood up, squinting. After almost a day in the odorous realm of Rodenthold, the air tasted as fresh and sweet as honey. In the distance he could hear car engines humming along, but the overgrown trees and landscaping around the old mall blocked his view even from the roof.

Olenthia and Zip Ric appeared from the darkness a moment later, holding their paws up to shade the sun from their eyes.

They re-fixed the lid on their escape hatch. Zip Ric checked the sun's angle and tasted the air before concluding which direction led back to the Ric Tree. They scurried to the roof edge and shimmied down a drain pipe to crouch in some shrubs below. The shrubs cast long shadows in the late afternoon's golden light. Their time in the prison cell had already snatched away most of the day.

Olenthia watched the roof lines for sentries or watch-rats. Finally she determined the coast was clear, and they dashed out into the open, to cross the vast parking lot toward the shelter of trees at the other side.

Side by side they scurried across the open ground, the asphalt warm under their paws after baking in the sun all day.

Sam looked back at Rodenthold shrinking away behind them. Daylight didn't make the old mall look any more welcoming. Even now it looked haunted, or like a scene from a zombie movie, eerily quiet and weed-strewn. If they didn't know better, no one would guess it housed a sprawling rat metropolis.

"I didn't think Rodenthold was so bad," Zip Ric said. "Certainly had its charms."

Sam's laughter was cut off by a bellow from the walls behind them. Though halfway across the parking lot, the voice of the Emperor's tiny assistant still reached their ears.

"There they are!" came the call from somewhere along the roof. "After them!"

A shout came from behind as a multitude of rat voices cried out in pursuit. Sam didn't need to look back to know there were a lot of them.

Without a word, Sam and his two companions ran harder toward the safety of the woods. He hoped the rats would surrender their pursuit at the tree line.

Sam, Zip Ric, and Olenthia reached the trees, but the rats weren't giving up. Sam heard their shouts and battle cries over his straining breath. His legs burned and his lungs felt like they'd pop if he tried to run any faster.

"They're… Nezearius's… Chosen…" Olenthia said between breaths. She was going as fast as she could, too, scurrying through leaves and over roots. "Vicious rats… cruel rats… the strongest… of Rodenthold."

Sam looked back for only a moment. He couldn't yet see their pursuers, but their shouts seemed to be getting closer.

"They… won't stop… never stop…"

He and Olenthia ran side by side, crashing through weeds and tangled sticks without slowing down. Zip hopped over them as they fled.

"Those brutes from the Vermin Keep?" Zip asked as he passed them.

Olenthia only nodded.

He paused to look back, reflecting. "But they'd seemed so lazy?"

Zip Ric charged forward again, easily staying ahead of the raccoon and rat, and led the way through the rows of planted trees that served as Rodenthold's border with the main woods. He'd dart ahead, stick to the side of a tree to pause and look back, and then burst forward again. Zip Ric's start-stop rhythm was as frantic as the look in his wide eyes.

"They're gaining on us!" he shouted. "Faster!"

"Could we," Sam's voice came out weak, "stand and fight?"

Olenthia shook her head as she ran on. "They're… too strong… and too many. Leave me… behind… split up… climb a tree…"

"We're not abandoning you," Zip called. "You saved us! We stick together!"

The woods thickened as they started downhill. Great trees blocked all but the last traces of Saturday's sunlight. Dusk gave the air a golden glow. Almost a whole day had passed since Sam and Zip had been beneath these very trees. Before long it would be nightfall.

But not too soon to stop the idea that suddenly popped into Sam's head from working.

Sam shouted to Zip, telling him where to lead them.

"Are you crazy? I was trying to go around."

"Just do it. Trust me." Sam said. Olenthia eyed him with curiosity as they kept running.

"If you say so…" Zip Ric said as he veered left. Then Zip's face lit up even as the day continued to darken. "Ooh, I think I understand. This way, follow me!"

The elite soldiers of Rodenthold, the Emperor's Chosen, were still out of sight, but would have no trouble following their change of course. For his plan to work, Sam was counting on their tracking skills.

After all, you couldn't lead someone into a trap without them first taking the bait.

CHAPTER SIXTEEN

All at once the trees parted for the rock-strewn stream bed to wind its way through the woods. The dry river bed looked innocent enough, but Sam and Zip Ric knew better.

Sam grabbed Zip's tail and dug in his own heels to stop. Olenthia huffed and puffed beside him. "We… must keep… going…"

Sam's eyes scanned the stony creek bed in the dying light.

"This way," he kept his voice down as he waved them further downstream toward a familiar bony, dead tree sticking up from the river bed. The same dead tree that he and Zip had found sanctuary in just 24 hours before. Its bleached trunk pointed at the sky as if reminding them of the time, telling them to hurry.

Sam stopped running, changing to a hurried walk, and told the others to stay off the loose stones. He whispered the rest of his plan as they quietly made their way toward the dead tree.

Olenthia's whispered question to the last part of his plan came out more like an accusation. "You want me to do what?"

"Just climb on. Trust me."

They reached the very spot Sam and Zip had crossed the river. Then Sam turned and tip-toed as well as he could with four paws across the loose stones. As much as he didn't want to deal with snakes again, he sure hoped that rattlesnakes kept the same dens night after night.

Zip Ric gulped down a yelp, pointing back at the trees.

Sam glanced back. A mob of rats streamed into view. Dozens of soldiers milled over each other as they scrambled to change course after the escaped prisoners and their traitorous general. Soon they'd be close enough for Sam to see their various scars and weaponry.

Sam reached the first boulder. Zip Ric hopped straight on top of it while Sam skidded to a stop.

"Hop on!" Sam tossed aside the parcel of rat food he'd been so careful to keep hold of. If it made him lose his balance and slip, it wouldn't get eaten anyway.

"This is lunacy." Olenthia protested as a mob of rats teamed toward them.

"No time to argue. You said it yourself, they'll kill us or drag us back to Rodenthold to rot. And either way, Zip Ric's home will be destroyed. This is our only chance."

She grabbed hold of Sam's fur and pulled herself over his shoulders, as tentative as a kid climbing onto a bicycle without training wheels for the first time. "I hope you know what you're doing."

Sam hoped so, too. He scrambled up onto the big rock, beside Zip Ric. He looked across the line of boulders casting long shadows in the stream bed and tried to visualize the route through the den of hidden snakes.

"Zip, lead the way. If we fall, you keep going, and don't stop running until you get home."

Zip Ric stood arrow straight and mimicked the salutes he'd seen in Rodenthold. The package of food on his back made him look like a tiny paratrooper.

"Here we go!" Zip Ric shouted. No more whispering. The plan depended on the snakes being alert.

Sam winced as Olenthia's claws dug into the scruff of his neck. The pain took his mind off the fear trying to bubble up from his gut, and he leapt for the next rock. For a moment his claws fought for traction before he pulled himself up. Zip Ric was already two stones ahead, but Sam couldn't help glancing back.

The rats were close enough now to see their waving weaponry as they veered into the river stones like a furious, furry tidal wave.

Sam continued to the next big boulder, and then across two more before he had to pause. His legs burned from their escape run, and the added weight of Olenthia made jumping more difficult than it had been the night before.

"Why are we up here? There must be a faster way!" Olenthia protested in his ear.

Sam didn't respond. He didn't have to. As he leapt to the next boulder, a sound he never thought he'd be glad to hear whispered in his ears. The hollow, dry sound of a lone rattle found its way through the din of rats clamoring over stones.

A rat sergeant somewhere behind shouted a frantic order to halt, just before a multitude of other rattles joined the chorus.

"Don't look down," Sam said more to himself than to Olenthia as more rattles joined the song.

The rats' war cries diminished and turned to frightened shouts of retreat. Adrenaline pushed Sam on, and in another few jumps his feet found soft ground on the other side of the river bed.

Zip Ric watched from the side of a peeling birch tree, looking back over the creek bed, a smile on his face. "They're fleeing!"

Sam stopped to look even as Olenthia leapt from his back. She spun and drew her sword in case any rats still followed. With no sign of pursuit, Sam collapsed to his side and gasped for air.

The creek bed rattled noisily, alive with more slithering snakes than Sam wanted to imagine. On the other side, the cluster of rats was disappearing into the safety of the trees.

"It worked, Sam!" Zip Ric hopped down from the birch and hugged Sam's shoulder. "You're a genius!"

Olenthia stood on her hind legs, sheathed her sword, and folded her paws. "Impressive, Sam. Using the rattlesnakes as a living, venomous wall to drive back our pursuers? A decisive, tactically masterful maneuver."

"It was amazing! Thought you'd gone cracked when you said to lead us to the snake den. Chikirith and the Four couldn't have come up with a better plan!" Zip Ric pointed with his thumb at where Sam was slumped on the ground. "That's raccoons for you. Clever as the summer day is long."

Sam's heart beat hard in his chest and he wanted to rest longer. Instead, he pushed to his feet and said, "Come on, before they regroup and realize they can cross the creek further upstream."

They hurried up the hill, beyond the birch trees, and deeper into the forest.

Zip Ric, untiring, encouraged Sam and Olenthia to press just a little further, just a little faster.

Twilight passed quickly, giving way to night. The last birds ceased their songs as crickets and tree frogs took over to continue the forest's soundtrack. There were still no sounds of pursuit.

A stern wind stirred the branches overhead, but felt like only a light breeze on the forest floor. Through the twirling branches, they caught glimpses of the bright moon.

Zip Ric's mood shifted as he kept glancing up to the sky. "Maybe we should hunker down and get some rest?"

Olenthia adjusted her sword belt and shook her head. "We should continue, take advantage of our head start."

"It's not safe to travel by night. What do you think, Sam?"

Sam sat down on the ground to catch his breath. A thought had been gnawing at him even as he'd struggled to keep up with Zip Ric.

"Do you think any of those rats got," Sam hesitated. "Killed? Eaten?" His stomach hurt, though he wasn't sure if it were out of nausea or hunger.

"Doubtful," Olenthia said. "I'd be surprised if those rattlesnakes killed even one of the Chosen. Those brutes shrug off wounds that would cripple other rats, and they bear the scars to prove it. My guess is that, after the snakes scared the frenzy out of them, the Chosen retreated back for further orders."

Sam hoped Olenthia hadn't just made that excuse up to make him feel better.

"What will they do next?" Zip Ric scurried to Olenthia's side as he asked.

"Their Emperor will likely send out search parties. That's why we need to keep moving."

"Wait, did you say *their* Emperor?" Sam repeated the strange choice of words.

Olenthia stood straight as she spoke, but Sam saw her eyes trembling. "Because of my actions, both in liberating you from prison and then leading the Chosen into ambush, there's little doubt that I shall be exiled. If I were to return to Rodenthold, it would mean my death."

Zip Ric gulped. "I'm sorry, General." He stood up on his hind legs and put his paw around her shoulders. "We didn't mean to get you in trouble, too. Honest."

"It's nothing," she patted Zip's paw gently. "Sometimes the right course of action is the most difficult. Aiding you was the correct choice. But now we must hurry, for if we don't save your tree, we'll both be without a home and all our perils shall be for nothing."

Sam got up, and thought of his home.

But it wasn't thoughts of his old life, the big city.

Instead his thoughts went to their house in Mapleton, backing up to the forest, that they'd moved into two weeks ago. He remembered how happy his parents had been to arrive that night in the moving truck. The excitement on their faces as they showed him around the house. He thought of his dog Winnie romping, chasing, and napping across every inch of their lawn. Before she'd tried to eat him.

If he ever made it home again, he swore he'd thank his parents for bringing him here, to this part of the country. And what a story he'd have to tell. If he could figure out a way for his parents to understand raccoon, that is.

"We've come this far." Sam said. "Whether it's old and familiar, or we've got to make a new one, home is important. But we're short on time to save Zip's, especially if we're going to implement a plan once we get there. Olenthia's right, it's time to get moving."

Zip Ric gave a thumbs up, Olenthia nodded once, and together the rat, squirrel, and raccoon set off through the darkness.

They trotted, steadily west and southward. Occasionally they'd stop for Olenthia to double back and mask their trail from any Rodenthold patrols that might be trying to find them.

For Sam and Zip, hunger quickly became a more immediate concern than bands of rats trying to find them in the dark. The last time they'd been full was from mulberries more than a day before, so while Olenthia worked, they snacked on any foods Zip could scavenge from their immediate vicinity.

Except acorns. When Sam bit into his first acorn, the pungent flavor nearly made him gag. He decided to stick with wild blackberries or the crispy and faintly sweet maple seed pods at the end of their helicopter wings, and leave the acorns for Zip.

They traveled for several more hours before Olenthia called for a break. The sky had clouded over, and even Sam's untrained nose thought the night smelled like it might rain.

"Let me see that pack," Olenthia said.

Zip Ric pulled the bag of supplies from over his shoulders. "So comfortable, I almost forgot it was there!"

Olenthia set it down and parted the folded seams as Zip and Sam looked on to see what delicious treasures might be inside. They recoiled when they caught sight of the contents; bits of dried bug legs, foamy chunks of fungus, and knobby pale grubs.

Olenthia paid no mind to their disgust. She held up a fuzzy chunk of something that could have once been a grape. "Care for a bite?"

Sam just shook his head while Zip Ric dusted off his shoulders at the thought of carrying the disgusting contents on his back.

"Suit yourselves."

Sam sat down on a bed of soft moss while Olenthia crunched away on bug pieces.

It felt good to be sitting still. All three wore an expression of relaxation and relief, despite the dangers still ahead and behind them. After a few quiet moments, Zip Ric sat up and snapped his fingers.

"This reminds me of a song," he said. "One that will lighten legs and calm hearts." He hopped up onto a tree branch, bare of leaves and likely soon to fall from its tree. Zip walked to its edge like a poet on stage before an audience, cleared his throat into a fist, and began singing in a clear, high-pitched voice.

Chikirith said to his sister Izel
Since you can fly, I'll ask you to tell
The lay of the land and the way we should go
Are there dangers ahead or are troubles below?

She leapt from the branch with her peeled eyes
And soared through the air, queen of the skies
With breeze she returned to Chikirith's side
And told what she'd seen from her vantage so high

The trees they go on, almost without end
Rivers they shimmer through narrow and bend
And trouble for squirrels, they are all around
But fear not dear brother, not as bad as it sounds

Together we two, plus our siblings make Four
Though beset by peril now 'n ever more
If we stick together, like stars on nights clear
There's nothing, dear brother, we ever should fear.

Zip Ric drew out the last few words, the song fading into night. Sam and Olenthia, who'd hung mesmerized with his simple tune, clapped in unison as they laughed. The verses of his tale, for a moment, had taken their fatigue and worries far away.

Zip Ric stood meekly, as if embarrassed by his friends' attention. He took a small bow, and then another. Sam thought if Zip hadn't had fur on his face, he'd see the squirrel blushing.

Then Zip Ric sat up arrow straight, like someone had called his name. Or like someone who'd heard the approach of pursuers.

"What is it?" Olenthia already had her sword in hand.

Sam listened to the night, but heard nothing.

Then Zip's eyes widened as a groan of brewing thunder swept through the trees. Not a storm, something else. Sam recognized what it had to be a moment too late.

"OWL!"

His shout had only just left his throat when a clap of wings broke from overhead. The world moved in a flurry of shaking branches, speckled feathers, and darting fur. A shriek filled the night, and then silence took its place. Even the crickets paused their melody.

It happened so fast, over in an instant, that Sam wasn't even quite sure what was going on until he stood up and looked around.

Olenthia was at his side, pointing her sword at the sky.

But there was no sign of Zip Ric.

CHAPTER SEVENTEEN

The tree branch that had been Zip Ric's stage still swayed from the impact.

"ZIP!" Sam screamed into the dark and empty night. Only his own echo responded.

He pawed at his face and covered his eyes. He shouted again and again, until his throat was raw from the wailing.

The commotion silenced the other ambient sounds of the forest, likely staying quiet in case this was some new predator.

"Easy, Sam, take a deep breath," Olenthia tried to sooth him. "And quiet, who knows what else might be out there."

Sam clenched his paws into fists so tight his fingers ached, and pushed Olenthia away. Then he did the only thing that came naturally to him in the face of danger and fear and sadness.

He fled.

Tired legs were forgotten, his racing heart ignored, as Sam ran from the scene. He rushed through weeds and flowers, briars and bushes, without trying to duck or dodge. He barreled through the forest like a linebacker lining up a tackle. The night became a blur as Sam raced to outrun his troubles, his pain.

Zip Ric. An owl. Of all the stupid ways to die. And after all they'd been through.

It was so unfair. Sadness and anger mixed to create an emotion Sam couldn't name. It ground at his stomach and made his whole body quiver.

And still he ran. Sam splashed through puddles and streams, and he couldn't tell if it was water or tears on his face.

There was guilt, too. It was growing, crowding out the other thoughts, and it hurt worst of all.

Zip Ric had warned that traveling by night would be dangerous. But they needed to make up time. Too long spent in Rodenthold. It had been Sam's call to keep going. Zip knew the forest better than Sam or Olenthia. If only he'd listened.

If only…

If only…

If only…

If only Sam had been paying attention, he may have noticed the huge tree root sticking out from the ground. It caught his foot as deftly as an eagle's claw and sent him flipping through the air. He landed tail first, soft leaves and slopping mud breaking his fall.

He collapsed there in a heap, like every bone in his body had been removed. His shoulders jerked as he sobbed quietly, alone in the mud.

He wasn't sure how long he laid there. It could have been minutes, it could have been hours.

Leaves rustled as something approached. Sam didn't move and didn't try to escape. He wasn't afraid, mostly he was just numb.

Olenthia's familiar round ears and the diamond shaped patch of white fur on her forehead appeared from the other side of the tall, gnarled root that had ended Sam's manic flight through the forest. She didn't say anything as she carefully climbed over roots and walked on two legs to stand beside Sam. Olenthia placed a paw on Sam's side but remained silent as she bowed her pointed face to the ground.

It was Sam who finally breached the silence. "He's gone. I can't believe he's gone." Fresh tears welled in his eyes as his words gave a new, sharpened edge to his pain.

Olenthia stayed quiet for several minutes as Sam wept. She patted his side and finally said. "Zip Ric was a rare squirrel. He was friendly to all, even his captors in Rodenthold. And he was brave. Few have the courage to venture into the unknown, travel so far from home on an errand that held little promise of success. But look how far he came! One brave squirrel, with the help of his raccoon friend of course, faced not one but two owls."

Sam sat up as she went on. He tried to wipe his eyes but only smeared more mud on his face from dirty paws.

"He escaped a snake's ambush, and had the courage to not question your idea to use it in our favor. He stood unwavering before Emperor Nezearius, a rat who makes even the stoutest of Rodenthold soldiers tremble."

"You didn't seem scared," Sam said, managing a weak smile, "standing before the Emperor and speaking on our behalf."

"Apparently I'm a better actress than I realized, because I'd felt that at any moment I might faint." Olenthia returned his smile.

"What I'm trying to say, Sam, is that the world can be a cruel place. Things happen for reasons we cannot begin to understand. All we can do is move forward, learn from examples set by folks like brave Zip Ric, and strive to make our actions honor their memory."

Sam stood up, feeling caked mud shifting through his fur. She was right.

"Thanks, Olenthia. I bet you were a great general."

She shrugged. "If you spent enough time around rats, you'd see they're eager to take orders. Directing them is easy. I imagine squirrels and raccoons are a bit more independent."

"So what do we do now?"

"It is up to you, Sam. I will follow where you lead. You know life in the woods better than I."

Barely. If she knew the truth, Sam doubted Olenthia would be so eager to follow him. But now wasn't the time. There was still work to do, and Sam felt his spirit sputtering to life again.

When he spoke, the words came out slowly, deliberately, and decided. "Zip Ric's home and his family are still in danger. We've got to do our part."

"Agreed," Olenthia said with a nod as she touched the hilt of her needle sword. "What is the quickest way to his tree?"

"Good question," Sam stood up and looked around, but was unable to get his bearings in the dark. "Which way did I run?"

"Well, if Zip was taking us by truest heading toward his home, you mostly went the right direction. A good thing too, for you covered some ground."

Sam tried to focus, thinking back to the previous day's travels and comparing it to the evening's trek. He had an easy time picturing the woods by day. In fact he surprised himself as he remember distinct paths they'd taken, when only a day or so before all the forest had looked the same to Sam's human eye. Now he imagined he could have found his way back by recognizing a familiar pile of rocks or a particular tree stump. However, he had difficulty trying to compare the sunlit images in his head with their wanderings through the dark.

"Alright." He decided. "Let's keep going in this direction. We'll know we're on the right track when there's a river or swamp to cross."

"Like this one?" Olenthia said, holding her paws up around them.

Only then did Sam notice their surroundings and he couldn't hold in the startled laugh.

Olenthia was right. They were standing in the very swamp where he and Zip had met Vera and Humphrey, the Wood Seer and her bumbling assistant. Stunted trees and marsh grasses were all around. He'd been here before.

But it wasn't just that. Sam's eyes followed the root that had snared his paw and sent him toppling. It led to a pale barked tree trunk that grew thick even in the marshy ground. Its branches spread out like a hundred-fingered hands, and its leaves drooped like a waterfall of tears.

They weren't just in Vera's swamp. He'd wept right beneath the Tearful Tree. If this wasn't a sign to keep going, Sam didn't know what was.

Sam thought for a moment about scurrying up the tree to see if Vera and Humphrey were there, but decided against it. The owls wouldn't be home. Surely, if they were around they'd have heard the commotion below, recognized Sam's voice, and come down to investigate.

Besides, Vera's murmurings about a secondary plan, with tasks for her and Humphrey, would have them occupied.

That was right, the Wood Seer still had a plan, didn't she? Though Sam and Zip had failed to raise an army from Rodenthold, all hope wasn't lost.

That made Sam's resolve a little firmer.

"Alright," he finally said. "I can't believe I'm saying this, but I know exactly where we are. We need to go that way," Sam pointed toward where the creek would be flat, meandering, and easy to cross. "Then we'll follow it upstream until we find a fallen sassafras. Then we'll turn back into the wood."

Olenthia scurried over to the base of the Tearful Tree. She pulled her sword from her belt and made four quick slashes.

"What're you doing?"

"Directions," she said.

"Directions?"

"I've been leaving them intermittently ever since we weren't being actively pursued. Clive's orders were to make his way back to the barracks, do his best to raise the Fourth Legion, and follow. If he's got any sense for timing, they'll have made their break when the Chosen were chasing us." She flicked her paw and scored another half dozen marks into the soft flesh of the weeping willow tree before tucking it back in her belt. "I've little hope he'll be able to raise even ten soldiers, but any reinforcements would be better than none."

"But what about the Emperor's Chosen? Won't they be able to use the markings to follow us?"

Olenthia shook her head as she sheathed her sword. "These symbols are a special cipher my captains and I developed. They will be meaningless to the Chosen, and I trust my soldiers to not reveal their meaning even under threat."

"I guess we are short on allies, and Clive was a good rat." Sam didn't ask how Clive and any other friendly rats would be able to get through the snake den or manage to find Olenthia's tiny scratchings in a forest full of trees. He scraped drying mud from his coat with his claws. His legs felt leaden, and then he yawned. His adrenaline was fading fast, and Sam began to feel the fatigue from his flight from the scene of the owl attack taking hold.

"Let's get going. If we sit still too long, I'm afraid I'll fall asleep."

Sounds of vegetation shifting and sticks cracking made them both jump.

It came from behind, back from the direction they'd fled. The noise grew quickly, the source of the sound getting closer. A metallic jingle that could have been weapons clinking together accompanied the noise.

"It's the Chosen," Olenthia hissed, keeping her voice low so it wouldn't echo over the marsh and betray their position. "Can you run?"

Sam's legs and feet ached from the miles and escapes and frantic retreats. It seemed all he'd done since being a raccoon was run. He shook his head. "I don't think so. I'm exhausted. They'd catch us in a heartbeat. Let's climb the tree and take our chances."

Olenthia glanced up into the web of branches above and nodded. "Alright, good idea."

Sam's whole body burned with fatigue, from his claws to the furry tip of his ringed tail, as he pulled himself up the willow tree. He got as far as the first thick bough five feet off the ground and then slumped there in exhaustion, tucking himself as deeply into the shadows as he could. Olenthia took position one branch over and crawled hand over hand further out away from the trunk to get a better vantage point.

This wasn't going to work. Even by the clouded, dark night, Sam could see raccoon and rat footprints in the mud below. If the Chosen had been able to track them this far through dense woods and despite Olenthia's attempts to mask their trail, the prints below would be as obvious as a neon sign on an empty street.

The noise kept getting closer. It sounded big, or maybe just clumsy. Maybe it wasn't the Chosen? What in the woods could make such a sound? Something big enough not to care who noticed its coming. A bear? A mountain lion?

Whatever it was, the jingling was also getting louder.

"Hello-oo," echoed a deep, singsong voice from the darkness.

It was a voice Sam had never heard, but somehow he recognized it instantly even before she came into view.

"Winnie?" He called. "Is that you, girl?"

CHAPTER EIGHTEEN

Any amount of stealth Winnie may have been attempting was abandoned. She crashed through the brush and into sight beneath the tree, her feet prancing in excitement the way the big dog always did when Sam's family returned home.

"Oh good!" She loudly bellowed, oblivious to what creatures in the dark might hear her. "I've been searching and searching. I'm sooo glad I found you!" A giant grin spread across Winnie's broad boxer head, which only accentuated her mouth full of sharp teeth that gleamed even without moonlight. Her tail waved so hard it circled like a helicopter's rotors.

"You know this creature?" Olenthia asked, her eyes wide in disbelief. Winnie kept skipping about beneath the tree. Her paws flung mud as she danced and spun.

"It's a long story," Sam said to Olenthia, and then called down to his dog. "Easy, Winnie, easy. I'm here in the tree with a friend. You won't recognize me, but you're not allowed to chase us. Okay?"

Winnie's back end sat down in the mud with a plop. She raised one of her front paws, as if ready to shake. "You have my word."

"Wait here," he said to Olenthia, "just in case her instincts kick in."

Sam crept slowly down the tree head first. If Winnie sprang forward, he was ready to turn tail and scoot back up to safety.

As she saw him, Winnie's tail swooped back and forth through the mud. She desperately needed a bath. Her white legs and feet were caked in mud, dark as soot in the clouded night. There were burrs and seeds, cottonwood and leaves sticking out from her amber flanks.

When Sam's feet touched the earth, Winnie dropped down onto her forepaws, chest on the ground like a canine sphinx. Sam had always thought of Winnie as a big dog. She was a solid 80 pounds of muscle, after all. But standing just five feet from her in his current raccoon-sized stature, Winnie looked as big as a grizzly bear.

Her face was wide in a silly, but also still scarily tooth-filled, grin as Sam met her stare.

"Good girl, Winnie."

Sam remembered back to what, at the time, he'd thought was a dream. Winnie's terrifying mouth coming toward him with those big teeth. His scramble through the house and escape through the pet door, the sprint through the yard and then the woods that led him to Zip Ric's tree.

"I've been looking everywhere for you!" Winnie's voice was deep and melodious, operatic even. Like the fat lady singing Flight Of The Valkyries.

"Did Mom and Dad send you? Are they alright?"

"They're fine, but were pretty mad about the mess! As soon as they opened the back door, I ran out after you. How come you ran so far away?"

"Because you didn't recognize me and were trying to kill me!" Sam exclaimed, remembering her teeth in the darkness.

"What!? Never! I just wanted to play, to wrestle." She hung her head in embarrassment. "I knew it was you by your scent."

Sam patted her side. "Sorry. I guess you just startled me, that's all. So how did you find me?"

Winnie sat back up straight. "It took a while to find your trail, but once I did there was no stopping Winnie! Give me a smell and enough time, and I could find just about anything in the forest."

"Is it safe to come down?" Olenthia clung to the side of the willow tree, still several feet in the air.

Winnie tilted her head to the side. "Who is this?"

"That's Olenthia, she's my friend from-"

Winnie jumped forward, faster than something her size should have been able to move. Sam barely had time to flinch as she expertly knocked him to his side with a swipe of her big head. Above, he heard Olenthia's alarmed squeak. He winced, waiting to feel Winnie's teeth bite down.

Instead, a wide wet tongue lapped across his face.

"You've made a friend? That's wonderful to hear!" Winnie said between excited slurps across Sam's face. "I'm so proud of you!"

"Stop! Stop!" Sam wrinkled his nose to try and keep some of the dog slobber out of his nostrils as he waved at her in vain with his paws.

After a few moments, Winnie contained her excitement and let him up. Sam spit out saliva, only some of it his own, with fresh mud sticking to his coat. "Thanks Winnie." He looked up into the tree. "Olenthia, it's safe, come on down."

"If I come down from the tree, will I be subject to that same treatment?" Her voice came from a hidden place among the branches.

Sam pointed a stern index-finger claw at the dog. "Winnie, relax. Say hello to my friend Olenthia."

Olenthia cautiously crawled paw over paw to the ground and gave Winnie a quick salute. She didn't draw her sword, but her paw hung close to its hilt.

"How do you do?" Winnie said very formally, sitting down again and bowing her head.

"I suppose you're here to take me home?" Sam asked.

Winnie shook her head and made her collar jingle. "Not yet. First, you have more to do."

"What's that supposed to mean?"

"While trying to track your scent, I met another friend of yours who wanted me to pass on a message. You're becoming so popular, Sam!"

Sure, he thought, with rats and squirrels. But he didn't interrupt. Winnie's next words surprised him.

"An owl named Vera. She's been looking for you to pass on further instructions."

Olenthia raised an eyebrow as she said. "First squirrels, then dogs, now owls? What other strange acquaintances do you keep, Sam?"

"You wouldn't believe me if I told you." Sam said quickly. "Winnie, go on, what did Vera say?"

"First she said it was difficult to find one squirrel and one raccoon in a forest teaming with life, but a large dog was out of place. At first I was hurt. I've always thought of myself as rather petite."

Sam stepped over to pat Winnie's flank. Despite her size, she always tried to climb on a lap or sit on a couch. "I'm sure Vera meant no offense. What else did she say?"

"She told me to track you down, and pass on this message. I had to recite it back several times. She said 'in hopeless causes, seek the help of a true bandit.' Vera repeated it three times, but I'll just say it once if that's alright."

Olenthia rubbed her chin. "The owl was right enough to assume our cause to be hopeless. But what is that advice supposed to mean? I'd heard that owls spoke in riddles, but had never been close enough to confirm. I assumed it was one of those things you only learn in your last moment, right before being eaten."

"She didn't explain it beyond that." Winnie leaned over to sniff Olenthia. "Speaking of being eaten, got any snacks?"

Sam repeated Winnie's message aloud to himself while Olenthia opened her pack to share some dried bug bits with Winnie. "In hopeless causes, seek the help of a true bandit." Something about the message sounded familiar. But he couldn't quite place it. He rubbed his face and covered his eyes, trying to concentrate and summon the memory back into his head.

"Are you alright?" Olenthia asked.

"Olenthia, have you ever tried to remember someone's name, and it's right there on the tip of your tongue but you can't quite remember it?"

Her whiskers twitched, thinking, before shaking her head. "No, I can recall the name and parentage of every soldier assigned to the Fourth Legion who's served under my command. Why do you ask?"

"Bad example. It's right there, I know what Vera's trying to say, but I can't quite make the connection. Like trying to remember the answer on a history test, or where you put an..." The words stuck in his mouth. "... overdue library book."

Sam clapped his paws and hopped in the air. Winnie and Olenthia's heads tilted in unison at him.

"Winnie," Sam said, pointing at the dog. "You said you could find anyone in the this forest?"

She nodded, her collar jingling like bells.

"Ok listen, we have to hurry. We're running out of time, and you need to find us a bandit."

CHAPTER NINETEEN

Winnie led the way through the swamp, her tail wagging as they followed a narrow brook's flow upstream. Sam struggled to keep up. His whole body ached from the long night and protested every step with a new twinge of pain. But there was too much at stake to slow down or take a break. Zip Ric's family was depending on them.

Olenthia, however, seemed in her element. She kept the bag of rat food, lightened from sharing its contents with Winnie, high on her shoulders as she marched along with a steady cadence.

"There's often little for Rodenthold's soldiers to do," she explained to Sam by calling back over her shoulder, "and most of the legions have grown lazy with time. To combat this, I've implemented a strict workout routine with the Fourth."

"This way!" Winnie's big, flowery voice said as they shifted course slightly to the right. She paused to let Olenthia climb onto her back before splashing across the narrow trickle of water. It was a much smaller stream than the one Sam had crossed on a fallen sassafras the day before, but still deep enough to soak Sam to his shoulders as his paws felt their way across slippery rocks in the dark.

After Sam had deciphered Vera's cryptic advice, Winnie said she wouldn't even need her nose to find his quarry, that she knew just the place to look.

They walked beneath maple trees and past closed up wildflowers. The flowers were awaiting daylight's return to reopen, only a hint of color now showing at the edges of their closed petals.

Before long the landscape changed again as the underbrush grew less dense and the trees more manicured. Sam recognized piles of decomposing grass clippings and raked leaves discarded between trees as signs of civilization being close by. The cloudy sky increasingly lightened as they continued through the forest, but not due to the sun rising. The pale glow of streetlights told Sam they'd arrived even before reaching the forest's edge.

A row of houses, their backs facing the woods, stretched out to the right and left. The houses were nearly identical in the darkness, casting long shadows over manicured backyard lawns from the streetlights up front. Chain link fences separated backyards and kept the woods at bay, as if protecting the grass inside from intruding trees. It looked almost like Sam's new street, if the backyards were a little bigger.

Only dark windows looked back at them as the Mapleton residents inside slept at this late hour. Sam fought down his jealously as his mind wandered to thoughts of warm beds and sleep.

Most importantly, Sam could see a green trash bin tucked to the side of each house.

"Good girl, Winnie." The dog leaned in as Sam patted her flank. He looked over at Olenthia, who was unshouldering her backpack. "You're coming with?"

"You think I'd stay here while you schemed without me?" Olenthia winked. "Of course I'm coming." She untied her sword belt and laid it along with the bandoleers full of pebbles on her backpack. Without her military gear, Olenthia looked like a plain gray rat with an unusual marking on her brow. She squirmed through the metal rungs of the chainlink fence and into the backyard lawn.

"I think I'll wait here." Winnie whimpered. "I don't want to say anything I don't mean in the heat of the moment. And I'd have to dig to get past these fences."

Sam didn't argue with that. There was no time to lose waiting on Winnie's tunneling efforts, and he didn't need her instincts kicking in when Sam found who he was looking for. It would be Sunday soon. Only one day to find Zip's tree and figure out how to save it.

He gripped the fence webbing, the metal cold as his fingers curled around it. The fence swayed as he climbed, making a light pinging sound as it bounced against metal posts and sagged beneath Sam's weight. Soon he was over the top and dropped to the other side.

"That wasn't the most graceful thing I've ever seen." Olenthia whispered as she started across the lawn.

The grass was wet, though it hadn't rained. Thick water droplets big as Sam's thumb-claw clung to the grass and soaked his legs. Dew. That meant dawn wasn't far off. They had to hurry. For Zip Ric's sake.

They reached the other side of the yard. Olenthia didn't slow as she hopped between the chain link fencing. Sam picked a spot to climb closer to a support post and made considerably less noise as he scrambled over.

The green plastic trash bin tucked in the shadows was identical to the one back at Sam's house. Rectangular and two-wheeled with its lid attached by a hinge. Sam looked around to make sure the coast was clear and immediately felt foolish. Who would be watching them at this hour?

His knuckles rapped lightly against the plastic, making a hollow, bass drum-like thump. It was louder than Sam intended. He flinched, waiting for a barking dog to sound the alarm or a sharp-eared early riser inside turning on a light to check on the commotion. No response came from the trash can or from the house.

"Let's try the next." Olenthia said, darting toward the fence.

Sam shook his head. "It'll be quieter if I go around front and keep off the fences. Meet you over there."

Olenthia followed him toward the front of the house. "Safety in numbers."

They used a wide flower bed as cover as they moved to the next house. Sam did his best to not disturb the landscaping, but trampled at least one fragrant clump of colorful flowers.

At the second trash bin, Sam used his claws to knock. They made a quieter clicking sound that didn't resonate like the thumping. But it wasn't silent enough.

Something stirred in the yard that Olenthia had nearly darted across.

Noise drifted toward them from the shadowed recesses of the backyard. Tell tale jingles and sniffing, the sounds of an awakened dog investigating an unusual noise. If it started barking, it would wake the whole neighborhood.

Sam and Olenthia crept back, away from the trash bin, trying to get out of sight of the investigating dog's yard. The sniffing became urgent, more hurried. Had the dog heard them? Sam glanced back and froze in place.

The giant frame and pointed ears of a German Shepherd came into view from the side of the house. It slunk through the shadows, just inside the fence. If Sam took another step, it would spot him and start barking. Or worse.

The fence looked tiny compared to the hulking shadow inside. With enough motivation, a raccoon out in the open like a sitting duck for example, the dog could likely jump the fence without much effort.

A drawn out, low sound met Sam's ears. It was coming from the woods, and repeating itself.

"...ll-oooo. Hellll-ooooo."

The German Shepherd stood up straight and swung its attention to the forest. It hustled with marching steps back to where the fence met the tree line and stopped short. Its tail began wagging excitedly, and Sam heard dog voices. They spoke too low for Sam to understand the words, and too quiet to wake the people in the houses. Sam saw a flicker of white fur from a wagging tail on the outside end of the fence, the culprit responsible for distracting the patrolling German Shepherd.

"Good girl, Winnie," Sam whispered to himself as he ran around the front to the next house. Olenthia was waiting for him beside a third trash bin.

"That was too close." Olenthia said. "Are you sure this is going to work?" she continued as Sam's claws clicked against the green plastic.

Sam wasn't sure of anything. No response came from inside the bin, even as he recited the message from Vera once more in his head. 'In hopeless causes, seek the help of a true bandit.'

It seemed like a lifetime ago, there at the school dance check-in table, but wasn't that what Ms. Quick had called raccoons? Bandits of the forest?

Sam had reasoned that finding a true bandit, a real raccoon, had to be the answer to Vera's riddle. Everyone kept saying how clever raccoons were. How Vera had guessed Sam wasn't a real raccoon he couldn't imagine, but he needed help from the professionals.

The problem was, Sam hadn't seen a single raccoon in the forest despite the miles he'd covered. Based on her own knowledge of raccoons, Winnie thought the best place to check would be trash cans and she led them straight to this neighborhood. But they were striking out.

Sam glanced at the sky. It could have been a trick of the street lights, but the clouded black sky seemed to be lightening on the horizon. "Maybe you're right. Maybe we're wasting our time, and should just get to the Ric Family Oak to do whatever we can to help them prepare." Even if Sam, Olenthia, and Winnie couldn't help Zip's family fight off the destruction, at least they could help with the evacuation.

"Alright," he went on, "Before turning back, should we try one more?"

"Try one more what?" said an unfamiliar voice. "Try interrupting another dinner?"

Sam and Olenthia spun around. Black beady eyes surrounded by a dark fur mask looked down at them from the lifted trash bin lid. The fingers of its front paws draped over the edges just beneath its chin.

They'd done it. They'd found a real raccoon.

"What do you want? Spit it out." It spoke with an accent that would have fit in better in New York City than in a small town trash can.

"Um... hello." Sam stammered. He hadn't really thought about what to say, so he just dove in. "We need your help."

"And I need you to get lost. I'm right in the middle of something," the raccoon snarled. "A pile of moldy spaghetti to be precise. You ever had spaghetti? Fantastic stuff. The fungus really brings out the flavor. Now beat it." The lid lowered as the raccoon ducked back down into the bin.

Sam's heart sunk at the dismissal. But Olenthia was not about to be ignored. Her paws closed into balled fists at her side as she stomped to the bin, pounded a paw against the plastic, and in a tone accustomed to ordering thousands of rats around at a time called "Your service is required! I, General Olenthia Von Brightwhisker of the Fourth Legion command you to come forth!"

The lid popped open as the raccoon's face reappeared. "Shuddup, would you? You'll wake the dog." The raccoon hissed the words as he gestured over his shoulder with a thumb toward the German Shepherd's house.

Olenthia put her paws on her hips. "Come down, and you'll see the dog has already been handled."

The raccoon craned his neck in the direction of the back yard, and his ears swiveled like furry satellite dishes seeking a signal. Apparently satisfied, the raccoon swung first its front paws and shoulders over the side of the trash bin before fluidly slinking to the ground without a sound. Sam instinctively retreated a step as the other raccoon got right in Olenthia's face.

"Alright, little rat. You got me down here. Now tell me why I shouldn't knock your head in?" He rose up on his hind legs to loom over Olenthia. The raccoon was huge, its coat thick over a solid muscled body. His ringed tail looked twice as big around as Sam's, and the rest of him was similarly proportioned.

Despite the size difference, Olenthia stood her ground and didn't flinch away from the bully.

"Calm yourself. We're not here for a fight."

"Oh yeah? Well maybe I am."

In that moment, Olenthia reminded Sam of Lia. It seemed like a lifetime ago, though it had only been two days. Lia had faced down Bradley Banks outside of Mapleton Middle School, driving off the big oaf, while Sam stood back and felt helpless.

The scene played itself out again, only now Bradley was replaced by a surly raccoon, and there weren't any adults nearby. It was just the three of them. The other raccoon could attack Olenthia, and there'd be no consequences for his actions here beside the trash bin. She was tough, but too small to have any hope alone in a straight up fight against the big raccoon.

But Olenthia was not alone.

The muscles in Sam's jaw tightened as his eyes found a focus that saw through all the fear and doubt clouding his thoughts. He stood straighter, and his rapid heartbeat steadied.

Sam took a step forward. "Stop it." His voice was flat and decisive.

"Oh, so now you want a piece of me too? Get in line, Kid."

"I said stop it." Sam would not be deterred now. "I don't know what your problem is, but cut it out."

"Now you're telling me what to do? Guess what, Hot Shot. You just moved to the top of my list." The other raccoon brushed past Olenthia with a dismissive shove to confront Sam. He stood more than a head taller than Sam, but Sam was past the point of being concerned about such things.

Sam stood up tall, straight but not puffed out. "After the day I've had, you don't frighten me. You're just a bully, and a blow hard."

"You got a big mouth." From this close, the raccoon's breath smelled like garlic from the spaghetti. "Tell you what, Shrimp. You can have the first shot, but then I'm shutting you up."

"Whatever." Sam ignored the threat, and looked past the other raccoon's shoulder to where his friend had regained her feet. "Come on, Olenthia. Turns out raccoons are just brawn with loud mouths, and that's not going to help us." Sam turned toward the front of the house, putting his back to the big raccoon.

"Oh, too scared to fight, eh?"

"No," Sam didn't turn around as he kept walking. "It's brains we need on this mission, not bravado."

"Now you're saying I'm not smart?" With each word the big raccoon's voice lost some of its edge. Like the question of his intelligence had left him hurt.

Olenthia joined in. "It's hard to tell when all you're doing is throwing around threats."

"Alright, wait, hold on. It was a misunderstanding. That's all. I'll listen. What do you want?"

Sam smiled as he stopped, but cleared his expression before turning back around to face the other raccoon.

"Really? No more threats? No more posturing?"

"Yeah, for sure. It's just, spaghetti, you know? Haven't had it in a long time. It's my favorite, and I got fired up for being interrupted."

Olenthia patted the big raccoon on the shoulder. "Well that was rude of us then, too. Let us start over with introductions." Olenthia bowed as she again repeated her name and title.

"Cranberry." The raccoon pointed at himself with the thumbs on both front paws. "Pleasure to meet you."

Had he said Cranberry? Sam almost laughed at the raccoon tough guy's silly name, but kept it down.

"I'm Sam," he said instead, sticking out a paw to shake, "pleased to meet you."

"Sam?" the raccoon, Cranberry, repeated and rubbed his chin. "Never had Sam before. In fact, never even heard of it. Is it exotic? You from around one of those ethnic food markets or something?"

"Um, I don't think so…", Sam responded, feeling more than a little confused.

"Doesn't matter. So what's up? What's this big score you need an expert's help with?"

Sam wasn't sure where exactly how to explain, so he just started at the beginning.

"Yesterday morning, a squirrel woke me up."

The the sky lightened by the minute, morning well on its way, while Sam talked as fast as he could. True to his word, Cranberry let him speak without interruption.

He told of the Ric Family Oak, the notes posted about the tree's slated demolition, and their mission to save it. He spoke about owls and snakes, Rodenthold and his unlikely rat ally. He had to fight down his tears as he spoke about Zip Ric.

The tale took several minutes as Sam tried to include details that would be important to both convince Cranberry to join the cause, as well as help formulate a plan. Cranberry's eyes widened as Sam spoke about how Winnie found then beneath the base of the Tearful Tree.

Sam finished by reciting Vera's riddle that led them to knock on Cranberry's trash bin. He left out the part about how an offhand comment by the eccentric old librarian Ms. Quick helped Sam decipher the clue, and any other references to being a boy and not a creature of the forest.

"Wow, Kid," Cranberry said, scratching his head after Sam finished, "that's one heck of an adventure you've been on. But I got a couple of concerns."

Sam gulped. Uh oh. Here it was. The moment of truth.

"First up, you say you need the cleverest raccoon plan we can concoct. Look, I don't know how to break this to you, but shouldn't that be where you come in? You are a raccoon, right? I'm thinking maybe you need to go earn your tail stripes. Sort this one out yourself. You can do it, Kid."

"I would, but," Sam hadn't told anyone of his predicament, of his true identity, not even Zip. And it was getting too close to morning to try and explain everything now. He decided in that moment to come clean to Olenthia and Cranberry when they got to the Ric tree, but for now just said, "I was raised by humans. In captivity. Only just recently escaped, and I don't know the tricks of the trade the way you do." It wasn't a lie.

"No wonder you've got such a weird name!" Cranberry snapped his fingers. "You're pretty balanced though, for growing up like that. Good for you. Knew another raccoon that grew up on a farm before getting turned loose. He could barely talk."

Olenthia put a consoling paw on Sam's shoulder. "I had no idea."

"It's alright, I'll tell you more about it later," Sam said to Olenthia.

Cranberry continued. "Hard hand you've been dealt, that's for sure. I get it. What you need is a mentor, a teacher, somebody to show you the true ways of raccoonism. And if I help you on this job, if you don't mind me saying, you'd be learning from the best."

"Oh please," Olenthia muttered, and Sam could almost hear her eyes roll.

"That all brings me to my second problem. If all goes right, a bunch of squirrels and rats and bats or whatever get their home back." Cranberry shrugged. "But, first lesson of being a raccoon- there's got to be something in it for you and me, right? Why should we stick our necks out to help when we could be scoring easy table scraps from this plump harvest of trash cans? So what's our angle?"

That was a question Sam hadn't thought of. His mind raced for an answer.

They were saving a tree that hundreds of squirrels called home, not attempting a bank heist where the spoils could be split up. There were no treasures at the end of this quest, not that a raccoon would have much use for gold or jewels.

Maybe the Rics would let Cranberry move in with them, pick a place in their oak tree to live?

That wouldn't work, either. Cranberry seemed more attuned to towns and trashcans than simple living in an oak tree. Raccoons were bandits, clever tricksters. Like a professional poker player or a conman. The thrill of the job was just as much of a payoff as the reward at the end. And, of course, there was the notoriety.

And that was just the ticket.

As Sam responded, he tried to think of himself as a rogue, a pirate, or even Robin Hood. "I'm helping because I want to stick it to the humans. Take them down a peg. Show them they shouldn't have messed with me or picked on a bunch of innocent squirrels. And for my friend. Zip Ric. He died on this mission, and I will see it carried through."

The big raccoon snorted. "You got guts, Kid, that's for sure. So where's my reward? What's in it for Cranberry?"

"How would you like to be a legend? Live on forever as the raccoon who saved the forest?"

As the thought seeped in, a seedy smile spread across Cranberry's face. "Cranberry, savior of the wood. You know, that has a nice ring to it. I think I feel a plan coming on."

CHAPTER TWENTY

While Olenthia dashed back through the fence webbing to find and update Winnie, Sam followed Cranberry in the other direction. "Come on, Sammy. Time for your first lesson."

Green and purple streaked up from the horizon into the dark sky, like oil paints onto a deep blue canvas. Almost sunrise. For now, the excitement of recruiting a real raccoon and the prospect of Cranberry's save-the-day plan fought off all Sam's fatigue.

Sam mimicked Cranberry, creeping low to the ground as they slunk around the side of one house and hurried past two more, passing under cold cars parked on concrete driveways and through more dew coated grass. In the early Sunday hours there weren't any lights in the house windows, but they still used all caution.

"Where are we going?" Sam whispered as they scurried beneath an SUV.

"Calling in some backup." Cranberry stopped, and pointed as he chuckled. "We're in luck."

A pair of crows sat in the middle of the quiet street. They pecked at the remains of an unfortunate and now unrecognizable creature that hadn't made it across the road. Their cackles were loud enough to echo. The crows were so focused on their meal that they didn't notice the two raccoons sauntering toward them from the lawn until Cranberry called out.

"Morning gentlemen."

The crows hopped into defensive positions around their find. "Go! Go!"

they called in unison, waving their sharp beaks like swords.

"Easy, boys. I'm not after any of your scraps." Cranberry said. Sam followed just behind as the real raccoon strutted out toward the birds.

"What! What! Do you want?" the crow on the left cawed.

"A proposition. How would you like to eat like a king... no, like a raccoon... straight from one of those?" Cranberry pointed across the road at one of the green trash bins.

The crows hopped in excitement toward Cranberry and Sam, forgetting their meal. "Yes! Yes! Tell us. How?" The other crow said.

"Why it's easy. I'll just tip one over for you."

"Yes! Yes!" They again shouted in unison with more hopping. "Now! Now!"

Cranberry held his hands up and gestured for them to calm down. "Not so fast. I need you to do something for me first."

The crows were silent. They swung their heads back and forth, looking at the raccoons with first a twitching left eye and then the right.

"Ready? Are you listening?" Cranberry leaned in, speaking softer, toying with the birds and piquing their interest. They trembled in excitement as he paused longer than necessary.

"Alright, I need you to do is spread a message to as many raccoons as you can find. And then, four sunrises from now," Cranberry held up four fingers for emphasis, "I'll tip over every trashcan on this street for you. Deal?"

"Deal! Deal!" The crows shouted triumphantly.

Cranberry outlined to the two crows exactly what he needed them to say when they found other raccoons, and made them repeat it back to him. "You got to do that today before the sun is at its peak. Got it?"

"Yes! Yes!"

"Alright then boys, that's it. Help us out, and all these garbage cans are yours. Don't mess up." Cranberry turned to go and get out of the street before any cars came along.

"Wait." Sam spoke up, a sudden idea coming to him. "There's one more message you need to carry."

The crows nodded and shook, waiting for the additional orders.

"After you rally the raccoons, here's what I need you to do…"

* * *

With Cranberry in the lead, the party moved quickly through the forest. He knew every bend in the land, guiding them around hills and to stream crossings with all the efficiency of an expert woodsman. The woods held a mystical glow as the sun rose and burnt off the night's leftover clouds. Morning sunlight found its way through the leafy canopy, making flakes of floating pollen and debris look like fairy dust, and buzzing gnats like tiny pixies.

Sam's legs burned with the miles, but it felt like the tide had turned. Momentum was suddenly on their side. As Vera directed, they'd found a real raccoon who had all the confidence and bravado to help them scheme their way to victory.

A prideful smile crept to his face again as he remembered Cranberry's compliment as they'd hustled to leave the street and houses behind, back toward the woods where Winnie and Olenthia were hiding.

"You're a fast learner, Sammy," Cranberry had said. "You knew we had those crows right where we wanted them. You could have asked them to fly to the moon and back, they were so excited about those trash cans."

Sam had shrugged at the compliment, but he did appreciate Cranberry's words. Now Sam just hoped his part of the scheme wouldn't backfire.

They marched in a line. Cranberry led the way, and he'd directed Sam to march right behind him to "see how it was done." Olenthia came up next, while Winnie trotted along at the back, happy to be part of a growing pack.

There'd been a tense moment when Winnie and Cranberry had met. A wild look came to Winnie's eyes, like she wanted nothing more than to bark and chase their new companion. At the same time Cranberry looked ready to scrap, his eyes narrowing and his mouth showing razor teeth. A few reassuring words from Sam was all it took to diffuse the situation, and soon Cranberry and Winnie were chatting back and forth with a mutual respect, like a couple of old sports rivals.

The woodland creatures regarded Winnie with curiosity as they passed. Rabbits flattened their ears with wide, shocked eyes and chipmunks stopped wrestling as she jingled into sight, not daring to move for fear the dog would give chase. Winnie seemed to ignore the attention, though Sam was sure she'd like nothing more then to tear through the dried leaves after them.

"So where'd you get the name Cranberry?" Sam asked. He stifled a yawn and hoped conversation would help him take his mind off the miles still left to cover.

"What's that supposed to mean? What kind of name is Sam? I've never heard of it, and certainly never tried it."

"It's what I've always been called. It was my grandpa's name."

Cranberry scratched his chin. "Were they both raised in captivity by humans too? Your mom and grandpa, I mean."

"Uh, yeah. I guess you could say that."

"Raccoons out here, we're named after our folks' favorite food. My mom was a nut for Thanksgiving leftovers, especially cranberry sauce. So me and my siblings are all named Cranberry."

"How many brothers and sisters do you have?"

Cranberry shrugged. "Dozen or so. Why?"

Twelve kids, all named the same? It sounded baffling. "How does anybody tell you apart or know which Cranberry they're talking about?"

"No reason to. Besides, it's easier to pull off scams if there are a bunch of other suspects with the same name."

For another hour they followed Cranberry. Sam's mind wandered as he walked. It was just his third day in the woods, but he noticed so much more than that first morning of blindly stumbling after Zip Ric.

Leaves, especially on the maple trees, were beginning to give up their green, edges just starting to show the crimson color that would soon dominate the forest. As cardinals and robins chortled overhead, their songs hinted at sadness for the passing of summer. Even the light breeze had a soft bite to it, a chill that seemed out of place on such a sunny day.

There was not enough time. If Sam and his crew of new friends couldn't prevent the destruction of the Ric Family Oak, there weren't enough summer days left for the Rics to both find a new home and gather the necessary supplies to survive the winter. They'd starve, perish, just like poor Zip Ric.

A pair of squirrels rushed through the limbs overhead. They didn't stop to assess the travelers as they busied themselves with some desperate errand. Then Sam saw two more squirrels clamor past, going the other way through the tree branches. Then another four.

"Hurry, it's just ahead." Cranberry said.

The forest stopped at the edge of a meadow Sam had seen once before under the moonlight in what he'd thought was a dream.

The Ric Family Oak rose above the meadow like a spire, easily twice the height of any tree Sam had seen on his travels. Its lower boughs, each as broad as another tree, spread wide over the earth before reaching back toward the sky and branching into hundreds of limbs and then thousands of fingers. Leaves glistened like emeralds as they caught the midday sun.

The first time Sam had seen the Ric's magnificent tree, he'd attributed its beauty to his own imagination. He'd thought something that awe inspiring and perfect could not actually exist beyond a dream as he'd joined in with the squirrels' joyful frolic.

Now, even beneath a cloudless noon sky, the mood had changed from a celebration to chaos.

The Rics ran in every direction, frantic and panicked, evacuating their home. They carried bundles of straw and twigs in their mouths along with food-stuffed cheeks. The squirrels did not seem to be following any kind of plan, other than to run away. Vera and Humphrey had been true to their word of bringing warning to the Rics.

"They aren't even running away from me," Winnie said as the squirrels only adjusted their course to avoid the big dog before carrying on with their frantic scampering.

The air buzzed with thousands of squirrel voices.

"They're evacuating." Olenthia said. "Making preparations to flee."

Olenthia was right. Berry bushes and thistle shrubs had been picked clean of fruit and seed. Sam didn't spy a single stray acorn on the ground. The whole of the Ric family had mobilized to retreat into the woods, taking as many provisions as they could from the place that had been their home for hundreds of years.

They reached the wide base of the Ric Tree, rising like a miniature mountain from the earth. At least twenty squirrel foremen circled around its base. A continuous line of squirrels ran in amber streaks up and down the tree trunk, pausing only to receive directions from the foremen squirrels before dashing away to collect another load of building materials or stored food.

"HOLD IT!"

The order rippled through the ranks, repeated dozens of times.

Every squirrel froze in place, like an assembly line when the electricity goes out. Whether mid climb, mid sentence, or mid hand-off, every Ric turned to see what the stop work order was about.

A lone squirrel moved through the throng straight toward Sam and his crew. He was missing half his tail, but this feature seemed to lend him an air of authority.

"Want. To. Chase." Winnie whimpered quietly.

Sam petted her side. "Easy girl, easy."

"Where are the sentries? How did two raccoons, a rat, and a DOG get through without warning?" The squirrel with half a tail said to any ear that could hear.

The response came from all around them, one at a time and rapid fire. Sam wasn't able to distinguish which squirrel each voice belonged to.

"The sentries are off scouting, Great Grandpa Ric!"

"Looking for suitable evacuation points."

"Yeah Gramps, it's all hands on deck for the retreat."

Great Grandpa Ric shook his head. "Still. Nobody bothered to pass back word we had visitors?"

"Too busy."

"Duty calls."

"Orders are orders."

More squirrels, returning from trips into the forest, gathered around the base of the tree. They gawked at Sam and his strange crew and joined in making excuses for how the intruders had gotten this far without so much as a warning.

Half-tailed Great Grandpa Ric hopped in place and quieted the chatter. "By the Fleet Feeted Four, they've got a giant DOG with them! It could have eaten somebody in one gulp!"

An outcry of voices all at once, pointing and blaming, defending and deflecting, and generally crying foul filled the air. Sam saw a few shoving matches break out, along with some tail pulling. The chaos made Cranberry roll his eyes while Olenthia's paw hovered over the hilt of her needle sword.

"Wait! Stop!" Sam's words were lost in the noise of the Rics' riot. Every squirrel had its own opinion, and the high pitched din was deafening. "We want to help you!" No one heard his protests.

"Oh nooo!" Winnie's voice, big enough to fill the meadow, rose in lament. "I didn't mean to cause such a fuss."

At Winnie's words, the squirrels froze again.

Winnie sat back on her haunches, the way she did when begging for table scraps. "There's no need to fight, and I'm not going to eat anybody. Don't you see? Sam brought us here to help!"

A murmur rose up from the gathering of squirrels. Whispers and gasps, but thankfully no fighting. Sam swore he heard his name uttered several times.

"Hold-it hold-it hold-it!" Great Grandpa Ric waved his hands over his head and jumped in place to quiet the gathered Rics. He hopped over to stand before Winnie. From close up, Sam saw the fur on Great Grandpa Ric's face was mostly gray. "Did you say *Sam*?"

Winnie's collar jingled as she nodded her broad head. "Yes. He's right there."

In one fluid motion, Great Grandpa Ric leapt in front of Sam and swept into the same low bow Sam recalled Zip Ric performing first before Humphrey and Vera, and then Emperor Nezearius in Rodenthold. Though Great Grandpa Ric's half-tail wasn't long enough to touch the ground above his head, it was still quite the elaborate gesture.

"Tales of your bravery precede you, Sam. We've been hoping for your arrival."

"Tales of my what?" Sam's eyes shifted around to the squirrels, who seemed to be gathering in closer around him. They bowed in the same manner, hundreds of tails sweeping forward to touch the ground just above their heads.

"Ten minute break!" Great Grandpa Ric shouted. "Then report back here for assignment updates."

Again, individual squirrel voices rose from the crowd.

"What about the evacuation?"

"I thought there was no time to waste?"

"You don't want me to keep dismantling nests for building materials?"

Again, Great Grandpa Ric waved his paws over his head to quiet them. "Change of plans everyone. The evacuation is postponed. Sam here is going to save our tree!"

As cheers and high-fives filled the meadow, Great Grandpa Ric gestured for Sam to follow him as he hopped toward the base of the mighty oak. "This way. Lots of planning to do, and there's someone who'll want to see you."

"Jeez," Cranberry leaned in to whisper in Sam's ear. "No pressure."

CHAPTER TWENTY-ONE

The squirrels went on break, while Sam and his friends followed Great Grandpa Ric up the tree. Well, all his friends except Winnie.

"Wait here, girl." Sam said. "I'll be back soon. Good dog."

Winnie whimpered as she laid down, covering her face with her paws. "It's taking a lot of self-control not to chase these squirrels."

"Just relax, you'll be alright."

"Hurry back!" she said as Sam followed Great Grandpa Ric, Cranberry and Olenthia up the tree.

Squirrels shot past him as they climbed, like cars passing on the highway. They called out with cheerful voices as they rushed by.

"On your left!"

"On your right!"

"The Rics," Olenthia noted, "are in remarkably good spirits for being on the edge of destruction."

Sam remembered Zip's unfailing optimism. Whether facing down snakes or imprisoned in an old mall bathroom, Sam had never seen the squirrel lose hope. "That's just their way." Even surrounded by hundreds of Zip Ric lookalikes, Sam felt a sudden loneliness as he remembered his first friend in the forest. No, his first friend in Mapleton.

They climbed through several forks in the tree as Great Grandpa Ric led them steadily up, up, up. Sam glanced back, out and through the leaves, at blue sky all around. They were already higher than any other tree ringing the meadow, and still they climbed.

At last Great Grandpa Ric's voice announced, "Here we are."

"Thank the rat gods," Olenthia's legs trembled as she walked out onto the branch, squeezing in next to Cranberry. "I thought my claws were about to pull from my paws."

Cranberry smirked. "Remember, you still have to climb down."

Sam was the last of the group to shimmy out onto the branch. It was wide and sturdy, but Sam was still careful not to look down.

Great Grandpa Ric pointed. "Stand over there, and I'll be right back." Then disappeared higher up into the tree.

To his surprise, Sam saw the Rics had built a wide platform between two branches from twigs, grass, and mud. Cranberry waved Sam and Olenthia past. "Rics are surprisingly good builders, but I'm a little thicker than you two, so I'll stick to the branch."

The real raccoon was right. The platform felt solid as a concrete floor beneath Sam's paws. He looked around seeing a number of similar platforms constructed between tree limbs and woven nest houses in the eaves of branches above, too many to count. The Ric tree swayed and creaked in the breeze, but even this high up Sam didn't feel uneasy. He still tried not to look down.

Hopping between branches and platforms, Great Grandpa Ric and another squirrel descended from above. The second squirrel was favoring its right front leg as it hopped, but otherwise it looked exactly the same as every other squirrel Sam had seen that day.

But somehow Sam recognized him as different. Sam's eyes widened. "It can't be…"

The second squirrel paused to wave at Sam before continuing after Great Grandpa Ric.

"Sam! Everyone! Good to see you!"

Zip Ric leapt into Sam's fuzzy chest and Sam squeezed him in a tight raccoon hug.

Olenthia smiled sagely while Cranberry blew his nose into a leaf plucked from the tree. "Aren't reunions beautiful?" he muttered to Olenthia, before putting his arm around her.

"You're alive?" Sam released the hug and wiped his eyes with his forearm. "How?"

"Let me field that question." A very proper and very accented voice boomed out from overhead. The unexpected sight of Humphrey's brown speckled form landed beside the teary party welcoming Zip back, and went on.

"It was all my fault. Apologies all around. Dreadful situation, dreadful night, and I was so dreadfully hungry. Dear Vera had me flying all about on errand after errand, all day and all night, and I simply forgot to eat."

"But you said we'd be safe, from you and Vera at least?" Sam asked.

"A moment of weakness, I'm afraid. Through the night, I zeroed in on young Master Zip, perched as though on a platter for me. Of course, I did not recognize him as the young Ric who'd sought my counsel the previous day, and despite my own misgivings, I fear my hunger overcame my oathes." Humphrey put the back of his wing to his forehead in a dramatic gesture and moaned. "I'm embarrassed to say instinct took over, and thinking only of my stomach, I swooped down to strike."

Zip petted Humphrey's feathers with his uninjured paw. "Luckily he recognized my voice when I screamed."

"Again, Master Zip, I do apologize. Hunger is no excuse for violating one's commitments."

"It's all forgiven, a misunderstanding." Zip Ric turned back to Sam. "He set me down in a big elm tree, but his talon nicked my shoulder so I couldn't come chasing after you. Humphrey went back to look for you and explain the mistake, but you'd already disappeared deeper into the forest. So he brought me back here, to join in the preparations."

Olenthia stepped forward and bowed her head. "It's good to see you again, Zip Ric."

Zip Ric swallowed her up in a one-armed hug. "Thanks for coming, General. We're in need of your smarts."

"Well, now just a moment," Humphrey snorted, "I thought it was I that would be looked to for wise council?"

"In your dreams, Feathers." Cranberry spoke up, pointing at himself with a thumb. "That's why they had to come recruit me."

"Do not think, raccoon, that you can barge up this tree and just take over!"

"Who's in charge here? I didn't know the King of Squirrels hatched from an egg!"

"Stop it!" Sam's voice came out louder than he expected. To his surprise, Cranberry and Humphrey paused their squabbling to look at him, as his shout echoed through the tree limbs. From the ground, a single loud woof from Winnie punctuated his words.

"We don't have time for this," Sam tried not to let his voice or his limbs quiver as he scolded the older, larger, creatures. "The Rics can't save their tree alone, and one owl or one rat or one raccoon isn't going to make the difference either."

"Are you saying it's hopeless, Sam?" Zip Ric asked.

"If we let stubbornness and egos get in our way, then yeah Zip, it's probably hopeless."

Cranberry and Humphrey, in unison, turned from each other and seemed to pout. But at the same time, they hung their heads, clearly recognizing their own arrogance was getting in the way.

"But if we all chip in, do our part, and play to our strengths, then who knows what we can accomplish. Does everyone understand?"

Olenthia stood straight and saluted Sam, and Zip Ric and Great Grandpa Ric copied her. Cranberry and Humphrey turned back to each other, shrugged, and Cranberry shook Humphrey's wing.

"Guess that answers that question," Cranberry said with a chuckle.

"Yes, as strong a case as I've heard presented," Humphrey agreed.

"Alright, Sam," Great Grandpa Ric stepped forward. "What do we do now?"

"Wait, me?"

"If we are to fight, we will need someone to lead us." Great Grandpa Ric looked Sam in the eye. "Sam, that must be you."

They all looked to Sam. Zip Ric, always happy and optimistic. Olenthia, practical and even-tempered. Humphrey, wise in his own way and encouraging, if prone to melodramatic fits. Cranberry, sarcastic and brash and outspoken, but clever and with a good heart. Below was Winnie, loyal and true. Great Grandpa Ric represented the thousands of squirrels that had ceased their evacuation plan with his arrival, and were now ready to fight for their home.

Sam finally saw his place on the team.

"Yes," Sam said, more sure of it than anything he'd ever said.

Great Grandpa Ric turned to each of Sam's companions in turn, asking if they'd fight.

Humphrey bowed. "My own efforts to find a mountain lion or black bear to aid in the defense were in vain I'm afraid, but Vera is still out there searching for help. Hope remains, and I shall fight until my last tail feather is bent and broken."

"A worthy cause, saving a home. I can think of no better fight." Olenthia declared. "Besides, I've got a thing for seeing humans turn tail and run."

Cranberry cracked his knuckles. "I like being an underdog."

A loud howl echoed up from the ground. "Me toooo!" Winnie's howl caused every speck of industrious amber fur in the field to freeze in place.

Sam smiled. "Sorry about Winnie. She has good ears."

Zip Ric's persistent smile didn't waiver as he asked, "So Sam, where do we start?"

Sam's mind raced as he looked out over the meadow and the ring of trees surrounding it. Trees formed a perfect circle around the field below, except for one bare place. Sam pointed at the gap.

"Is that where the men brought their dragon?"

Great Grandpa Ric shuddered. "I'm afraid so. It's foul, what's happened there. Ripped up, empty and ugly."

"At least we know where they'll be coming from." Sam muttered, before speaking more decisively. "Olenthia. No one here has the experience you do repelling invaders or managing troops."

She nodded, hand on her needle sword.

"And these squirrels have never fought anything except when they've wrestled each other. The Rics are going to need some quick combat training. They need a crash course on throwing acorns, how to use their teeth, and anything else that will help them fight and survive the day."

"We start immediately," she said. "Great Grandpa Ric, if you would be so kind as to help me assemble our army?"

"Right this way, m'lady," he said, before they dashed down the tree toward the meadow.

Sam glanced out again at the broken gap in the tree line. "The rest of you, come with me."

They started the long descent down the Ric tree. "Where are we going, Sam?" Zip Ric asked. He was still an excellent climber even with only three uninjured paws.

"I want to get a look at this dragon of yours."

* * *

The swath of cleared trees was easily forty feet across. Sam, Cranberry, and Winnie climbed over unnatural furrows and ruts in the ground. The earth had been scored and gouged by machine tracks, heavy boots, and uprooted trees.

"We watched as the dragon roared and pushed the trees over, roots and all. Then it dragged the trees back that way." Zip Ric pointed with his good paw before grabbing hold of Winnie's collar again. Winnie proved a good steed for the injured Zip, and he was almost camouflaged against her fur.

Humphrey swooped in and landed on a slender maple tree that had been damaged during the demolition, half its branches ripped away as other trees had fallen around it. The maple bent beneath Humphrey's weight.

"I have seen Zip Ric's dragon, and it is terrible to behold!" He put the back of his wing over his forehead for emphasis.

"He's going to get a cramp if he keeps doing that," Cranberry muttered.

Seeing the destruction, Sam had formulated a guess as to the true identity of Zip's dragon but said nothing.

The cleared swath stretched out before them a hundred yards or more, and then bent at an angle to the right. Though all he could see was tilled earth and bordering woods, the distinct sound of passing cars carried over the remaining trees and grew louder with each step down the cleared corridor.

The strange mix of animals moved in silence, navigating the unnatural terrain, mud, and earthen ruts with caution. The disturbed topsoil had a foul and rotting smell to it, like passing a dairy farm with the car windows down on a warm day.

Here and there a bit of green remained from the former section of forest floor. A lone fern frond or the last loping blades from a wild daffodil. But mostly, the path was dirt and mud and scoured clean of vegetation. Even beneath the warm afternoon sun it gave Sam chills, and he thought it might be less unnerving to walk through a graveyard by moonlight.

They reached the turn in the cleared path, and they all stopped in their tracks. There was Zip Ric's dragon.

In fact, there were two, slumbering side by side, beneath the shade of some still untouched trees.

"Oh no!" Zip Ric whispered. "The dragon has multiplied!"

They were enormous and identical, covered in yellow armor plates that were scratched from years of hard use. The beasts' mouths gleamed silver, and great nostrils stretched up toward the sky.

"Those aren't dragons at all," Sam said without a bit of relief. "Those are bulldozers."

The machines were parked in a wide, cleared staging area set up for the construction project. Gravel had been dumped in the clearing, and spread out to give a harder surface for men and machines to maneuver. Tools and other equipment were scattered around. An empty flatbed trailer waited behind the bulldozers to usher the large machines away after their destructive work was done. The gravel continued out the other side of the clearing, and to a distant roadway where Sam saw cars rushing past.

The smell of fresh mulch filled the air, and a pile of ruddy wood chips steamed beside a square, green wood chipper. A stack of logs and branches waiting to be disposed of was all that remained of the cleared section of trees.

Cranberry whistled in awe. "We're going to have our work cut out for us, that's for sure."

"Shh…" Zip Ric put a finger to his mouth. "You'll wake them."

"Don't worry, little squirrel," Winnie cooed. "Without a person around, I don't think the machines can wake up."

Sam imagined the bulldozers' shining front blades ripping through the soft ground of the meadow as they methodically lumbered forward. How were squirrels, rats, and a pile of thrown acorns supposed to fight against that? Emperor Nezearius had conquered a mall, but surely even the conquest of Rodenthold hadn't had to face a machine as powerful as a bulldozer, let alone two.

Though he hated to admit defeat so quickly, Sam didn't have any idea what to do. "If we can't figure out a way to stop those bulldozers," he said, "we may as well give up now."

"Alas, the moment looks dire." Humphrey landed a few feet off and then waddled along the gravel ground to stand beside them.

There was a rustling noise, from near the bulldozers, that made Sam jump.

"They're waking up!" Zip Ric said as he buried his head in Winnie's fur.

The noise startled Humphrey too, and he lifted up from the ground with a thumping of wings.

Only Cranberry seemed unfazed. He punched Sam playfully on the shoulder and winked. "Finally! Reinforcements."

Out from the forest beside the bulldozers appeared the black masks of four raccoons.

"It's about darn time." Cranberry's shouts echoed in the cleared meadow. "What part of 'get to the Ric tree as fast as you can, big job' did you not understand?"

One of the raccoons gave a disinterested wave at Cranberry, and together the four raccoons slunk across the gravel yard toward Sam and company.

"Yeah yeah yeah," one complained, "what did you expect? Crows are the worst at relaying messages. Took him twenty minutes to get to the point. After I introduced myself, the bird just kept squawking my name."

"Well, Corn, you should know better then to distract such a simple minded creature with pleasantries."

"Hey, not all of us are mannerless savages like you, Cran. Just saying, if it's that important, send a better messenger next time."

Cranberry stalked toward the other raccoons until he stood face to face with the four. "I had limited options and was in a hurry. How about next time I send a woodpecker to drive the message through your thick skull?"

They traded a few more barbs and insults, and it looked like any second Cranberry may come to blows with the other raccoons.

But then, almost in unison, the raccoons began to laugh and playfully grab each other in hugs and headlocks before ambling back to where Sam stood watching.

"Sam, everyone, meet my team." There was Corn, who seemed to be second in command, two siblings both named Taco, and French Fry. They seemed pleasant enough, for a band of thieves.

"So what's the job?" Corn asked.

Cranberry waved off the question, and turned back to Sam. "You help whip those Rics into fighting shape and prepare the defenses, and just leave those dragons to us."

The raccoons got busy strategizing how to disable the bulldozers. They were climbing all over the first machine, pulling at tubes and inspecting pistons and gears, when Sam turned to head back toward the meadow with the others.

Humphrey muttered something about scouting and the need to keep a lookout, yawned, and flew off.

Sam wasn't paying attention as he led the way back into the meadow, and nearly fell face first into a freshly dug hole. His front paws caught the edges of the pit and just barely helped him keep his balance.

"Careful Sam!" cried Winnie.

A startled trio of squirrels, covered head to tail in dirt, stared up at him from the bottom of the hole. It was almost two feet deep and they must have worked fast to dig it in the short time Sam had been gone from the meadow.

"Well, it works!" laughed Olenthia. The rat emerged from behind some tall grass. "Humans rarely watch where they're walking. If they get this far, these holes will slow them down."

Behind each clump of tall grass and berry bush, another team of squirrels toiled away digging the booby traps. It was a smart move if the workers came on foot, but the holes would have little effect on a pair of bulldozers.

Winnie stuck her nose into a shallower hole. "It looks like you could use some help down here. Hold on tight, Zip." Her front half disappeared into the ground and a split second later a rain of dirt flew back behind her. Squirrels from other holes popped up to watch Winnie's digging prowess. Soon cheers and applause rose from the squirrels ranks.

Sam turned to Olenthia. "I've got some bad news," he started to say. Olenthia shushed him, grabbed his arm, and led Sam away from the teams of squirrels watching Winnie's digging skills.

"The first key to commanding soldiers," Olenthia said as they walked toward the Ric tree, "is keep their moral up. Give them tasks to tackle, like hole digging and ammunition gathering, and they'll stay focused and confident. Let the command staff worry about the big stuff. That means don't deliver bad news in front of the troops."

"Sorry."

She looked around, saw the coast was clear and stopped in the shadow of a wild blueberry bush, picked clean of all but a few last berries. "So what's the bad news?"

Sam told her about the pair of bulldozers. He kept his voice low to prevent others from eavesdropping, despite how unlikely it would be for a squirrel to hear him as they raced past on errands and missions.

Olenthia rubbed her chin with two fingers. "But the raccoons say they can disarm the machines?"

"They seem to think so. I'm not so confident."

"We'll just have to take them at their word. No sense doubting before we've given Cranberry and his crew time to show their mettle."

Just then a call rippled through the ranks of darting squirrels.

"More visitors from the forest!"

"More strangers coming!"

"It's rats!"

"Rats!"

Olenthia's eyes widened.

"The Chosen?" Sam asked. "How did they find us?"

Olenthia grabbed his paw. "Come on."

They ran as fast as they could to the Ric Family Oak, asking passing squirrels which way the rats were attacking from. It took several relayed messages, but they got the story.

The rats weren't attacking. In fact, they seemed friendly and had stopped at the meadow's edge. Sam and Olenthia changed course toward where the squirrels said the newcomers had arrived.

It was no Legion, and it was not the Emperor's Chosen. The band of rats, less than a hundred, were dropping packs of food and gear as they collapsed in exhaustion at the tree line.

A big rat, scarred with a notched ear stood wobbly and managed a weak salute. Then Clive barked an order at his fellows. "Show the General some respect, you louts!"

The disbelief was apparent on Olenthia's face as she saluted Clive back.

"Sorry, ma'am," Clive said, "this bunch was all that managed to fight through." Then he sagged to the ground like a deflated balloon and began snoring.

CHAPTER TWENTY-TWO

"To be honest, it wasn't easy," Clive said. He looked refreshed after just an hour's rest.

The big rat picked at his teeth with a pine needle and leaned lazily against a rock as the rest of the rat soldiers strapped on gear to do their part in the defense of the meadow. Sam had just asked Clive how he'd convinced the rats to leave Rodenthold, and how they'd managed to find the Ric Family Oak.

Clive was basking in the attention and milking a dramatic pause when Olenthia's stern voice snapped him out of it. "No one likes a boaster. Answer Sam's question, and then there's work to do."

Clive popped to attention at the General's orders, and quickly recounted what had happened.

There had been grumbling in the Fourth Legion's ranks over the way Emperor Nezearius had treated their general. To a rat, every member of the Vanguard present at the hearing before the Emperor had been ready to march out and aid Zip's cause. They'd decided Olenthia was right, and the opinion was quickly taken on by the rest of the Fourth. Rodenthold was crumbling around them. They had to do something.

That meant Clive's job convincing the Fourth Legion had been easy. They'd marched out from the walls, but had no luck with their timing. They ran straight into the returning Emperor's Chosen as they'd fled from the snakes. A fight broke out in the parking lot.

"We gave them a good thrashing, but they outnumbered us. Had to call a strategic withdrawal." Clive pointed at the assembled rats. "This lot was all that could get away, and follow me to the trees. The Chosen didn't give chase. Seems they'd had enough of the woods for one day, but most of the Fourth got pinned down in the fighting. Hope them blokes are alright..."

"But how did you find us?" Sam wondered. "You've never tracked anything through the woods before."

"First part was easy. The path was pretty beaten down, up to where the Chosen had to turn back. Leading them into a snake ambush? Brilliant."

"So how did you and all these other rats get past the snakes without any casualties?"

Clive chuckled. "Didn't try to go through at the same place, that's for sure. Those buggers were still riled up and rattling when we arrived. We followed the creek bed till the rocks weren't big enough to hide more than one or two snakes. And when you get enough rats with enough teeth and pointy things," Clive hefted his spear, "even snakes will decide to wait for easier prey."

"Then we doubled back, and a scout found one of the General's scratchings. Followed that for a while, but in the darkness we got a bit turned around. Luckily, we had a visitor to help steer us here. You got some strange friends, Mr. Sam."

"You don't know the half of it. Who was-"

At that moment, Winnie, with her snout covered in dirt and Zip Ric sitting tall on her back trampled through the bushes toward them. Surprised rats lunged for weapons, but Olenthia quickly barked for them to stand down. Rat soldiers warily backed away as Winnie sat. Zip Ric climbed off Winnie's back and dashed over to hug Clive in reunion.

The momentary distraction hadn't stopped Sam's mind from puzzling. Who could have guided Clive to the Ric Tree? As Olenthia loudly introduced Winnie to the remnants of the Fourth Legion, Sam pulled Clive over to ask who'd helped guide them.

"An owl. Gave me and the troops quite a fright when she came swooping down from the trees. Like a bright white ghost, even with the moon all cloud covered. Said her name was Vera."

"Vera? You're joking."

"No sir, would never joke about an owl. Terrified us, she did. But told us where to go, and told me to pass you a message."

Clive thought for a moment, and then went on. "She said to stay the course, fight with courage, and she'll be here to join us quick as she can to strike the decisive blow." Then Clive shrugged. "Any idea what she's got planned?"

Sam shook his head. "None."

Clive shrugged again, then dashed over to where Winnie was surrounded by awed rats.

Sam sat down, feeling like his head was swimming. First Vera had found Winnie, and given the hint of finding Cranberry. Then she'd steered Clive and the remaining troops to their door. What other tricks did Vera have up her wings?

* * *

Squirrels, rats, raccoons, and a dog toiled away with a singular purpose under the afternoon sun.

Clive and the other Rodenthold veterans served as drill sergeants over battalions of squirrel recruits, while Zip Ric stayed nearby to offer encouragement. They practiced marching, battle maneuvers, and acorn tossing.

Zip Ric relayed the story of how Sam had thumped a rattlesnake from ten paces with a stone, and the rats insisted Sam step in and give everyone tips. After reviewing proper pitching form with the rats and squirrels, it seemed like the thrown acorns had an extra zip behind them.

Humphrey reappeared after a few hours, apologized that he'd actually stopped to take a short nap and overslept most of the day way, and then served as messenger between the preparations happening in the Ric Tree meadow and where Cranberry's raccoons were formulating a plan of attack against the bulldozers.

"Master Cranberry says they are making progress," Humphrey reported in to Sam with a salute, "but that they've not yet struck the deathblow on the foul machines. The hulls are proving impenetrable."

A small handful of squirrels requested to stay on digging detail, and

Winnie happily joined them to lend extra muscle. She dug tirelessly, and by the day's end most of the squirrels were just watching and cheering her on rather than tending to their own pits.

It seemed Olenthia was everywhere at once. She saw to the overall logistical operations, directing lines of squirrels and rats carrying projectiles and gear to the trees lining the cleared swath that connected the meadow to the construction staging area. She reviewed attack formations and fall back points with her squad leaders. And she instructed teams of squirrel blacksmiths on proper weapon and armor construction as twigs were gnawed into sharpened spears and acorn tops became helmets.

Great Grandpa Ric had taken charge of the evacuation. The Rics too old, too young, or otherwise too injured to fight were falling back to a long-branched pine tree a mile deeper into the forest. It would not serve as a permanent home, but if the coalition forces of Squirrel, Rat, and Raccoon were unsuccessful in fighting back the humans, the hope was that beneath the pine's boughs the Rics could survive the winter.

Sam split his time among the different tasks and made sure everyone kept cooperating, helping where he could throughout the meadow, but it was with the evacuees that he spent most of his efforts.

The sun continued its relentless march. There was not enough time for all the training Olenthia would have liked and, even with the help of all the rats and squirrels, not enough hands to finish preparations.

Sam kept watching the sky. As dusk settled in over the meadow, giving the world an orange tinted glow, there was still no sign of Vera or the additional help she'd assured them was coming. Every time Sam looked up he expected to see her soaring into the clearing leading a squad of mountain lions, red wolves, or black bears, and every time he was disappointed. There was no trace of her. Humphrey had even quizzed passing birds, hoping for some news of her coming, but none had caught a glimpse of the Wood Seer's ghostly visage.

"It's alright, Sam," Olenthia patted his shoulder as he looked skyward. The sun was slipping beneath the tops of the trees and would soon disappear over the horizon. "We've done much today to prepare."

"Will it be enough?"

The rat general only shrugged. "All will be decided with the new day. Come on. The work is wrapping up, and we're having a final strategy session before some much needed rest."

Sam followed her through the meadow. Adrenaline, wonder, and terror had pushed him through the last few days with little sleep or food. At Olenthia's mention of rest, fatigue hit him all at once. His legs felt heavy as the Ric Tree as he trudged past Winnie-dug ditches, stockpiles of supplies staged for the front, and groups of squirrels and rats getting in a few last round of sparring practice.

They gathered beside the Ric Tree's trunk. Assembled were Olenthia, Clive and the other rat captains, Great Grandpa Ric with a few other graying squirrels Sam hadn't met, and Humphrey. Winnie arrived a moment later with Zip Ric sitting like a knight on her back. He was clearly getting used to having a noble steed, just as all the Rics and Winnie were getting used to each other. Winnie wasn't trembling excitedly like she wanted to pounce, and the squirrels didn't even flinch at the sight of the big dog.

Olenthia clapped her paws, quieting conversation. "Alright. Let's keep this short and to the point everyone. We've done some good work in a short amount of time, and we're all going to need our rest for tomorrow. Great Grandpa Ric, how is your people's morale?"

"You don't have to worry about us," he replied. "We're as cheerful and optimistic as they come."

"Good to hear. We're honored to make your acquaintance and fight on your behalf. Clive, same question for the Fourth."

Clive glanced back at the other captains, who thumped fists together and grinned as they clutched spears and swords. "After that long march to get here, we're all itching for a fight."

"And training operations? Will the Ric soldiers suffice?"

"Are you kidding? Have you seen one of them Rics jump? Just you wait, General. The strike teams will execute those new maneuvers you dreamed up better than imagined."

"Excellent," Sam thought he heard a hint of excitement in Olenthia's voice. She turned then to Winnie. "All trenches and pit traps completed?"

"Yes ma'am!" Winnie howled, waving her paw at the air like she wanted to shake, Winnie's own version of a salute. "As deep as you wanted and then some!" Her white fur was stained the same brown and red as the dirt and clay. Winnie definitely needed a bath.

Olenthia turned then to Humphrey. "What updates do you have from the raccoon's efforts against the bulldozers?"

"Let me field that one," Cranberry said, dusting his paws off as he stomped over on hind legs. The other raccoons Corn, French Fry, Taco and Taco followed just behind. "Those bulldozers are locked up tighter than a chained on garbage lid. We've been trying all day to jimmy the locks open to get at the controls, but no luck. We did chew up a bunch of exposed rubber tubing, but that probably won't do much."

Olenthia raised an eyebrow. "So you spent the day trying unsuccessfully to get inside the bulldozers? How does that help us stop them? If those machines are brought into the fight, we may as well sound the retreat now."

"Hold on, did I say I didn't have a plan? Because let me assure you, I got a plan. It's just a little more risky and less covert than I might have liked."

It sounded to Sam like Cranberry might be bluffing. If in a half day the raccoons hadn't been able to damage the bulldozers enough to stop them from running, what other ideas did they have?

"Well," Olenthia said after Cranberry paused for several seconds, "go on."

"You're kidding. You want to hear it all spelled out, right now? Where's the dramatic tension in that?"

Olenthia nodded. "Coordinating efforts and understanding everyone's role is the purpose of a war council, after all."

Cranberry rolled his eyes and twisted his face, but Olenthia didn't back down.

"You know, Olenthia, you're tough, for a rat. I like you. Fine, here's what me and the crew are going to do."

Based on the elaborate and precise plan Cranberry proceeded to outline to the group, Sam felt bad for ever doubting the big raccoon.

When Cranberry finished speaking, Olenthia thanked him for detailing his team's efforts, and volunteered two squads of squirrels to assist them with the necessary diversions.

"Yeah," Cranberry rubbed his chin. "Thanks. A few dozen extra sets of hands would be helpful when it all goes down."

Olenthia ran through a few last details, such as where to assemble in the morning and reminding everyone to allow time for breakfast beforehand.

With a long bow to the assembly, Humphrey volunteered to keep watch through the night for Vera, other reinforcements, or potential approaching dangers. "I can also sound the wake-up call, if you like."

"Now everyone, get some rest," Olenthia said, "and make sure those under your command do the same. We've accomplished much today, but it will all be for naught if we're unable to perform our duties tomorrow due to exhaustion. If there are no other questions-"

"Pardon me, ma'am, but I had something to add," Zip Ric said, hopping down from Winnie's back. He still didn't put much weight on his injured front leg, but he looked to be feeling better even since the morning and moved almost as quickly as he had before the injury.

"The last few days have been crazy, and today was no exception. Before I set out with Sam, I hadn't ever been more than a few hundred yards from my home. Now I can say I've traveled to Rodenthold and all points in between, that I've been carried first by an owl and then by a dog, and that I've survived more dangers than any squirrel has right to."

"But the most important thing that happened along the way is making wonderful new friends I never expected to have. And you're all here, ready and willing to fight for my family's home. We Rics are just simple and silly squirrels. We don't have much to offer, but if there's any way we can ever repay you, just ask."

"Here here!" agreed Great Grandpa Ric, and the other squirrels in attendance cheered along with him. The meeting dispersed as squirrels, rats, and raccoons patted each other on the back and congratulated one another on the excellent preparation work. Cranberry even grabbed Zip Ric in a hug, and then lifted the squirrel high over his head. A few bold squirrels climbed onto Winnie as she danced and bounced playfully. Olenthia leaned against the Ric Tree's trunk as Clive and the other rat captains admired Humphrey's wing span that he was proud to open wide for them to examine.

Sam could only smile. In that moment, the danger that was to come and the lingering uncertainty of how he would ever get back to his old life was forgotten, replaced by the warm feeling that only comes from being surrounded by friends.

Olenthia had to shout to get everyone's attention again and break up the festivities. Everyone needed their rest. The squirrels climbed up their tree to the multitude of dens nestled in the branches, while Sam, the rats, and other animals drifted into the meadow to bed down for the night. Zip Ric didn't follow his family members up the tree, choosing instead to trot alongside Sam and Winnie.

The three wandered to a patch of grass on the far side of the meadow. There hadn't been much paw traffic here, and the grass was still standing tall and untrampled. They were far enough from the Ric Tree that no branches stretched above their heads to break up the view of the sky. Winnie spun around three times like she always did before laying down, and slumped into a heap that started snoring in only seconds.

Sam laid back on the soft earth with his paws beneath his head. The moon was round and full, looming in the night sky larger than Sam could ever remember, and looked so close he thought he might be able to touch it if he reached his fingers far enough. Zip Ric nestled in beside him, curling up in a ball in the crook of Sam's arm.

Tomorrow morning, the fate of the Ric Tree would be decided. The thought made Sam's heart race. As tired as he was, he wasn't sure how he'd be able to sleep with that on his mind.

"What makes this tree so magical, Zip?"

Zip Ric shifted, but didn't sit up. "Nothing," he said through a yawn, "but everything. Every tree, every blade of grass, has a voice, and they all have in them their own wonder. Here has been our home for over five hundred generations of Rics, and that itself brings a kind of magic."

"But what made this tree so special," Sam asked, "all those generations ago? Almost three hundred years back, even this tree couldn't have been much more than a sapling. Why didn't the Rics pick a big tree to live in?"

"The Rics started as a small family. Why would they need a big home? This tree was perfect. It grew with us, and we aided each other. It gave us shelter from the elements and predators, and we in turn planted the meadow."

"Are you telling me squirrels are farmers now?"

Zip Ric chuckled, "Planted out of sheer forgetfulness. Stockpiled acorns are easy to find, dig up, and eat. But berries get squishy, and before you know it new plants start popping up…"

Sam gazed up at the sky and felt as far from sleep as he was from home.

The stars were innumerable and so bright they didn't look real. The biggest, brightest stars formed shapes Sam recognized from astronomy books and from the city skies. Constellations they were called, named after all sorts of ancient heroes, gods, and monsters. Other stars, thousands, millions that he'd never seen before because of the ambient glow of the city, filled in gaps between the main constellation points. Some were so dim he had to stare at their square of sky for a moment before his eyes could focus on their faint point of light.

But still, the constellations stood out and declared their mighty presence, just as they had thousands of years ago, before great city lights could drown out the smaller, more distant and dimmer stars. The Big and Little Dippers, Draco the Dragon, and, Sam's favorite, Orion the Hunter.

A thought came to him. "Zip, didn't you once say that a starry night meant for good luck?"

Zip didn't reply. He'd already fallen asleep.

Tomorrow would be a big day. Either they would succeed and save the Ric Tree and the meadow, or they would fail and a parking lot would take its place.

The stars, though, they would shine on. Somehow that gave Sam comfort as he stretched out and yawned beneath that ocean of twinkling lights. The morning promised chaos, battle, and destruction. For a little while, in the meadow's serenity, all that slipped away from Sam's thoughts. Before he even felt it coming on, Sam fell into a deep, dreamless sleep.

CHAPTER TWENTY-THREE

A cold, wet something nudged Sam's face. He swatted sleepily at the air like he was shooing away flies, but didn't open his eyes. He rolled over. All he wanted was a few more minutes of sleep, but just then the nudging started again.

"Wake up, Sam," cooed Winnie's sing-song voice, like a mother calling her child out of bed for school.

Sam's eyes snapped awake, his consciousness rousing his sleepy brain and the urgency of that morning waking him up.

Today was for all the marbles.

Today was the Battle of Ric Tree.

He sprang to his feet and immediately realized how stiff he was. Muscles in his shoulders, legs, and back ached from the miles walked, trees climbed, and battle preparations over the last three days. But there was no time to worry about that. He set off at a run with Winnie right at his tail.

The sky was washed in strange colors. The sun hadn't yet risen but already it chased off the night. Deep violet retreated along one horizon from a burning orange growing on the other, as streaks of olive and deeper greens in the cloudless sky overhead separated the opposing colors. The sun was unstoppable and always won that battle. That made Sam think of relentless bulldozers, and he had to push the image from his mind.

Commotion filled the meadow. Animals scrambled to battle stations or with final evacuation errands.

Sam passed a pile of berries and seeds, harvested and being carried off by squirrel teams on evacuation duty, and stuffed a handful into his mouth. It was all the breakfast he'd have time for. Winnie didn't even sniff the food. "I'm too nervous to eat," she moped, but stuck with Sam as he continued on.

As Sam and Winnie ran beneath the Ric Tree, a group of twenty squirrels lining a wide branch saluted and cheered. Sam smiled at the gesture but didn't slow as he ran toward the meadow's far edge and to the cleared path leading to the sleeping bulldozers.

A great wingspan appeared overhead and descended in a circular pattern. Humphrey landed in a jog beside Sam. "The workers are arriving, dressed in hard hats and orange vests just like you guessed. I count eleven of them."

"Any sign of Vera?" Victory was a long shot. But if the wisest owl in the wood said she had reinforcements coming, Sam wasn't about to give up on her.

Humphrey shook his head. "None. But there are other humans, too. They actually got here first, while it was still dark, but waited in their cars until the workers began arriving. Now they're all shouting at each other. They don't seem to get along much at all. Maybe we can enlist their help?"

That was news Sam hadn't expected to hear. More people at the construction site?

Then he remembered something Dad had said in what seemed like a lifetime ago. The newspaper article Dad had been reading about the new mall construction mentioned an organized protest. Sam's pulse quickened. Were these the protesters? Maybe his Dad was among their ranks?

"Thanks," Sam said as he started hopping trenches Winnie and squirrels had dug. "Sounds promising. Hope they're on our side, but can't count on it. For now, stick with the plan."

"Aye aye, sir Sam. Wise advice." Humphrey spread his wings. "I'll check in with the other commanders and report back in when I know more. Good luck."

"You too."

With the cleared pathway at her back, Olenthia stood atop a tall pile of debris pointing and shouting orders. Bands of squirrels, each with a small smattering of rats, were organizing into their assigned units. While the rats wore the same equipment they'd brought from Rodenthold, the squirrels were fitted in new helmets made from acorn caps, tied around their chin by a single blade of grass. Some clutched tiny spears while others lugged pebbles, acorns and other ammunition.

"Hickory Team Two, form up and fall out!" Olenthia's voice rose over the din. A chunk of the mob broke away from the main group and slipped into the trees.

A paw smacked Sam on the shoulder. "Exciting, isn't it?" Clive said. The big rat was dressed the same as the other troops, but with an oak leaf over his shoulders like a backpack to denote him as a squad leader.

Before Sam could respond, Olenthia called for Oak Team Six. "That's my cue," Clive said, before raising his spear in the air and shouting. "Alright gang, let's do this!" To wild applause he led over a hundred acorn-helmeted troops into the underbrush beside the cleared area to their designated ambush location.

"Sam!" Cranberry called from the other side of the troops, waving him over.

Sam turned to Winnie and petted her nose. "I've got to go. Be a good girl, Winnie, and stay safe." Her eyes were long and sad. She had to wait for Olenthia to call for Thistle Team, the animals assigned to medic duty.

"Be careful, Sam," she whimpered, laying down so he could scratch her ears with his claws.

Sam darted over to where Cranberry and another of his raccoon gang waited along with around twenty squirrels and a pair of rats. The two rats were as scarred as Clive, and the squirrels hopped in place ready for action.

Cranberry motioned all to follow, and they hugged the edge of the cleared swath toward where the bulldozers waited. The sun rose up over the trees and Sam had to squint.

As they approached the construction staging area, Sam heard human voices for the first time since Bradley and Mitch had been driven off from Rodenthold. The memory of those creeps getting what they deserved made him grin. It served them right for stealing lunch money, intimidating other kids, and of course the bathroom sink dunking. Olenthia, Clive, and the other Rodenthold rats had put them in their place.

Today there were more than bullies to chase off. The stakes here were life and death, homes and hope. And this time, Sam was part of the fight.

They took cover in the underbrush and stayed hidden as they scurried to where the other raccoons were already lying in wait within the trees, near the bulldozers. The raccoons, squirrels, and rats high-fived and patted shoulders as they hyped themselves up for the mission.

Cranberry and Corn crawled forward to the edge of the tree line, and Sam followed their ringed tails. He shouldered up beside the two bigger, boss raccoons, staying as low to the ground as he could, and peered out into the cleared gravel area.

Gathered around the construction yard were many more people than Sam had expected.

The construction workers, eleven of them, just as Humphrey had reported, wore dusty yellow hard hats, orange reflective vests, flannel shirts, jeans, and wide work boots. It was Monday morning and no one looked excited to get to work. Their cars were parked around the edge of the clearing, while a shiny black pickup truck sat idling in the middle of the gravel area.

Beyond them, two uniformed officers stood with hands on their hips beside their parked squad car. The police officers were facing a crowd. The crowd numbered fourteen and they carried signs and banners reading '*Save the Trees*' and '*Mapleton Doesn't Need Another Mall*'. Protesters, for sure, though Sam didn't see his father among their ranks. He felt guilty, knowing his father was no doubt too preoccupied with trying to find his son to have contacted anyone about joining in on the protest.

Further back behind the protesters, all the way to where the gravel driveway intersected the highway, a big white van rolled to a stop. A satellite dish stuck up from its roof and a navy blue graphic plastered to the side read "News Channel 9" in bold letters.

"Cranberry, look," Sam said, pointing at the van as a cameraman climbed out and started unloading equipment. "That's the local news. You're going to be famous."

"In some circles," Cranberry winked, "I already am."

The door of the black pickup opened, and another man emerged. He was lean and tall, dressed very differently than the workers. His khaki slacks, polo shirt, and loafers looked more like what Sam's dad wore to work than clothes suitable for a construction site. He too wore a hard hat, the only thing that suggested he belonged. His hard hat was white, though, and shiny - with writing too small for Sam to read from the trees - rather than scuffed and yellow like the other workers'. Sam decided he must be the foreman.

That meant in the battle to come, this man was the enemy's general.

The foreman unrolled a set of blueprints on the hood of the pickup and waved over three of the workers to review the plans with him. The other workers seemed to keep their distance from the foreman, drifting away to drink coffee and smoke cigarettes. The faint smell of cigarette smoke made Sam's nose twitch involuntarily.

For several minutes Sam and the others waited while the foremen pointed at things on the plans. The protesters tried to get a chant of "No New Mall!" going, but they had a hard time keeping it up when the only ones listening were apathetic construction workers and the police. Sam thought they'd probably try harder once the news camera was rolling, but the News Channel 9 team seemed in no hurry to get set up.

The breeze stiffened, rustling the set of plans the workers reviewed and the yellow tree clearing notices tacked to the trees. Sam shook his head. To think, one yellow sheet of paper had been the catalyst for his whole adventure.

Well, that and a silly, childish stocking cap.

Overhead, Humphrey wheeled into sight. He circled through the morning sky above the construction area once, twice, and then a third time.

Sam's heart thumped so strong he could feel it in his throat as he nudged Cranberry. "That's the signal. Everyone is in place. Operation Stout Oak is a go."

Cranberry looked back to where the other raccoons and the two squads of rats had crept up behind. "You heard the kid. Time to make some mayhem."

Taco and Taco fist bumped and then, waiting until there weren't any workers looking, darted out into the open and under the nearest car. They disappeared into the shadows and waited. The squirrel squads split up, each led by a rat, but stayed in the trees as they peeled off to get into position. Cranberry, Corn, French Fry, and Sam stayed in place, waiting for the workers to move toward the bulldozers.

Cranberry rubbed his paws together. "Oh the waiting is the hardest part."

After a few more tense minutes, one of the workers took a jingling set of keys from his pocket and started toward the giant machines.

"Here we go," Sam said, readying himself.

"Kid, there's something we need to talk about." Cranberry put a paw on Sam's shoulder. "Sam's no name for a raccoon."

"What do you mean? That's what I've always been called."

"Look, this is important. I don't have any kids of my own, and if I don't make it through today, I want you to carry on my legacy, and accept my namesake."

"You want me to be a Cranberry?" Sam was sure if his cheeks weren't covered in fur, he would have blushed bright red. He had never felt so honored. That's why it was a surprise when Cranberry made a disgusted face.

"What? No! Cranberries are terrible! They're tart, sour. Yuck. No man, I want you to be named Spaghetti. It's my absolute favorite food. Nothing better. Now wait here and watch this."

The worker with the keys took a long step up onto the bulldozer tread. He fumbled with the key ring for a moment before selecting the right one, fit it in the cabin lock, and pulled open the glass door.

"NOW!" Cranberry shouted, then leapt from the woods with Corn and French Fry at his heels.

The three raccoons sprinted together toward the bulldozer, all thoughts of stealth abandoned. Two raccoons scrambled into the bulldozer's cabin, while the third climbed the now shrieking man.

The raccoons in the cabin bit and clawed and pulled and tugged. They shredded the upholstered seats and pushed buttons, punctured cables and bit through electrical wiring to render the bulldozer obsolete.

With a shout of surprise, the other workers rushed toward their assailed coworker. The man who'd unlocked the bulldozer jumped back to the ground even as the raccoon assailing him, Corn, jumped off the man's shoulders. Corn sprinted the other way with something jingling in his mouth.

"It's got the keys!" someone shouted.

Two workers turned to run after Corn before leaping back in surprise. Ten screeching squirrels burst from the woods to cover Corn's escape. It was a sight the pair of workers clearly had never anticipated, and they jumped back with their hands in the air and their eyes wide.

"Hurry!" Sam yelled as he saw men grab shovels and hammers to deal with the assault. Cranberry and French Fry finished their destructive work in the bulldozer cabin and fled before the workers reached them while Corn and the squad of squirrels retreated into the woods.

A loud cheer went up. Sam was startled by how human the squirrel, rat, and raccoon voices were. Then he realized it wasn't his comrades cheering for victory, but the protesters.

The camera crew was hustling now, pulling battery packs, cables, and cameras from the van, no doubt regretting they hadn't been faster to catch the sudden act of wildlife defiance from the raccoon demolition squad on tape. Sam knew if they hurried, there'd be much more for them to record.

Cranberry appeared at Sam's side. An oily liquid stained his cheeks, possibly hydraulic fluid. "How'd we do, Kid?"

"Incredible," Sam looked around Cranberry to French Fry, who had developed a twitch. "Is he alright?"

"Yeah, just got a bit of a shock on an electric wire. She'll be fine." Cranberry patted the other raccoon hard on the shoulder. "Shake if off, Frenchie." Then he pointed back out at the staging area. "Ready for Phase Two?"

The foreman had moved over first to the bulldozer. While he stood with the workers, hands on his hips and shaking his head at the wanton destruction from a few raccoons, the Taco twins slipped out from their hiding place. They ran straight toward the now untended plans sitting on the hood of the black pickup truck. One Taco leapt up and grabbed the plans, while the other neatly caught them.

Together they expertly rolled the large stack of papers and bound them closed with a rubber band they'd pilfered from who knows where. They carried the plans over their shoulders like two lumberjacks hefting a fallen log and disappeared into the trees before the foreman or workers saw a thing.

The protesters, though, witnessed it all. They provided more whoops of encouragement, like fans at a ball game cheering for a home run. Some had their phones out to record the antics of the animals. The police, whose backs had been to all the action, turned from the protesters and tried to figure out what they'd missed.

At the cheers, the foreman stomped back to where his plans had been. He threw his hands up in surprise and, after using some words that would have gotten Sam grounded, spiked his hard hat to the gravel with a hollow thump. It bounced and spun, and landed with its logo upside down but facing Sam. It read *Banks Development Company,* and that made Sam grin.

Now, hidden in the trees, Taco and Taco would have already rendezvoused with the second squad of squirrels and be shredding the plans into unidentifiable pieces.

"Who has the spare bulldozer keys?" the foreman shouted. Workers checked their pockets and shrugged. They were busy checking the man that Corn had jumped on for bites, and seemed less than enthusiastic about approaching the second bulldozer. Nervous eyes scanned the tree line, likely expecting more squirrels and raccoons to come bursting out any moment.

The foreman's face turned red. "Fine." He barked, "Get your saws. Now!"

Sam turned to Cranberry as the workers went to gather tools. "I need to get to the next front. If they find keys for that second dozer, can you take it down?"

"Spaghetti, my boy," Cranberry winked, "It would be my pleasure."

Sam scurried through the underbrush toward the cleared swath that led to the meadow. As he left Cranberry and the rest of the bulldozer strike team behind, he felt his confidence grow. So far so good, the animals had won this round.

Before he'd gone far, he heard the first of the chain saws rattle to life behind him. Sam gulped, and realized there was still a lot of fight left.

CHAPTER TWENTY-FOUR

Sam swiped aside fern fronds and weeds as he ran from the first battle field. Startled insects buzzed through the air as he hurried past. Behind, all the while, the throaty sound of chain saws grew.

There was no need to see the staging area to know what was happening. Each of the workers were grabbing tools of destruction and soon they'd be stomping through the swath where their bulldozer had already cleared and heading toward the Ric Family Oak. Sam smiled to himself as he hurried. If the workers were surprised by the sudden raccoon hi-jinks, they hadn't seen anything yet.

He didn't slow as he reached a thick elm tree bordering the cleared swath. With all his might, Sam leapt against the elm and stuck like velcro, the way Zip Ric and the other squirrels always did. He was getting the hang of this being a raccoon thing.

Sam shimmied ten feet up the trunk before stopping and looking down to the ground were Winnie and Zip Ric were crouched in the dried leaves, trying to stay hidden. Winnie's eyes rolled up at him and she whimpered nervously.

"Good girl, just wait there, I'll be back," Sam said before shooting the rest of the way up the tree. He heard Winnie's tail wag and scatter some of the dried leaves around her while Zip Ric rubbed her leg.

Squirrels saluted as they moved aside for Sam to pass. He found General Olenthia keeping watch from a high elm branch that leaned out over the cleared alleyway. Without looking back at Sam, Olenthia pointed. "Here they come."

One by one the men trudged into view.

Three lugged unwieldy chain saws, six more had pickaxes, and one huge man with a thick, red beard carried a shovel. There was no sign of the foreman or the eleventh worker, the one Corn had stolen the keys from.

Olenthia issued a few last minute directions to a trio of squirrel messengers. They dashed away to deliver the orders. Then Olenthia raised her left paw in the air while putting two fingers from her right in her mouth. She issued a whistle that filled the clear morning air.

If the workers heard Olenthia's signal, they made no indication. They continued down the alleyway in clumps of two and three men. Several were smiling, laughing, and probably joking over what had just happened with Cranberry and the raccoons. Sam couldn't hear them. The idling growls from chain saws drown out their voices.

"Steady," Olenthia said mostly to herself, her left paw still raised and quivering. A dozen commanders and captains, hidden along both sides of cleared alley, would have their eyes on her, awaiting the signal.

The workers were a third of the way down the alleyway. They didn't even glance at the trees to either side of them. Their destination was clearly the Ric Tree.

One man, a few steps ahead of the others, took an awkward step and almost fell. The Winnie-dug trenches, disguised by pine boughs and long grass blades, were impossible to see among the rutted ground if you weren't looking for them.

The first worker found his feet and stepped out of the hole when two more almost fell, the ground disappearing beneath them. Each held a chainsaw and lost their grip on them as they slipped. Moments later, two more men stumbled in another of the booby traps. The third chainsaw hit the dirt when the worker carrying it set the tool down to help the others out of the trench.

"Now!" Olenthia shouted, dropping her arm.

A chittering battle cry from the throats of a thousand squirrels filled the air. The workers froze in place and looked up at the trees as they righted themselves. The hair stood up on Sam's neck.

As the battle cry stopped, the sky darkened.

Squirrels lined every tree branch within range of the workers, and now they flung all manner of acorns, pebbles, and other projectiles at the startled men below.

Most squirrels threw using the instruction Clive and the other rat captains had shown them, with some minor tweaks to the pitching mechanics provided by Sam. A few had mastered a new technique. Some squirrels had discovered that, by spinning a certain way and by gripping an acorn in their tails just right, they became living slings, firing on the men at incredible velocities.

The workers cowered and ducked beneath the acorn barrage. Acorns left welts on skin and thumped hard hats, making a sound like rain on a metal roof. The men swatted at the air around them, as if shoeing away hornets.

Men flinched and flailed and ducked their heads against the onslaught. They stumbled forward and tripped into more trenches. That was when Olenthia began waving her paws over her head, signaling the next phase.

From the both tree lines, squirrels and rats poured from cover. They shrieked a blood curdling shout as they charged. Sam saw Clive down there, several steps out in front of his troops.

As the furry creatures reached the terrified and confused men, the squirrels leapt and attacked from above while the rats came in low, just like they'd practiced.

The animals washed over the men like a crashing ocean wave. They poked and bit and shrieked while the men flailed their arms and legs to get the wild creatures off. Squirrels were flung from the men's arms, and rats were shaken free from their legs or kicked off by heavy work boots. They needed Thistle Team, Sam and Winnie's squad, out there.

"Got to go," Sam said, and hurried down the tree face first.

"Be safe, Sam!" Olenthia called after him.

Sam dropped from the elm tree beside Zip Ric and Winnie. They were still hiding in the trees. Zip Ric was in position on Winnie's neck, while Winnie trembled.

"Are you two ready?"

"Ready!" Zip said, without taking his eyes from the battlefield.

"I'm ready, Sam, but very nervous," Winnie whined.

Sam patted her side. "C'mon, just like we practiced. You've always wanted to catch squirrels, right?"

Winnie sprang to her feet. "Yes! You're right! Hang on Zip Ric, here we gooo!!" she howled, and burst from the trees. Zip Ric leaned against the wind and pointed his tail straight back like a jockey in a horse race. Twenty squirrels appeared from their own hiding places and followed the big dog and brave Zip Ric toward the fray. These squirrels still had dirt under their claws from spending the last day digging under Winnie's direction. They'd quickly become the dog's loyal followers, and they'd been eager to join her on medic duty.

Sam did his best to keep up with Zip Ric and Winnie's squad of medics as they dashed out onto the battlefield. They weren't a moment too soon.

Men flailed, animals charged, the melee had broken into chaos. The man with the red beard swung his shovel in long arcs, wielding it like a broadsword. Rats ducked beneath the swipes and went for his shins only to be kicked aside by work boots.

Winnie and her squirrel medics ducked beneath the shovel swings to rescue the fallen soldiers before they got stepped on and more gravely injured. They grabbed rats and squirrels under the armpits to drag them to safety while Winnie carefully mouthed three rats in her muzzle before dashing toward the opposite tree line.

A pair of squirrel soldiers went tumbling past Sam, tossed from a worker's shoulders. They landed in a heap. Sam moved without thinking, and scooped the pair of squirrels under his arms. He hustled on two legs towards the safety of the trees.

The squirrel under Sam's left arm winced in pain. "I think my tail is broken."

"Grandma, is that you?" said the squirrel under Sam's right, looking up at Sam with dazed eyes beneath a cracked acorn helmet. "Wait, who am I?"

"You're a hero, that's who," Sam said as he set the squirrels down on a soft bed of moss beneath the trees, beside the three slobber covered rats that Winnie had rescued.

Sam tried to keep up with Winnie as Zip Ric maneuvered her around the battlefield. Zip kept her clear of the men and steered her to those who needed help most. Most of the wounded she grabbed gingerly in her mouth, but some were able to cling to her fur and ride her flanks as if she were a big fuzzy bus.

The battle became a blur as Sam did his best to avoid the workers while saving injured allies. Once, he thought he saw Clive darting through the chaos. The rat tumbled into sight, bruised and bloodied. Then Clive laughed, rolled to scoop up a discarded spear and charged again.

Sam ducked beneath the wild swings of the red bearded worker's shovel and grabbed a rat who's front arm was bent at an unnatural angle. Something stung Sam's ear, a bee or a wasp he thought. The pain made him stumble and almost drop the rat. Sam grit his teeth, kept his feet, and pulled the soldier to safety.

A shadow swooped in from overhead. Sam's eyes widened. Could it be Vera and her promised reinforcements?

No, it was Humphrey joining the fray as he dive-bombed the workers. Humphrey wheeled and dove again, this time knocking a hard hat aside. Then a strike team of songbirds swooped in to harass the un-helmeted worker. It hadn't been part of the plan, but it was effective.

Sam sat watching the birds for a moment too long. A steel toed boot caught him square in the ribs and sent him flying backward.

He tumbled across the dirt, landed in a lump, and gasped for breath he couldn't find. One of Winnie's squirrel medics was with him in a heartbeat. The squirrel rubbed his shoulders ineffectively while Sam's eyes rolled back in his skull. The edges of his vision blurred dark.

Finally, after what seemed a lifetime, his lungs remembered how to work. He gulped that first breath like a diver coming up from the bottom of a pool, and then he felt the pain in his ribs. With each inhale the pain renewed. He rolled to his side just as Winnie and Zip Ric arrived to check on him.

"Sam! Are you alright?"

He struggled to his feet to face the battlefield. The pain was intense but standing seemed to make it fade. "I think so," he lied through clenched teeth.

The animal allies, for all their ferocity, were being driven back. Their numbers dwindled as rat commanders withdrew their forces as the casualties mounted. Clive still led his team in the melee, whirling like a vermin tornado from one worker to the next, but even he could not fight forever.

"Bombardiers!" Came a shout from the trees overhead. Olenthia. "To the ground!"

Branches shook as squirrels descended. Olenthia was going to lead a second charge into the rear flank of the men.

"Come on guys, we're joining them." Sam said.

Winnie looked out over the carnage of the battle, at the moaning and unconscious squirrels, at the rats limping away from the fight, and whimpered. "I'm more of a fetcher than a fighter, Sam. I'll keep getting the wounded to safety. You'll have to take care of the other stuff." Sam winced in pain as he reached up to scratch Winnie's ears. She didn't have a vicious bone in her body.

Zip Ric shrugged. "I'd just slow them down. Me and Winnie are better off sticking to what we know."

"Ok you two, but hurry." Sam said, and then winked like Cranberry would have. "We're about to send these guys packing. Get everyone out of the way so they don't get trampled."

Winnie howled as she and Zip barreled back out onto the battlefield to collect the wounded. Her team of squirrels followed close behind in her wake.

Sam could see Olenthia, across the way at the opposite tree line, step to the head of a mass of squirrels at her back. As she drew her needle sword it caught the sunlight, and she spoke words too distant for Sam to hear.

A shout went up from the squirrels behind Olenthia that made the hair on Sam's haunches stand up. These squirrels were too small to join the initial fight so had been assigned to throwing duties. But it was now or never.

The workers had chased off the last of the animal defender's first wave and now stood with their hands on their knees gasping for air and wondering what had just happened. They also looked on in confusion at the sight of Winnie retrieving rats and squirrels.

Olenthia pointed her tiny sword toward the men. As one, a multitude of fluffy tails charged. The squirrel faces were grim and determined. As they approached, Sam thought they sounded more like a stampede of bulls than a band of tiny forest creatures.

The first squirrels leapt with all their might onto the closest worker's back. They stuck to his orange vest and bare neck like pins on a cork board. He howled and spun, dropped his pickax, and flailed his arms like a boneless puppet before turning and fleeing.

Sam fell in line beside Olenthia, both running on all fours. "That one," She gestured with her nose. It was the huge worker with the shovel.

The man had a great red beard that resembled a Viking's. With hands as meaty and big as bear paws, his muscles bulged to fill the reflective vest. His face was intense and focused as he grabbed squirrels from his shoulders to fling them back toward the woods.

It could have been because Sam was now only a foot tall, but he thought this might be the scariest person he'd ever seen. And yet somehow, the man's face looked vaguely familiar. Sam couldn't place it, and it didn't matter anyway.

The Sam that had last rode the school bus would have veered away.

The Sam that had hid in the library during lunch would have gone back to the trees, found a log to hide under, and waited for the battle to end.

The Sam that had gone to the school dance would have figured scary men would eventually lose interest and go away, the way jerks like Bradley eventually always did.

Except these men would only leave after Zip Ric, his family, and the Ric Family Oak were destroyed. They'd plow and pulverize the meadow to make way for some stupid shopping mall. In the last few days, Sam had found something that he hadn't realized was inside himself.

Was it confidence? Was it courage?

It didn't matter what it was called. All that mattered was that Sam grabbed hold of the new feeling and it propelled his leap. He arced over the swinging shovel to land upside down on the back of the man's tree-trunk like leg. Sam dug his claws into jeans and hamstring as the man tried to shake him off. But Zip Ric had given Sam expert tree climbing instruction, and this was no different than a swaying branch in a storm. Frankly, the man's leg and pants were a bit easier to grab hold of than willow or oak branches.

Sam held on tight as Olenthia led another pack of Rics up the man's other leg, biting and clawing. Sam thought what the heck, and bit his long fangs into the man's calf.

That was all it took. The man howled, finally dropped his wicked shovel, and spun away. He took a few awkward hops on one leg before breaking into a run.

The impact of those first steps was too much for Sam's aching ribs, and he dropped to the ground. Sam spit the taste of dirty denim from his mouth as he watched the red-bearded man fleeing. The man tripped over another of the trenches, but scrambled to his feet and kept running. Squirrels hopped off his back to land lightly on the ground.

Cheering erupted all around. Sam looked back and saw the giant, Viking-like man with the shovel was the last of the workers. They'd done it. Somehow they'd won.

As squirrels and rats hugged and high-fived all around him, Sam felt a twinge of remorse. The red-bearded man disappeared around the corner into the staging area. He realized the men they'd been fighting had just been a group of guys going off to work. They weren't any more wicked or evil than a school teacher or the mail man or his own parents doing their jobs.

And the workers would be back. The battle field was full of limping, celebrating squirrels and rats. They'd won, but had taken a beating. How many more times would they have to fight this battle? How many more times could they hope to win?

For now, it didn't matter. They'd done it.

Clive, limping and grinning, staggered to where Olenthia was surveying the battlefield and barking out commands. His fur was streaked with blood, both his own and others'.

"Well General, it worked. Don't know how we pulled it off with an army of loopy squirrels, but it worked."

Olenthia paused. She had already begun issuing orders for restocking ammunition supplies, assessing the wounded, and reforming into fighting squads. In a most un-Generally move, she threw her paws around Clive's shoulders and hugged him with all her might.

Zip Ric reined up beside Sam. Winnie panted, her tongue fat as a lillypad, but she smiled wider than Sam could remember.

"Look! Look!" she jerked her head toward the woods. "We got them all out of the way!"

Packs of wounded and woozy Rics and rats stood at the treeline, waving and giving thumbs up.

Humphrey landed and was immediately swarmed by squirrels hugging his legs. "Well done! Well done everyone!" He stretched his wings wide and hugged fifteen members of the Ric family at once. "Bravery and courage and a large helping of acorns have won the day! The poets shall sing of this victory for ages to come!"

The ground was littered with acorns, discarded tools, and hard hats. And in a few places, a stone-still squirrel or rat that would not move again.

"They made the ultimate sacrifice to protect this place," Olenthia said as she stepped to Sam's side. Sam tried to blink back the tears from his eyes, failed, and had to wipe them away with his furry forearm. "Battles often claim the bravest among us, and it never gets any easier."

Winnie, Zip Ric, and the other squirrel medics pulled their fallen comrades from the battlefield and back to the serenity of the trees.

Great Grandpa Ric joined them from where he and the other elder Rics too feeble to fight had watched from the Ric Family Oak. He clutched his half-tail somberly. "They will be forever remembered. For as long as we call this meadow home, their names shall echo through the oak branches with the same reverence we give the Fleet Feeted Four."

As his adrenaline faded, Sam's pain returned. He felt like he'd been hit by a bus. His ribs were likely broken, each breath ragged and raw, like he was getting kicked with each inhale. His head ached too. He reached up to feel at his ear, where he'd felt the sting, and it came back damp with blood.

"It seems you took a nasty wound in the fight, Sam," Olenthia said. He crouched down for her to examine it. "There's a ghastly gouge on of the side of your ear. You're lucky not to have lost it. We'll need to get you stitched up back at the Ric Tree."

Sam guessed the swinging shovel had nicked him when he'd been pulling the wounded to safety. It quickly took Sam's attention away from his aching side as the pain in his ear started to throb.

But, at least for today, they had won. Sam would have taken twice the pain to save his friends.

At the back of the cleared swath-turned battlefield, Sam saw the News Channel 9 team finally had their camera set up. It was trained on the celebrating animals. A man in a suit with a microphone faced the camera, his back to the meadow.

Sam could only laugh. The news had missed filming all the action, but Sam still might get on television for the recap on the evening news. He waved and stuck his tongue out, the way people in the background of newscasters always did, though he was probably too far away for the camera to see him.

And then he thought of his mother and his father. His smile faded. This was the fourth morning he'd been gone, and they were no doubt sick with worry over what had happened to him.

"Winnie!" he called. Winnie was laying on her back getting her belly scratched by a mob of squirrel hands, and didn't seem to hear him.

He had to get home, and Winnie would know the way.

"Winnie!" he shouted again, but his voice was overpowered by another voice.

"Run! Retreat!"

Cranberry burst from the trees, frantically waving his paws. He had something streaked across his face. It was thick and red and matting down his fur. Not hydraulic fluid this time, but blood.

The other raccoons hurried behind him, similarly battered, hobbled and limping.

Sam grabbed Cranberry by the shoulders. "What happened?"

"There were more of them, and they were ready for us." He panted. "We've got to get out of here."

Olenthia stomped forward to meet them. "Report!"

In response came a great bellow echoing through the trees. Like the roar of a dragon.

CHAPTER TWENTY-FIVE

"Fall back to the trees!" shouted General Olenthia.

From the edge of the tree-lined corridor, the second bulldozer appeared. Smoke billowed from the exhaust stacks and its metal-toothed treads clanked as they tore at the earth beneath them. The machine threw tilled ground behind it in clumps, like a bull readying a charge, as it turned to square up with the cleared swath.

Humphrey took to the skies, calling for the wounded to follow him to safety and out of the way.

Sam froze there, watching the machine line itself up. Zip Ric rushed to his side with Winnie just behind. Zip's eyes were wide with terror while Winnie tried to hide her face beneath a paw. All around them a wave of rats and squirrels ran from the bulldozer.

Clive came limping past. "Hurry, lads! Let's go go go!" he shouted at the members of his squad, the remnants that hadn't already been carried off injured from the battlefield. Sam grabbed Clive's paw as he passed.

"What do we do? What's the plan?"

Clive looked back at the rumbling bulldozer. "Sorry, mate. There's no plan." He patted Sam on the shoulder. "We did what we could. Time to retreat."

"No…" Sam said, as Clive dashed away, joining the flow of animals running toward the Ric Family Oak. Zip Ric scrambled up Winnie's side, and they turned to follow. All able bodied animals would grab a load of supplies and fall back to the designated pine tree, where the juvenile squirrels had already been evacuated. That was the plan from the beginning, should the defensive operation fail.

Sam's eyes searched the crowd. Everyone was running with all haste to the Ric Family Tree, except for one rat. General Olenthia stood in the midst of the retreat, directing traffic and shouting encouragement. Sam ran to her.

"What do we do?"

"We run, Sam. Cranberry and the raccoons spent most of yesterday trying to sabotage the machine and failed. It has no weakness. There's no fighting that thing."

Olenthia jerked her head toward the Ric Family Oak. The last of the animal soldiers were running and limping past to join the evacuation. "Come on, there's last minute work to do."

"No." Sam looked back at the bulldozer, idling beside where the cameraman had set up. Its glass windshield reflected the sun, and from straight on looked like a single eye staring down at Sam, a menacing yellow cyclops. Its broad metal blade looked like a solid set of bared teeth sneering, the way bullies always seemed to. "I'm not quitting. There must be a way."

"Don't be foolish Sam. You accomplished much. We nearly won the day, thanks to your planning, quick thinking, and ability to bring this strange assortment of animals together. But now we have to admit when we're beaten."

"I said no. You can run if you want, but I'm stopping that thing. Even if I have to do it alone." He turned his shoulders to face the bulldozer. Its diesel engine revved up, as if accepting his challenge.

Olenthia hung her head. "I must go, Sam. There are duties and coordination I must see to for the sake of the others. Be safe, be smart, and please retreat when you know you're beaten. See you at the fall back pine." She dashed away to follow the last creatures running toward the Ric Family Oak.

With another roar of its engine, the bulldozer lumbered forward.

Sam dug his claws into the ground and looked all around. The sky was a clear, crystal blue. His fingertips were damp from soft earth, and the trees bordering the cleared swath swayed easily in the breeze, oblivious to the fate that would soon befall them.

All that stood between the smoke belching bulldozer and the destruction of these trees and the Rics' home was a small, frightened raccoon. He wasn't even full grown, and didn't even bear a true raccoon name. But, after the last three days, what Sam lacked in size he made up for in courage.

Sam ran straight at the bulldozer. He didn't have a plan, he just knew he couldn't quit.

The bulldozer raised and lowered its blade menacingly, as if taunting the tiny creature that dared challenge it.

There had to be a way to stop it. While gigantic, intimidating, loud and stinking, it was just a machine. It didn't have a spirit or courage or resolve.

Machines could be broken. Shut down. Turned off.

Cranberry and his band had proved that when they'd disabled the first bulldozer. All it took was chewing a few of the right tubes or stealing the keys.

Sam dug his heels in and came to a stop. He was close enough now to see it was the foreman in his shiny white Banks Development Group hardhat behind the controls of the bulldozer. The man had closed himself inside the glass cabin and no doubt locked it up tight to keep out unwanted woodland creatures.

The bulldozer pitched and lurched over the uneven ground. Thrown acorn ammunition, and discarded spears and helmets were ground to dust beneath its treads, and he watched a dropped chain saw wilt beneath the grinding machine. The bulldozer tipped itself up as it rose high over a bump in the cleared alleyway, and suddenly Sam had an idea. If they hadn't been able to take out the machine from straight on, maybe its weak point would be underneath? He also wished he'd thought of it yesterday when the machine was safely sitting still.

With the timing of a base runner stealing second, Sam sprang forward. He leapt beneath the gleaming steel blade mounted to the front of the machine and landed between the pair of churning metal tracks. He pressed himself flat to the ground as the bulldozer passed over him. The machine blocked out the sun and Sam had to squint to make out any features. Pistons and gears and all manner of mechanical parts crunched and pumped deadly above him. The slick scent of grease and oil filled his nostrils and Sam had to force down a cough.

While he lay there stone-still, afraid that the slightest movement would pull him into the maze of moving gears and grind him to a pulp, his eyes raced, searching for some weakness. Just one tube or a single rubber belt or some other vulnerable piece of this damned machine was all he needed to find. But there was just metal and more metal.

Sam reached up at one line that looked promising, but found it too was metal. And scalding hot. It burnt the pad of his paw and Sam almost bit his tongue in surprise at the pain.

The sun reappeared, almost blinding, as the bulldozer passed over him and continued its deadly march to the Ric Tree.

"Well that was stupid." Cranberry said, running out from the trees and pulling Sam to his feet. "Brave, but stupid."

Sam watched the back of the bulldozer as it kept lumbering on. "I thought I could disable it from underneath, like you did from inside the cabin."

"Good thought, Sammy Spaghetti, but we checked that angle yesterday. As you saw, it's no good."

The Channel 9 News crew hustled toward them across the tilled earth, stepping over tree debris and mounds of chewed up underbrush to follow the bulldozer. The reporter's fancy shoes slipped on the damp ground, and he fell on his butt in the mud.

"Serves him right," Cranberry scowled back at them as the cameraman tried to pull the reporter to his feet. "Come on, Sam. Let's go help with the evacuation."

"No. We can't quit." Sam took one step and nearly toppled in pain. He looked down at his front paw and saw the once black skin was pink and tender from where he'd touched the belly of the beast. Sam grit his teeth and said it again. "We can't quit."

Winnie burst from the trees. Her tail stuck straight out behind her as she galloped at full speed to Sam.

"Whoa, girl!" Zip Ric said as he reigned her in by the collar to stop on a dime beside Sam and Cranberry.

"Climb on, Sam!" Zip Ric whooped like a cowboy.

"I'm not running," Sam said, taking a labored step toward the back of the bulldozer. The machine was only a minute from breaking into the meadow.

There had to be a way. They just had to buy more time. Where was Vera? And where was that silly second crow?

A wide paw reached out and rested itself square between Sam's ears. "Neither are we!" Winnie barked.

Sam looked up at the big mutt. She licked him full on across the face. With his good paw, Sam grabbed hold of Winnie's collar.

Winnie bolted forward before he was ready. Zip helped haul Sam onto Winnie's back as she closed the distance to the bulldozer.

"Traveling by dog is pretty fun, don't you think?" Zip Ric asked. Zip Ric's optimistic attitude was as certain as the sun rising in the morning.

Winnie ran up beside the bulldozer, just inches from the churning teeth of the metal track.

"Now's your chance, Sam!" she shouted over the noise of the engine and the clanking treads. "We know you can do it!"

The bulldozer's metal tread rumbled like a deadly conveyor belt. Sam knew that what he was about to do was incredibly stupid, but couldn't think of any other way.

He leapt with all his strength, landing on top of the track. His aching ribs, his throbbing ear, and his paw all screamed in unison, but Sam had no time to notice. If he didn't move fast, he'd be swept under and chewed up by the tread. The Spaghetti name Cranberry had given him would be all too fitting. Sam jumped to his feet and ran on the bulldozer track like a treadmill, looking for what to do next.

The startled foreman looked over with wide eyes and a gaping jaw at the daredevil raccoon that had just boarded the dozer. Sam jumped to grab hold of the lever that opened the bulldozer's glass cockpit. It turned easily in his paw and wasn't locked after all. Sam pulled it all the way down and pushed with his legs against the metal frame around the door.

The door swung open several inches before the foreman grabbed an inside handle and slammed it shut. The impact nearly made Sam lose his grip, but he held on. The lumbering tread brushed his tail. If he fell, Sam would either bounce helplessly over the side or be pulled under the bulldozer. Neither sounded appealing.

Sam saw the foreman flinch, followed by a loud crash. A baseball sized stone bounced onto the tracks. Cracks in the bulldozer's windshield spread like spiderwebs out from the point of impact as Sam saw Humphrey wheeling away to find another stone. It felt good to have help, but they were running out of time.

With a bump that almost made Sam slip, the bulldozer rolled over the last two saplings that had separated the cleared tree alley from the Ric's meadow.

If he could only get inside the cabin, Sam was sure his adrenaline, claws, and teeth would quickly convince the foreman to give up, but his attempts at the door and Humphrey's rock throwing only seemed to have made the foreman angrier. The man's teeth were clenched and his gaze fixed forward on the great oak tree.

The shrubs, long grasses and Winnie's trench network between them slowed the bulldozer more than Sam would have expected.

Humphrey reappeared, this time landing on top of the glass cabin.

"Troubling development, Master Sam."

"Yes, I'd say that's one way to describe all this."

"Oh, no no no. Not this. Though you're right, you are currently in a less than enviable spot."

"Get to the point," Sam grunted. He was beginning to really notice the pain in his paws from hanging onto the door handle.

"It seems there's another army of rats that's just arrived. Thousands of them, easily ten times what Master Clive led here. A grizzled rat named Emperor Nezearius leads them. Would you believe he had the audacity to laugh in my face when I suggested they come and help our efforts? Instead, I'm afraid, he's calling for your blood."

Sam's eyes widened. The second crow had done it. Sam's message had been delivered.

"Humphrey, as fast as you can, go tell Nezearius exactly where he can find me."

His plan, somehow, was working.

CHAPTER TWENTY-SIX

The bulldozer's tracks chewed away at the ground beneath them, churning the earth like a blender as they pushed the massive machine forward.

It's blade was unrelenting as it tore over berry bushes and left a tilled brown gouge in its wake. The foreman pulled at levers and adjusted switches as they went, careful not to bury the blade too deep but also keeping an eye out for the loose foliage so it wouldn't tangle in the mess of gears beneath the machine.

All Sam could do was hang on to the door lever, hope, and wait.

They were getting closer. In another minute they'd be beneath the shade of the Ric Tree. The foreman kept glancing over at the curious raccoon, clinging so desperately to the door. Now and then he'd bang a closed fist against the window to try and startle Sam and break his grip.

Though Sam's fingers ached and his burnt paw was almost numb with pain, he knew his only hope was not letting go. Everything depended on his grip holding and staying on top of the bulldozer.

The cameraman was close behind them, carrying a shoulder mounted television camera. Surely, with his strange raccoon behavior, Sam would be making the evening news now.

"Sam! What are you doing!?" shouted Olenthia from just ahead and above. She'd wandered as far as she dared out onto a narrow branch of the Ric's tree, clinging with wobbly legs to the swaying leaves around her. "Are you trying to get yourself killed? Nezearius has come, we have to escape!"

The bulldozer bounced into the dappled shade cast by the Ric Family Oak's ocean of fluttering leaves. The emerald oak leaves glittered in the morning sun, and then dulled as the smoke stack passed beneath them to belch acrid smoke over their delicate forms.

"No time to explain!" Sam shouted back. "Keep everyone away from Nezearius and his army! Make him focus on me!"

The bulldozer's cabin was directly beneath Olenthia when she dropped onto its roof. She peered over the side, the white blaze on her brow flashing. "If you wish to ensure he comes for you, I suppose I'll be joining you on this infernal machine. Can't say I understand your plan, but I guess Nezearius will just have to come and get us both from up here."

A dozen more rats dropped onto the roof from another branch. Olenthia sprang up, ready to fight, but Sam saw Clive's familiar, scarred face through the glass. A moment later, Clive too peered over the side.

"Wish I had some means of pulling you up here to join the party, mate."

"Just glad you could come."

Clive winked. "You just keep hanging on, we'll fight at the General's side up here."

Sam looked ahead at the dwindling distance between the bulldozer's blade and the Ric Family Oak's trunk. "If it comes to that, we've lost."

Then, a squeaking sea of silver and brown fur broke around the base of the Ric's tree. It flowed like a river around a rocky outcropping. Above them was Emperor Nezearius.

The rat ruler rode on a litter borne on the shoulders of eight burly rats, bigger than Clive, near the front of his force. Before him were at least a hundred thick rats with stout spears, and at his back came an uncountable number of similarly armed vicious vermin. They were charging the bulldozer head on.

"He's gone mad, and brought the entirety of his personal army," Sam heard Olenthia say from the rooftop, over the roar of the bulldozer engine. "That must be every member of his Chosen force, and more!"

Sam met Nezearius's mad gaze. The Emperor stood up from his seat and hopped in place. He could hear the foul rat's voice even above the groan of the bulldozer. "There is the invader who dares taunt us! Get him! Find a way up! And make him regret every inch as we drag him back to the dungeons!"

The Emperor's Chosen shrieked a battle cry and picked up speed. The army of rats narrowed at its middle as the first ranks dove beneath the gleaming bulldozer blade just as Sam had minutes before, waving their spears with blood lust in their eyes.

"Forward fools! Forward!" Nezearius shouted, snapping with the end of his tail at the rats carrying his litter. They followed the first of the troops under the bulldozer, beneath the blade, and to the dark space full of whirring gears and throbbing pistons.

The foreman's face twisted up in disgust as the rats poured beneath the machine. More rats followed Emperor Nezearius's lead to disappear from sight before a sizable portion of the rat army held back, dug their heels in, and now ran the other way. It seemed not every rat that had accompanied Emperor Nezearius was quite ready to charge into the jaws of death.

A new smell displaced the diesel fumes and grease stench filling the air. This was one of gears straining against resistance, malfunctioning machinery, and worst of all, burning hair. There was no sign of Emperor Nezearius or his Chosen emerging from the other side.

The bulldozer lurched, sputtered, then died with one last loud pop. The sudden stop made Sam lose his grip, and he fell to the stilled metal tread.

The foreman tried the key three times and banged against switches and levers, but the bulldozer would not come back to life.

Sam rolled to his back, looked up at the patches of blue sky making its way through the green canopy of the Ric Tree, and tried not to think about Emperor Nezearius's vengeance-fueled charge or the rats' gruesome fate. He felt sick in his stomach, sore throughout his whole body, and weary from everything that had happened both in the battle and in the journey leading up to it. He just wanted to shut his eyes and rest, and then find his way home.

A loafer kicked open the bulldozer door. The foreman stuck his head out and swung his gaze around until he found Sam, laying helpless and battered on the bulldozer tread. The man grunted, tossed his hard hat back inside the bulldozer's cab, and revealed a head of spiky blond hair that looked an awful lot like Bradley Banks'. The foreman landed on the metal tread with a thunk.

As hard as he tried, Sam couldn't lift himself to escape. The foreman towered over Sam, his brows furrowed and angry. He raised his foot. Sam closed his eyes. This was it.

"Agh! Eh!" he heard the man's surprised grunts. Sam opened one eye and saw acorns ricocheting off the foreman's face and polo shirt.

"Don't let up! Keep firing!" came Zip Ric's familiar cry from somewhere above. "Let him have it!"

There was more commotion from above, this time from the roof of the bulldozer. Olenthia led the way, with Clive and the rest of the squad right behind, as the rats went airborne. They disappeared beneath the foreman's shirt as he tried in vain to swat them off while shielding himself from the acorn attack.

His rage against Sam forgotten, the foreman jumped off the bulldozer and stumbled away, trying to get clear of the tree and its vengeful squirrels. Sam rolled to his side to watch.

"Get him team!" came Cranberry's shouts from somewhere in the bushes. Seconds later three raccoons latched onto the foreman's legs. "Poor fool is going to need a rabies shot tonight!"

The camera man watched in bewilderment as the foreman ran past. He kept the camera trained on the action, though he no longer looked through the eye piece. The reporter was hurrying toward the commotion, still dusting himself off from his earlier spill. The protesters were at the edge of the meadow now too, issuing mixture of laughter and shock at the scene.

Sam closed his eyes and rolled to his other side. They'd won. For real this time.

He could have fallen asleep right there, if not for Winnie's operatic voice below. "Sam! Do you need help getting down?" She stood up on her hind legs against the quieted bulldozer tread and licked Sam's face right as he opened his eyes. He grabbed her around the neck and Winnie carefully helped Sam to the ground. She carried him away from the bulldozer and commotion to the same patch of soft grass on the other side of the meadow where he'd slept the night before.

Sam stretched out on the grass, and tried to fight sleep so he could savor what victory felt like. Yet his eyes were so heavy he couldn't resist.

He saw a peculiar sight as he drifted in and out of consciousness. Silver wings, followed closely by squirrels that almost looked like they could fly.

Vera?

"I must already be dreaming," he muttered, before actually falling to sleep.

CHAPTER TWENTY-SEVEN

When Sam finally stirred it was already dusk.

He sat up and immediately regretted it. Every inch of him hurt. Sam imagined this must be what it feels like to be hit by a car.

"He's awake!" shouted Zip Ric. The squirrel squeezed Sam in a hug that made Sam's eyes tear up. His ribs were most certainly broken.

"Hurray!" Winnie exclaimed. Judging by the matted grass, they'd both been laying nearby keeping watch over him.

He was surprised to see his burnt paw caked in mud and bound between a stack of oak leaves, and felt a similar poultice had been applied to his sliced open ear.

Sam leaned against Winnie with his good paw as she helped him back to the middle of the meadow, toward the Ric Tree and the abandoned bulldozer. There were no signs of construction workers, protesters, or the news crew. They'd all left a while before, after all the action died down, Zip Ric and Winnie explained.

A number of uninjured rats were carrying all manner of nest materials, food, and other supplies in every direction through the meadow. They looked unreasonably happy. When Sam asked about them, Zip Ric laughed.

"Oh, them? That's the rest of Olenthia's Fourth Legion! She tried to keep a stern face when she ordered them to brief her, but you could tell she was happy to see them."

"It seems after they got roughed up outside of Rodenthold, when Clive and a few others managed to get away to come join us, Emperor Nezearius dragged them along as punishment when he marched out to come find you. He didn't even recognize he was bringing the very backup we'd originally requested!"

"And," Zip went on, "Olenthia said that since they were late for the fight, they're to help get things back in order for the 'Heroes of the Meadow'. That's what she called us all! Can you believe it?"

Sam smiled and rubbed his head. "What else happened while I was out?"

"You'll see!" Winnie howled. "It's a surprise!"

At the base of the Ric Tree, Cranberry and the other four raccoons were lounging beside a pile of ripe mulberries. They'd cleaned themselves up, and looked no worse for wear.

"Hey! There he is! Sammy Spaghetti!" Cranberry said through a mouthful when he caught sight of Sam. "Welcome back, sleepy head."

Sam was the center of attention as they talked over each other, telling him just how brave and stupid he'd been. They also couldn't believe his cleverness, using Nezearius's likely embarrassment for losing prisoners to bait him into unwillingly helping to save the day.

"What was it you said to that other crow, Spaghetti?" Corn asked.

Cranberry slugged Corn in the arm. "I already told you, leave the kid alone."

"No offense, Cran, but sometimes you ain't the most trustworthy. We just want to hear it from him."

Sam thought, trying to remember exactly what the message had been. "Well, I figured the Emperor had to be mad that we'd escaped his dungeon, evaded his patrol, and stole off with one of his best generals. So I had the crow fly to Rodenthold and tell all the rats on patrol that Sam was building a new rat kingdom, that one day we'd come to take over Rodenthold, and had the crow tell them exactly how to find the Ric Family if they wanted to come stop me."

"Nice," one of the Tacos said, nodding.

"Smart," said the other.

Sam shrugged and then continued. "Then I just hoped Nezearius would find his authority challenged and seek to snuff us out. It worked, and whether he wanted to or not, Nezearius saved the day."

"He may have unwittingly saved the day," Olenthia said, leaning against a spear and smiling, "but something else won the war." Sam hadn't seen her approach while he'd been mobbed by the raccoons. "This way, Sam. I'll show you."

Sam, Zip Ric, Winnie, and the raccoons followed her around to the other side of the tree, where the bulldozer had finally come to rest. Perched on its roof and overseeing an assembly line of rats dismantling the bulldozer from the inside out sat two familiar shapes.

The first was Humphrey, who bowed when Sam came into sight.

The second was Vera. She nodded her head and pinched her black eyes closed in hello as Sam approached.

"It is good to see you, Sam," she said.

"I saw you, just before I fell asleep, didn't I?" Sam said, and then suddenly annoyed asked, "where were you? We needed your help."

"My assistance was delayed more than I'd have liked. However, the promise of help seemed to be enough to win the fight. It hardened your resolve, and saw you through to the end."

Sam looked down at his paw and felt at his ribs. She was right. If he hadn't held out hope for Vera's help, Sam would have given up just as everyone else had. And where would that have gotten him? Certainly not hanging onto the side of a bulldozer as a target for an army of vengeful rats, that's for sure.

Zip Ric chimed in. "And in the end, she came through! Squirrels saved the day, just like you said, right Vera?"

She only nodded her somber and quiet gesture.

"What do you mean?" Sam asked.

"Look up above you," Zip Ric pointed.

Sam stared at the branches of the Ric tree. It teemed with squirrels, hurrying between nests, and settling back in after their scare from the last few days. Everything looked ordinary. At first.

Sam squinted. He thought it was his imagination, but then he saw a second, then a third, squirrel glide between the boughs. "That was too far to jump…" his voice trailed off.

"That's right!" Zip Ric agreed. "Vera found some descendants of Izel and brought them here to live with us!"

Flying squirrels, hard to count because they moved so fast but at least ten, flitted through the tree branches. The descendants of Izel, the fourth of the Fleet Feeted Four, who Zip had said was magical.

"This tree," Vera said, "will not be going anywhere. It seems the Rics' flying cousins are endangered, and as long as they're here…" Vera's voice trailed off as she pinched her eyes closed.

"They can't bulldoze this meadow." Sam finished her thought. "Brilliant. Vera, you really are the smartest creature in the woods."

"Maybe," Cranberry said, "but can she tip over a trash can?"

* * *

As evening arrived a celebration erupted. Beneath the moon the squirrels danced as they had that first night when Sam found them, in what he thought was a dream. Rats, raccoons and even a big dog joined the festivities. Humphrey rounded up a group of crickets and sang with a deep baritone voice in accompaniment to their creaking.

The flying squirrels entertained everyone with aerial acrobatics, swooping and soaring through the night sky.

Winnie was a celebrity all night. Everyone wanted a turn riding her around the meadow. "You have to pay me in belly rubs or snacks," she informed each squirrel and rat that stood in line.

Olenthia sat in a circle with Clive and six more of her most trusted captains. When he saw Sam watching them, Clive scurried over.

"Rodenthold is without an Emperor for the first time since its founding. We're outlaws now, every rat of the Fourth, but we'll come up with a plan to win the city back and put things right. Well," Clive shrugged, "at least Olenthia will. The rest of us will just follow orders."

"That's exciting, good luck."

"It'll be one heck of a grand campaign. Couldn't have done it without you!" Clive thumped Sam on the back. "Whoops, sorry," he said when Sam winced.

The Rics, meanwhile, had decided they needed to spread out a little. It had never occurred to them that some disaster, man-made or otherwise, could have endangered their whole family's existence. It was therefore decided that Great Grandpa Ric would oversee colonizing the empty pine tree where most of the young Rics had sought shelter during the battle.

As the festivities began to die down, Sam saw Vera sitting on the ground, alone and away from the ruckus of merry making. Her back was to him as she stared up at the sky.

"Hello, Sam," she said without looking.

"Vera, there's something else I need your help with." His voice almost caught in his throat as he spoke.

"You want to go home. To your real home." She turned her gaze onto him. The stars reflected in her deep black eyes.

Sam looked to each side, making sure none of his friends were there to overhear. "Yes. How did you know?"

She spoke, but did not answer his question. "It is a testament to your goodwill, compassion for your friends, and perseverance that you haven't gone back already."

"What do you mean?"

"Going home is easy, Sam. All you had to do was fall asleep with the thought in your head that you'd had enough, that you were ready to return to your old life." She bowed her head. "Instead, your bravery saw you through to the end. This tree would not still stand without your courage and sacrifice. You're a hero, Sam, to everyone here in this meadow. On behalf of all of us, thank you."

"You're welcome, I guess." He didn't feel like a hero, he'd just done what was necessary to help his friends.

"If you're ready, lay your head back on the ground, and home will find you with the morning."

It sounded kooky, but after everything Sam had seen, he didn't doubt her words. "Ok," he simply said, settling down on the grass, beneath the moonlight.

The moon's face was smaller than it had been the previous night, and would start dwindling over the days ahead. His eyes again felt heavy, so much so that keeping them open was harder than anything he'd ever tried, either as a raccoon or as a boy.

CHAPTER TWENTY-EIGHT

The first thing he noticed was the smell of disinfectant. A lemony, soapy scent. Like nothing he'd perceived in the forest.

The next was how smooth his body felt where it lay. Sam shifted his arm but didn't feel the bristly fur that he'd gotten used to.

Noises were different too. He heard the hum of an air conditioner, the sound of water running, and a beeping somewhere nearby.

Sam rolled over and felt a tension in his arm, tugging at his wrist. He slowly opened his eyes to see a white room with a morning sky outside. A muted television on the wall was showing a laundry detergent commercial. Tubes and wires and instruments were all around, and at first he thought he was at the dentist's office. Then he saw the IV tube connected to his arm and heard his Mom's excited voice.

"Sam! You're awake! Oh thank God, you're awake!"

His parents took turns hugging him tighter than he could ever remember. Mom had tears in her eyes and Dad's face was drained with relief.

He looked down at his fingers when she let go. He was in one piece, and could see his own skin rather than a coat of charcoal fur.

"What happened?" His voice came out weak and scratchy.

His parents continued to fawn over him, but eventually Sam got the story.

The night after the dance, some manner of creature had gotten in the house. A raccoon or opossum or some other animal, probably through the dog door they guessed. Winnie had chased it off with much fanfare, but when the commotion didn't wake Sam up, his parents checked in on him to find Sam burning up with fever.

"102.8 degrees!" Mom exclaimed.

"And you wouldn't wake up." Dad said. "We were terrified, so we rushed you right here to the hospital."

The doctors thought he had pneumonia, but couldn't figure out why Sam remained unconscious. He'd been in the hospital for four days, with one or both of his parents by his side the whole time.

He'd had other visitors, too. There were balloons tied to a chair and several get well cards standing up on a table beside his hospital bed. One had an owl on the front. Another had a pair of squirrels high-fiving each other.

"From your friends that stopped by." Mom said as she straightened one of the cards. "That Lia is a sweetheart, and Charlie is a character. We're proud of you for making friends so fast. They each came by a couple times."

Next to the cards was an empty cardboard pizza box with a moustache twirling cartoon chef printed on the top. Pizza Pete's, though obviously not from their Rodenthold location.

Was there really a Rodenthold? The thought popped into Sam's head suddenly. Had his adventures through the woods all been a dream? Could he have imagined it all while unconscious? Was it all a product of his fever, of friends stopping by, and hearing the television in his sleep?

The memories were vivid in Sam's head, unlike most dreams that faded away as soon as he opened his eyes.

A dream would make more sense than warrior rats, Winnie-riding squirrels, and all manner of talking animals. Of course. It must have been a dream.

When the nurse came in she listened to his chest, checked his breathing and temperature, and measured his blood pressure. She was bewildered when all his vital signs were completely normal.

"You gave us quite a scare, young man. Not sure what was wrong with you, but now everything seems normal." She turned to his parents. "We'll keep him overnight to monitor, but tomorrow morning he should be all set to head home."

Sam sat back and looked up at the television, which was silently playing commercials, while his parents thanked the nurse profusely and went over what symptoms they needed to monitor for.

He wanted it all to be real. Zip Ric, Olenthia, Rodenthold, everyone, everything. He wanted to be courageous and brave, and not just in his own imagination.

The nurse turned to leave. "If you need anything, just hit the button. I've been too swamped today to even drink my coffee."

She was halfway into the hallway when she said something that made Sam sit up.

"I've never used this many needles in one day. Seems everybody suddenly needs a rabies shot."

Dad chuckled. "Poor guys. I guess they shouldn't have messed with the forest."

"What are you talking about?" Sam asked, suddenly suspicious.

"Oh, it was awesome, Sam," Dad stood up to get the television remote. "Let's see if they talk about it on the news again."

Dad turned the television to channel nine and sure enough, they were still discussing one of the strangest things to happen in Mapleton in years.

The television showed an abandoned bulldozer sitting beneath a big oak tree as they panned across an open meadow. If they'd filmed any of the action leading up to that point, they didn't show it.

"Yesterday, during a scheduled tree clearing, eyewitnesses claim to have seen flying squirrels living in this oak tree." The news man explained to the camera. "State employed naturalists are being brought in to investigate the area. The flying squirrel is an endangered species in North Carolina and normally only found in the mountains. It would be exciting to welcome them to Mapleton."

Dad squeezed Sam's shoulder. "Pretty cool, eh?"

The newsman continued. "In related news, the group of construction workers that were savagely attacked by a marauding pack of raccoons are in good spirits and expected to make a full recovery. Back to you, Susan."

They turned off the television, and Dad went down to the cafeteria while Mom waited with Sam.

It was too weird, but it didn't prove anything. He could have heard the news in his sleep, and his imagination could have filled in the rest. Right?

"Oh, Sam, I almost forgot," Mom said, going to her purse. She reached inside and pulled out a familiar mass of yarn and felt. The button eyes reflected the overhead fluorescent lights. "Where did you get this hat? You still had it on when we found you, sick with fever." She tossed it onto his bed.

Sam picked it up from the sheets and turned it over in his hands, as if he were looking the raccoon face in the eye.

"No way..."

Sam touched the side of his head. He could clearly recall the pain from having his ear nearly severed as he dashed about rescuing rats and Rics from the battlefield. So too could he remember the sting of his burned palm when he'd foolishly dove beneath the bulldozer and mistakenly touched a boiling hot piece of metal. The pain of both was gone now, replaced only by an aching stiffness from being in bed for the last four days.

But the stocking cap told a different story.

At the end of a paw-like tassel, the felt and yard was blistered and crisp, like it had been melted beneath the heat of a match.

And then there was the left ear. It hung from just a few remaining strands, like it had been snagged on something. Or grazed by a shovel.

CHAPTER TWENTY-NINE

They went home on a Wednesday, and Winnie got a much needed bath.

It turned out she'd been missing, wandering the woods since the night Sam got sick. Dad had found her, filthy and happy, Tuesday night after Sam was awake when he'd gone home from the hospital to grab a few things.

Sam stayed home from school on that day, but by Thursday morning, he was standing outside at the edge of the driveway. His parents had offered to give him a ride into school, but Sam insisted on taking the bus.

A whole lot had happened in the week since he last headed into school. The trees behind their house no longer looked quite so scary or ominous, and Sam didn't feel even a hint of the usual dread that usually accompanied the start of a school day. He watched the long grass at the other side of the street for the squirrel he'd seen one week ago, but there was no sign of it. All the seeds from that area were already harvested, he guessed, and any squirrels would be off working somewhere else.

The bus pulled up and Sam climbed the stairs. It stank even more strongly of diesel fuel than he remembered. Or maybe, after being so up close and personal to a bulldozer, Sam was just more sensitive to the odor.

As he shuffled down the aisle, he saw several familiar faces. The first was Lia's, and she waved at him to come and sit down.

"You're back!" she said as Sam paused in the aisle next to where she sat. "Have a seat, Sam."

"Thanks Lia," Sam said, his eyes trained further back in the bus. "There's something I need to do first."

A few seats back, Charlie, from the dance dessert table, was sitting straight backed and trying to ignore Bradley Banks as the big kid kept punching the back of Charlie's seat.

"It's a bumpy ride, Chubby Charlie!" Bradley taunted, saying, "Bump! Bump! Bump!" with each punch. Bradley's fan club was laughing along with the blond haired oaf, though it seemed pretty forced.

Bradley wasn't so scary. Snakes? Now those were scary. An army of rats? Chainsaw wielding men? Hanging from the side of a bulldozer? All that was much more terrifying than some overgrown, privileged idiot with peach fuzz on his face.

"Leave him alone." Sam said as he stepped into Charlie's seat.

"Oh, is the sick little baby feeling better?" Bradley pouted his lips and rubbed his eyes like he was crying. "Did you catch a cold from getting all wet?"

"You know, Bradley, you're going to feel really stupid when..." Sam deliberately let his voice trail off. Then, forcing his eyes wide and trying his best to act startled, he pointed at Bradley's shoulder and shouted "Oh my gosh! Is that a rat!?"

Bradley bolted up from his seat like he'd been stung. "Get it off me! Get it off me!" His hands were a whirlwind as he spun and flailed and tried to brush off a rodent that wasn't there. Sam had to duck to not get inadvertently smacked.

Bradley's entire crew of underlings started laughing again, but this time it was at him. When Bradley realized Sam had tricked him, his face blushed bright red and his former friends laughed even harder. Bradley stomped away to the back of the bus to sit by himself, but not before promising that Sam would pay for that.

"Whatever," Sam said, then he sat down next to Charlie. "How's it going?"

"Thanks Sam. He was starting to make me motion sick, and I'd hate to have thrown up my pancakes."

"No problem, it was the least I could do. My parents said you came to see me in the hospital. Thanks."

"Twice," Charlie said, holding up two fingers. "Once over the weekend, and once on Monday when my dad went in to get some shots. A raccoon bit him at work!"

Sam's voice was low as he realized why he'd recognized the man with the shovel. "Is your dad a big guy, with a red beard?"

"Yeah! How'd you know?"

"Uh, I think my parents saw him at the hospital," Sam fibbed, "yesterday. Sorry. Was he mad? About getting bitten?"

Charlie shook his head. "Nope, he said it was the craziest thing ever. A bunch of squirrels attacked him and he had to fight for his life! Now he gets the whole week off, paid. He spent most of yesterday sitting in our hot tub."

"Cool," Sam said, and then changed the subject for the rest of the ride in.

The bus parked. Lia waited at the bottom of the steps for Sam and Charlie. "That was really nice of you," she said to Sam, tilting her head at Charlie, "sticking up for him like that."

"No kidding!" Charlie said.

Sam shrugged. "Thanks. I guess I just needed some practice."

The three joined the rest of the kids milling around the outside of Mapleton Middle School. After being around thousands of rats and squirrels, this crowd didn't seem quite so big.

The warning bell rang as they walked past towering Mrs. Betty Banks. Her smile faded when she saw Sam. Apparently she'd decided to hold a grudge for Sam trying to tell on her son. He didn't let her spoil his mood as he waved goodbye to Lia and Charlie as they went the other way down the hallway to their lockers.

"Oh, Sam, Charlie," Lia said, turning back. "Want to sit at my lunch table today?"

* * *

When the lunch bell rang three and a half hours later, Sam again found himself dashing through the hallway. This time he wasn't trying to hide from anyone, but he did have a few questions before going and joining his new friends in the cafeteria.

Ms. Quick was sitting at the library table where he'd eaten his lunch at a week ago. She looked lost in thought as Sam approached before snapping to and looking up at him through her spectacles.

"Sam! Wonderful to see you've made a full recovery, and glad to have you back."

"Hey Ms. Quick. I had a question," Sam said, as he dug into his backpack. He pulled out the knitted raccoon stocking cap. "This hat… where did you get it?"

"You know, Sam. I'm not sure I recall." Ms. Quick said with a smile. "When you get to be as old as I am, you tend to forget things."

"Huh," Sam said, turning the hat in his hands again. Mom had stitched the left ear back down with green thread, the only color she had in the house. He stared into the raccoon's button eyes. They seemed to swirl in the lights.

"Has the hat brought you courage, confidence, and cleverness, Sam?"

"Strangely enough, I think it has. Thanks again, Ms. Quick."

"You know Sam, I have many names and titles. But after all we've been through, and with the future adventures we'll no doubt undertake, you should just call me Vera."

She winked an eye that, through her glasses, almost looked like an owl's.

THE END

THE BANDIT MASK

ACKNOWLEDGMENTS

Writing a book was much harder than I could ever imagine, and you wouldn't be holding it in your hands without the help of some amazing people.

I could not ask for more supportive parents or parents-in-law, always interested in hearing about the process and offering encouragement along the way. I do have to apologize to both dads for the species of the story's protagonists... squirrels and raccoons run rampant in their yards.

Anne and Thomas listened to me verbally outline The Bandit Mask's plot long before anyone had read a word of the story, and gave great feedback throughout the process. They're also my go-to for all things technical, including websites, mailing lists, and formatting review.

Dave might be the fastest, and thus most widely read, reader I know. He was the first to complete the beta-reader review when I initially sent out the first manuscript to trusted friends, and provided great story notes.

Thank you to Dan and That-Kate for having several children all willing to read the manuscript! It was amazingly helpful to hear story evaluation from a span of ages.

I'm so thankful that Jacob took on the role of editor, something he always talks about pursuing, and was a big help finding my (many) grammatical mistakes. All errors currently in the story are due to me making last minute changes that did not pass beneath his watchful eye.

Laurie and Renee were absolute heroes throughout the entire process. They were involved in every step along the way... From big picture things like helping find character motivations, identifying the boring parts, and pointing out where to flesh something out more to get the plot dialed in, all the way down to red-lining spelling and grammatical mistakes. The Bandit Mask wouldn't be half of what it is without the amazing talents, help, and guidance of these two ladies.

Speaking of heroes, Jeff designed a cover that shocked me both in quality and in creativity. Just when I thought the book was done and ready to send out to the world, Jeff blew me away with his artistic interpretation of the story, and made me circle back one more time through the book to try and make the words worthy of his cover art.

Thanks to BREW, a local Raleigh coffee bar. It was there that the plot went from a jumble in my brain to a complete outline, and a good chunk of the story's first draft was written within their walls.

And of course the biggest thank-you goes to my beautiful (and patient!) wife Kate for not just believing in my crazy dream of writing a book, but being the most supportive, wonderful, and amazing partner I could imagine. I'm so blessed to be with you and I love you so much!

There's many others who deserve a thank-you for their words of inspiration, support, and enthusiasm along the way, but this book already ended up way longer than I ever expected. Just know that I am incredibly blessed to have you as friends, and I look forward to the next adventure!

-Justin Biegler
January, 2017

ABOUT THE AUTHOR

Justin Biegler lives in Raleigh, North Carolina with his wife Kate, three cats, and a dog named Winnie. When he's not writing, Justin likes to be outside exploring both far-off places and locations closer to home. Winnie, however, is much less adventurous and far lazier than her fictionalized counterpart.

Go to www.JustinBiegler.com for the latest updates on new projects, side stories, and other fun. And if you enjoyed this book, please consider leaving a review on www.amazon.com, www.goodreads.com, or any of your other favorite reading sites to help others discover this adventure.

Thank you so very much for reading!

And as for you, brothers and sisters, never tire of doing what is good.
-2 Thessalonians 3:13

62115814R00134

Made in the USA
Lexington, KY
29 March 2017